Pandemonium reigned in the Communist camp

As soon as all the men were accounted for, Gerber ordered them to move on. As they fled the area, the small-arms fire behind them increased in volume.

They moved swiftly, the need for speed and silence outweighing the necessity for caution. If they encountered a Communist patrol, they would have to shoot their way through. There was also the risk of walking into booby traps or mines, but they could not afford to crawl along looking for trip wires.

After pushing hard for more than two hours through the dense bush, Gerber finally slowed the pace. They walked quickly now, stopping every few minutes to listen, but there was no sound of pursuit. Gerber was almost ready to call a halt and give his men a break to catch their breath.

Then in the far-off distance, they heard that sound most feared by reconnaissance patrols deep in enemy territory.

The baying of hounds.

VIETNAM: GROUND ZERO®

RECON

ERIC HELM

A GOLD EAGLE BOOK FROM

WORLDWIDE®

TORONTO · NEW YORK · LONDON · PARIS
AMSTERDAM · STOCKHOLM · HAMBURG
ATHENS · MILAN · TOKYO · SYDNEY

First edition September 1990

ISBN 0-373-62727-0

RECON

VIETNAM: GROUND ZERO®

RECON

For Mom, who taught me to love books and told me to come home with my shield, or on it.

For Dad, who understood better than I the horrors of war and who recognized early that I was a writer but had the good sense to let me discover it on my own.

For Shannon, who when I was depressed gave me her love and encouraged me to press on.

For Mary Ann, who also gave me her love and understanding and forced me to sit down at the keyboard and write.

For Bill Fox, Clarence Andrews, Bob Tucker and all the rest, who taught me the tricks of the trade.

For Sharon Jarvis, my agent, who stood by me through thick and thin.

For all the vets, especially those who gave their all and made the ultimate sacrifice so that America could remain free.

And most important of all, for all the readers, who stuck with me for so very long.

PROLOGUE

THREE RIVERS SECRET
ZONE SOUTHEAST LAOS

Sergeant First Class Craig Barnes of the U.S. Special Forces sat on the floor of the UH-1D Huey slick, his feet hanging out the open doorway, feeling the cool wind rushing past the helicopter at three thousand feet slowly drying his sweat-soaked, tiger-striped jungle fatigues. It had only been a little past nine o'clock in the morning when the choppers had picked them up at the MACV/SOG pad near Kontum, but the day was already hot, and the two-hour wait for their air assets to arrive—caused by some bureaucratic foul-up—had left the whole team stewing in their own juices.

Barnes always considered a late start to be a bad omen for a mission, whether the insertion was scheduled for first light or the middle of the night, and he was getting too damn short on his second and last tour to be beset by bad omens. In another thirty-four days and a wake-up, he'd be on his way back to Fort Bragg, North Carolina, where Ellie and the kids would be waiting.

Barnes shifted his gaze away from the scenery passing beneath his feet and looked ahead. Out in front he could see their escort—two Charlie-model helicopter gunships riding shotgun for the insertion. Somewhere to the rear of his own aircraft,

Barnes knew, would be three other UH-1Ds; one with his one-one, or assistant team leader, Jack Searsboro, and five indigenous mercenaries on board; another with Captain Al Kellog in the C and C ship; and a third with Special Forces medic Tom Gibson riding chase in the Medevac bird. If things went to hell in a handbasket during the infiltration, Tom was as good a man as any to have around.

Barnes's attention was brought back to the interior of the helicopter by the crew chief, who tapped him on the shoulder and held up five fingers twice, indicating they were ten minutes out from the target area. Barnes reached into a pocket of his fatigues and took out a 30-round magazine loaded entirely with tracer ammunition. Most of the magazines the team had were the older, 20-round model, but Barnes had managed to scrounge enough of the new 30-round mags so that everyone in his team had at least a couple for use during insertion and extraction, when the team was most likely to come under sudden fire. He kept one of the magazines loaded entirely with tracers to mark targets for the gunships if the team was ambushed going in or had to extract under fire. It was one of the little tricks he had learned in recon.

Barnes reached over and tapped his one-two, Sergeant Tim Chelsea, flashed him a smile and help up the magazine. "Time to lock and load."

Chelsea returned the smile, cupped a hand to his ear and shook his head, indicating he hadn't been able to hear his team leader over the helicopter's engine. Nevertheless, he dug out a 30-round mag and popped it into his CAR-15, nodding to show that he had still understood the instruction. Both men then tapped the indigenous troops seated on either side of them and pointed to their weapons, indicating to the mercenaries that it was time to load up.

The small, dark-skinned Sedang tribesmen glanced nervously up at their American one-zero and his RTO, saw their reassuring smiles and smiled back without really knowing why. They saw what Barnes and Chelsea were pointing at and obediently dug out their own 30-round magazines and inserted them into their M-16s, each man drawing back the charging handle to chamber a round after making sure the safety was set, then closing the dust cover over the bolt.

Each man except for the Blooper Man, that is. Blooper Man, a seventeen-year-old Sedang kid with two years of combat experience already under his belt and an almost totally unpronounceable name, broke open the breech of his M-79 grenade launcher and dropped a canister round into the chamber before snapping it closed. The safety of his M-79 came on automatically as the breech was opened, but he still checked it when he had finished loading, the way the big noses had taught him. Blooper Man always put a canister round, essentially a 40 mm buckshot shell, up the spout for insertion and extraction in case some NVA decided to pop up out of the grass in front of him. If he needed a high-explosive round, there would be time enough to change the load.

The crew chief tapped Barnes again and held up five fingers. Five minutes to go.

Barnes felt as much as heard the change in pitch of the helicopter's rotors and felt the air change from cool to warm and sticky as the helicopter began its descent. He mopped at his face with the cravat bandage tucked into his shirt collar and let his hand rest loosely on the quick-release buckle of the broad nylon strap running across his legs, which kept him and the Sedang sitting on either side of him from falling out the doorway as the chopper banked sharply to one side. The gunships had already broken off with the Medevac ship and the C and C bird to hold in a tight orbit outside the range of small-arms fire, but near enough to help in a hurry if needed. The two Huey slicks holding Recon Team Florida continued downward alone.

The air washing through the open cabin of the Huey was warm and thick with humidity now. Everyone was sweating, both from the hot, moisture-laden air and the natural fear and uncertainty that accompanied every combat insertion. A hundred thousand "what-ifs" always ran through everyone's minds in the final moments before landing, but Barnes knew there was really only one question that mattered significantly in the next ten to fifteen minutes: would the LZ be hot or cold?

The pilot had the chopper at minimum altitude now, flying almost in the trees. The deck lurched sickeningly as the helicopter jerked left and right or zoomed up suddenly to clear a ridge line or hill, then plunged again like a roller coaster. Just when Barnes felt sure he was going to lose his breakfast before they got to the LZ, he felt the nose pitch up sharply as the tail boom slewed around and the helicopter dropped off both speed and altitude in a gravity turn, then rolled out level and settled into a low hover barely above the tops of the elephant grass.

"Goddamn chopper jockeys!" Barnes growled. "They all think they're some kind of cross between Steve Canyon and Sky King."

He yanked the release on the buckle, tossed the web strap to one side and balanced momentarily on the skid before dropping the four feet through the grass to the ground. The two Sedang tribesmen dropped into the grass beside him as the helicopters thundered away.

Barnes moved directly to the west side of the LZ and into the trees, where he paused for a moment while the rest of the team gathered in so he could count noses. Then he sent Searsboro and his five indigenous mercs a hundred yards ahead to make a sweep through the trees. When they reported back the all-clear, he nodded to Chelsea, who radioed a brief situation report to the C and C ship, while the insertion birds made another of the three dummy runs into alternate LZs designed to confuse any enemy observers.

"Florida is down with twelve and cold," Chelsea whispered into his handset.

"Roger, Florida," Kellog acknowledged tersely. "Capital Center standing by."

That was Kellog's way of letting them know that the C and C ship, Medevac and, most importantly, the two helicopter gunships, would remain on-station in their holding orbit for another twenty minutes before returning to base. That would give Florida a little more time to get settled in and check out the immediate area in case the bad guys were hiding somewhere in the bush, waiting for them. After that, Barnes and his men would be on their own.

Chelsea relayed the message to his team leader. Barnes nodded a silent acknowledgment, then said, "Go ahead and check in with the AB Triple C."

Chelsea changed frequencies on his radio and keyed the handset again. "Hillsboro, Hillsboro, this is Florida. Operational radio check, over."

He got only a burst of static in return, waited a few moments and tried again. This time the answer was almost instantaneous.

"Florida from Hillsboro. You are five-by-five on the active, over."

"Thank you, Hillsboro. Florida out."

Chelsea whispered to Barnes, "Radio check complete. We're on the active board."

"All right, then," Barnes said, "let's have a little look around the neighborhood, shall we?" He turned to one of his Sedang scouts. "Papa-san, you take point. Take us out about five hundred yards west, nice and slow, then wait. If we don't find anything, we'll go north half a klick and then try west again."

"Aye-aye, Sergeant Craig," Papa-san answered. The old family man of the Sedang mercenaries at twenty-five, more or less, Papa-san was a little vague on exactly when he had been born, as were most of the Sedang. He started to go, then paused for a moment. "Sergeant Craig, what we look for?"

"Anything," Barnes told him. "Any sign of Charlie at all. That'll do for a start."

Papa-san nodded and started off, with Cheo, Barnes's best tracker, taking the slack position behind him. When the two Sedangs had moved out, Barnes, carrying the team's camera and the smaller of their two pairs of binoculars, followed. He was trailed by Chelsea with the radio; Kue, their interpreter and the indigenous team leader; and Blooper Man, acting as tail gunner.

Searsboro kept the rest of the team a hundred yards to the rear and seventy-five yards out, where they could cover Barnes's left flank and be in a position to pivot behind Barnes's group and hit the enemy on their left flank should trouble come from the right. It was impossible for the two groups to keep each other in sight, but since Barnes and Searsboro had already discussed the intended route, it was simple enough for Searsboro and his native troops to follow a parallel course. If either group found anything interesting, they would alert the other using the small HT-1 AM radios.

They had gone only a hundred yards when Cheo dropped back to report that he and Papa-san had found something: a small but well-traveled dirt path running at an acute angle to their course and apparently paralleling, roughly, the edge of the tree line running along the western boundary of the LZ they had used for infiltration.

Barnes contacted Searsboro on the HT-1, telling him to hold his position, then brought the remainder of his half of the team forward cautiously for a closer look.

It was a footpath, less than a yard in width, but made of well-packed dirt. The fact that the floor of the trail was dirt, with no vegetation growing on it, told Barnes that it had seen extensive use.

"Sergeant Craig, you look here," Cheo whispered excitedly. "You see what we find."

He pointed to a small scrap of paper, such as might have been torn from a notebook. The paper was creased, as though someone had torn it quickly from the pad, and it had two small, yellowish spots near one edge.

Barnes nodded and whispered to Chelsea, "Somebody, presumably Chuckie, has been along this trail in the past twenty-four to seventy-two hours."

Chelsea arched an eyebrow. "How so?"

Barnes smiled indulgently. Tim Chelsea was a good soldier and a good RTO, but he was new to recon and not yet adept at reading signs.

"It's like this, Tim," Barnes whispered. "Sunlight bleaches and discolors light-colored paper and cloth, turning it first yellow and then eventually completely white. Paper will start to yellow after twenty-four hours. This piece is just beginning to turn, so we know it's got to be at least twenty-four hours old, but probably not real old yet. So we know someone was down this trail at least a day go, but probably not more than three."

"No more than two days," Cheo insisted. "Paper not yellow enough for three days."

"All right, two days, then," Barnes agreed. He turned back to Chelsea. "That kind of precision estimate comes only from experience, and Cheo's good. One of the best. If he says two days, you can believe him. Therefore, we know this trail was in use yesterday or the day before at the latest."

Chelsea nodded, filing the data away in his brain for future use.

"Let's move on and see what else we can find," Barnes said. "Everybody be careful to watch for trip wires crossing the trail. Blooper Man, you be sure and rub out our tracks. I don't want one of Chuckie's trackers discovering we've crossed his trail."

Blooper Man flashed a quick smile. "You no worry, Sergeant Craig. I no leave zip for Chuck to find."

Blooper Man took out a small folding pocketknife and opened the blade. Stepping back a couple of meters from the trail, he cut off a small, leafy sapling with which to dust the trail once they had crossed, being careful to make the cut below ground level, where the white inner wood exposed by the slice wouldn't show if someone happened along the same spot. Once he had swept the trail clear of their tracks, he would retain the brush until he was well clear of the trail and then discard it under a bush, sticking the raw, cut end back into the ground so that it wouldn't show. The severed sapling would thus blend in with its new environment until it began to wither

in a few days, by which time RT Florida would be well clear
of the area.

Barnes then radioed Searsboro on the HT-1, cautioning him
about the trail, and the six men crossed the path in single file,
stepping carefully in one another's prints to make as few tracks
as possible and hide their number, should Blooper Man not
be completely successful in his efforts to obliterate their footprints.

They needn't have bothered. By the time Blooper Man had
finished sweeping the trail smooth behind them, the only trace
of human passage left on the pathway was a tiny, yellowing
scrap of paper.

1

NHA TRANG, RVN

Colonel Alan Bates, director of special operations for MACV/SOG, sat behind the desk of his Nha Trang office and pondered the significance of the report he had just finished reading. In his mid-forties, Bates wore his graying, sandy-colored hair in a crew cut and looked as though he should have played college football, which, in fact, he had, though there were no trophies or pigskins in his office to mark it. He was a man who should have earned his own stars several years ago, but had got involved with Special Forces, and like many really good officers, hadn't had the good sense to get out after one tour, thereby assuring his promotion to brigadier general would come slowly, if ever.

Bates pulled the stub of a cigar from between his teeth and discarded it in his ashtray. Then he took a fresh cigar, his last, from the pocket of his jungle fatigues and placed it in the corner of his mouth.

The report in front of him was a standard Intelligence synopsis of MACV/SOG cross-border reconnaissance operations run out of Command and Control Central at Kontum. Bates had circled one paragraph with a yellow highlighter. It concerned an increase in enemy activity in the Three Rivers Secret Zone across the border from Kontum in Laos. Long known to be a sanctuary for the NVA Tenth Infantry Division, the Three Rivers Secret Zone was so called because it was roughly bordered by the Se Kong, Se Kamene and Khampho rivers, which also separated it from the Bolovens Plateau. The only sizable town the area contained was Attopeu, which had an airfield, but the Ho Chi Minh Trail ran smack through the territory, and traffic along the Trail was of considerable interest to MACV.

The fascinating thing was that the new activity didn't seem to be associated with routine traffic down the Trail. C and C Central had infiltrated three different reconnaissance teams in recent weeks, and all three—RTs Illinois, Louisiana and California—had made heavy contact with NVA patrols, but hadn't noted any unusual levels of truck or elephant transport. RT Florida was in there now, trying to make some sense of things.

However, Bates found the report interesting for a more personal reason than was to be found in the handful of neatly typed words. The area near Attopeu had once been the scene of an attempt at more or less direct involvement in the Indochina war by the People's Republic of China. Acting under high-level orders from MACV, Bates had scotched that attempt by sending a hand-picked team into Laos to assassinate the Chinese officers involved, along with a few highly placed NVA and Pathet Lao officers. The mission had been successful, but the team had got shot up pretty badly getting out. Now, for no other reason than a familiar feeling in his gut, Bates couldn't help wondering if the Chinese Reds were again up to something in the area.

He picked up the receiver of the black phone on his desk and pressed the intercom switch, then set the receiver back in its cradle, got up and opened the door instead. Sergeant Major Taylor was at his desk, typing up some requisition forms, a large china mug of steaming black coffee near his left elbow. Taylor heard the door open and turned in his seat. "Yes, Colonel, something I can do for you?"

"As a matter of fact, Bob, there is," Bates said. "Would you ring down to the operations office and see if Captain Mauraides is in? If he is, ask him to come down here for a moment. Then get me Derek Kepler over at the Intel shop, and see if you can get a call through to Charlie Khan out at the Kontum FOB on the scrambled line. I'd like to ask him a few questions. When you've done all that, please put on a fresh pot of coffee and ring down to the PX and see if they've got any decent cigars."

Taylor smiled, opened a desk drawer and took out a flat wooden humidor. "I think you'll find these satisfactory, Colonel. Help yourself to a handful."

Bates took a half-dozen cigars, checked the label and raised an eyebrow. "I didn't know you smoked, Bob."

"I don't, sir. I had Alice send these over for me. She had a hell of a time finding your brand."

"Thanks, Bob." It was rare to find an administrative aide who took such good care of his commanding officer, Bates mused, and he wanted to do something nice for Taylor in return. "Why don't you take the rest of the day off once you've taken care of those phone calls for me?"

"What, and miss out on the opening scenes?" Taylor said in mock horror. "I wouldn't dream of it, sir."

"Opening scenes of what?"

"Whatever operation you've got in mind that we're about to field, sir."

"And just what makes you think I've got anything in mind?"

Taylor's grin broadened. "I've worked with you on two tours now, sir. I think I know you well enough to know that when you have me start calling in the S-3 and S-2 and making calls to the CO of C and C Central on the secure channel, something's in the works."

It was Bates's turn to smile. "Nothing's in the works yet, Bob. Right now I'm just looking for a little more information on a report we got out of Kontum. It's just a feeling I've got. Nothing more."

"A feeling, or *the feeling*, Colonel?"

Bates scratched his belly and then rubbed a hand over the short bristles of his crew cut before answering. "All right," he said at last. "*The feeling,* although I'm damned if I can tell you why."

"Yes, sir," Taylor said. "I'll make the coffee extrastrong."

RECON TEAM FLORIDA was having a busy day. The whole area was a veritable rabbit warren of trails, pathways and roads, nearly all of which had seen recent use. Moving with great stealth and caution, RT Florida had covered only about four square miles by midafternoon and had found no less than five trails and three dirt roads. The roads had been cleverly camouflaged by tying together the overhead branches of trees growing along either side, creating the effect of the roadway passing through a living tunnel and effectively concealing it from observation aircraft that might pass overhead. It wasn't a new trick, but one which the VC and NVA had used with good results in the past, and here they seemed to have taken unusually good care in the construction.

Less time had been taken with the trails, but then less effort was necessary. Varying in width from only a couple of feet to a couple of yards and winding in among the trees, they took advantage of the natural camouflage offered by overhanging branches. Two of them had been constructed as all-weather trails and laboriously decked out with split wood and bamboo flooring. The others were simply well-trod dirt and would quickly turn into muddy quagmires when the rains came. The well-maintained nature of all of the trails indicated that they were in current use.

The most fascinating find had been made on one of the dirt roads. A series of well-defined tracks pressed into the dirt, coupled with several large piles of dung, indicated that a group of elephants, perhaps as many as twenty, had recently traveled the road. The NVA were known to have used elephants, both in timbering operations for construction and for moving heavy loads, and to an experienced jungle hand like Sergeant Craig Barnes, the data added up to the Intelligence that Charlie had either been moving a lot of supplies along the route, or some unusually heavy equipment, possibly antiaircraft guns or fieldpieces. The technique had certainly worked well enough for General Giap at Dien Bien Phu. It was an unsettling idea, because it led to only a limited number of possible conclusions.

First, it might just be that whatever the items were, Charlie was simply moving heavy stuff through the area on southward. That was bad enough news, since it would mean either the NVA had expanded the Ho Chi Minh Trail network farther eastward than ever before, or they were moving a lot of additional supplies into the area in preparation for a new offensive across the border in the Central Highlands of South Vietnam.

The second possibility was that the equipment being moved by the elephants actually *were* fieldpieces. That not only presented a grave, immediate danger to RT Florida, should the enemy discover their presence in the area and be able to fix their location with sufficient accuracy to shell them, but could also indicate the NVA were bringing in 85 mm or 122 mm guns with the intent of shelling targets across the border in Vietnam, indicative of a change in enemy strategy, and once again, possibly the precursor of a new offensive by the NVA.

The third possibility was that the elephants had been used to transport antiaircraft guns into the area. That could indicate that the enemy had something important enough located here to consider it worth going to extraordinary measures to protect. It left unanswered the question of exactly what that something was. It would have to be more than just a small NVA base camp. It might be that the NVA Tenth Infantry Division had decided to relocate its divisional headquarters to the area. It might even be the secret POW camp for holding American prisoners in Laos that Intel was always hearing rumors about, although Barnes tended personally to discount that idea. Based on what little he knew about enemy POW procedures, he figured the NVA would be more likely to keep prisoners dispersed in several smaller camps in order to increase the

psychological effect of isolation on the individual prisoners and
to minimize the likelihood of a surprise U.S. raid freeing all of
them at once. Or it might be something entirely different that
no one had even considered. Whatever it was, it was up to
Barnes and his team to find out.

Barnes took several photographs of the dungpiles and elephant prints for the Intel boys to ponder over, being careful to
take multiple exposures of each subject, intentionally over-
exposing and underexposing the shots as well as snapping the
pictures at the shutter speed and aperture setting indicated by
the light meter as ideal. He was equally careful to include a familiar object in each photograph for size comparison: a CAR-
15, a canteen, a 5.56 mm cartridge—whatever was handy and
would fit in the frame. Having such an object included with
the subject being photographed, the size of which was known
or readily determined, would allow the Intel photographic in-
terpreters to develop estimates of the size of the elephants by
providing a rough measure of the length of their stride. They
could get some idea of how heavy a load the beasts had been
carrying by the depth of the depressions made by their footprints, and by estimating the size of varying prints and com-
bining them with the length of the stride, could even make an
educated guess as to the sex of the animal. Barnes also took
pictures of the surrounding terrain and vegetation, which
would provide the experts with other clues, such as an estimate of the compressibility of the soil and potential food
sources for the pack animals. He used two rolls of film in the
process and then decided to follow the road for a bit to see if it
led to anything interesting.

Barnes was far too intelligent simply to stroll along the trail,
following the spoor. That kind of careless action could lead a
man straight into a carefully arranged ambush. Instead, he
moved the team a few yards off the trail and had them parallel
it, stopping every fifty yards or so to send Papa-san and Cheo
back to the trail to make sure it hadn't turned off somewhere
and that the elephant tracks were still on it. Searsboro kept his
half of the team some distance behind and on the opposite side

of the dirt track, where they would be in a better position to outflank the enemy should an ambush occur.

With almost excruciating slowness, they carefully followed the road throughout the afternoon until around 1600 hours. Cheo and Papa-san returned from checking the trail to explain excitedly that it had junctioned with another, wider trail. This new trail was different in construction, they explained. It was covered with small round rocks.

Curious, Barnes went forward himself to see what his scouts had discovered and was astonished to find a well-maintained, recently graded surface covered with pea gravel. RT Florida had blundered onto the apparent Ho Chi Minh Trail equivalent of Interstate 80. The well-worn wheel tracks where the gravel had been crushed by the weight of heavy vehicles indicated that not only elephants but military trucks had been along the road. That kind of traffic indicated that a lot of troops and supplies had been in the area. A whole lot of troops and supplies. Barnes began to have the uneasy feeling that perhaps RT Florida had discovered something too big. With that many NVA around, Florida could be in deep trouble.

Barnes considered the situation, trying to decide if they should stay and watch the graveled trail for a while or get out now. He knew he was on the verge of something important, but he still didn't know what. Every new discovery raised more unanswered questions. Barnes felt sure that the only way he was going to get any answers to those questions was to get his hands on a prisoner. The road itself, though, was unlikely to provide an opportunity to snatch someone. Any enemy traveling down it would likely be either in a vehicle, which would itself most probably be in convoy with other vehicles, or be marching in such a large group of men that it would be dangerous to attack them. This was by no means a certainty, however, and it was possible that a small patrol taking the easy route home, or a security team conducting a dawn or dusk sweep of the road, might provide a target of opportunity that could be quickly neutralized and allow a prisoner to be taken. Even if no such opportunity presented itself, it was possible that much valuable information about traffic on the road could be gleaned from simply watching it for a day or two or, more likely given the enemy's preference for the cover of darkness, for a couple of nights.

Barnes made his decision. He still had six days left to complete his mission. There was no sign yet that the enemy was aware of Florida's presence in the area. He had a lot of questions, but no real answers. And he wanted that damn NVA prisoner. For the time being, RT Florida was going to stay right where it was. He would set up an NDP nearby, get the claymores in place and establish an OP to watch the road. Once they had an idea of the amount of traffic using it and the schedule of any patrols, they'd set up the ambush and make the prisoner snatch, then get the hell out before Charlie got wise and dropped a world of shit on them. It called for pinpoint timing, but that was nothing new for Florida. They'd done the job many times before.

Barnes started back through the bush along the edge of the road to give the others his decision. As he passed the spot where the dirt road intersected the gravel, the faint glint of something shiny lying in the dust caught his eye and he halted. He squatted alongside the intersection, studied the dirt path for several minutes and decided the shiny object was something metallic. But it was too far out in the road for him to see it clearly.

Suddenly inspired, Barnes took out his camera and attached the 200 mm telephoto lens. Then he took another look at the object through the camera. With the telephoto, he could make out what looked like a cartridge case, but unless part of it was buried in the dirt, it seemed a bit small for a rifle cartridge, too small even for the 7.62 mm round used in the AK-47 or SKS.

After studying the cartridge for a moment or two, Barnes made a decision to take a risk. Checking the trail carefully in all directions, he stepped out onto the roadway and walked to the center. He had intended to step out quickly and scoop up the round for examination, then retire to the cover at the side of the trail to look it over, but when he stopped to snatch up the object, something else caught his eye and he paused. For a full three seconds he stood in the open, staring at the strange print beside the cartridge and wondering what it meant. Then, snapping out of his trance, he quickly took a couple of pictures of both the cartridge and the print, changed lenses and snapped a couple more, then picked up the cartridge and hurried back to the bush, taking a few seconds to rub out his own prints as he did so.

In the less-exposed but still questionable safety of the bush lining the roadside, Barnes took a moment to study the small cartridge. It was a pistol round about the size of a 9 mm but a little bit shorter. It wasn't quit small enough to be a .380 ACP, however. It seemed familiar, but in a vague, indistinct sort of way, and Barnes took a few seconds to place it. After all, he had only seen one round like it before, and that had been several years ago when he'd undergone foreign-weapons familiarization as part of his basic course of instruction at Fort Bragg. Barnes couldn't be positive, but he was reasonably certain that it was the 9 mm intermediate round used in the Soviet Makarov pistol that had pretty much replaced the Tokarev as Moscow's standard side arm.

Maybe the Russkies were providing the NVA with a new pistol, he thought. Maybe, but Barnes didn't think so. The smudged print he'd found in the dirt near the cartridge had been that of a hobnailed boot. To the best of his knowledge, the NVA wore canvas-and-rubber boots similar to a tennis shoe, and the VC favored sandals soled with the tread of worn-out tires. The print of a hobnailed boot and a new Soviet pistol cartridge were just about the last things Barnes had expected to find in the Laotian jungle, but then he hadn't expected to find a gravel road, either.

The Special Forces sergeant hurried back to the others, even more excited than Cheo and Papa-san had been about finding the gravel road. "Tim, get out your cipher pad and encrypt a message for Hillsboro to relay to the FOB," Barnes told Chelsea. "Give them our coordinates and tell them this: 'Have

found many recently used trails and roads, including one sur-
faced with crushed rock. Also found what appears to be 9 mm
Makarov round and print of hobnailed boot. Will watch road
for traffic.' Get that off as soon as you've encrypted it.''

Barnes knew he was taking a risk, although he felt it was
really only a small one. Anytime you transmitted using a PRC-
25, there was a chance the enemy RDF teams might pick up
the message. But a short transmission was difficult to pinpoint, and he judged the information to be worth the risk. If
there were Russian advisers in Laos, the military bigwigs
would want to know pronto.

2

THREE RIVERS SECRET ZONE

After a long, uneventful night spent on uncomfortably hard ground in a well-secured thicket, Barnes was awakened by Papa-san gently shaking his shoulder as the Sedang tribesman cupped a hand over the Green Beret's mouth. Barnes opened his eyes and nodded, and Papa-san took away his hand, then leaned close to whisper in the American's ear. "Sergeant Craig, we got *beaucoup* trouble. Chuckie come. I think maybe he look for us."

Barnes sat up, fully awake now. "How many? Where? How soon?"

"*Hai muoi,* maybe *hai muoi lam.* They follow our trail. Be here pretty quick. Maybe ten minute, tops."

"Twenty or twenty-five, huh?" Barnes said, glancing at his wristwatch. "What makes you think they're looking for us? It could be just a routine morning patrol."

"Negative, Sergeant Craig. Chuck looking for us. I sure. I wake early and think maybe backtrack, look see nobody leave trail for Chuck to follow. Make very sure all tracks wiped out. Blooper Man do good job, but maybe he miss something. Either that or Chuck have very good tracker. They move very slow. Study ground much, but follow route we take here almost exact.''

"You actually saw them, then?"

"Affirmative."

"Were they VC or NVA?" Barnes asked.

"They NVA. Wear uniform and canvas shoe. Have funny hat to keep off sun. The one like helmet, but weigh nothing. One man not same-same all others. His uniform different, made no-see-me like ours but not like same-same. Wear hat like you, like other Americans, only blue."

"A beret? He was wearing a blue beret?" Barnes asked. "Did you see this man well? What did he look like? Was he Chinese?"

"Yes. He wear blue beret. I no tell if Chinese. Not want get that close. He have face cover with paint same-same us."

Barnes turned to Searsboro, who had been awakened by their whispered conversation. "Jack, get everybody up. Roll up the claymores and be damn quick about it. We've got company coming. Papa-san thinks they're looking for us."

"What about the trip flares?" Searsboro asked.

Barnes glanced at his watch. "Screw the trip flares. We haven't got time. Just roll up the mines and let's get the hell out of here. We've got maybe eight minutes before they get here. I want to be gone in under five."

As Searsboro and the others scurried off, Barnes thought hard. What did it all add up to? Heavy traffic, hobnailed boots and a Soviet pistol cartridge. And now trackers and a soldier in an unusual camouflage uniform with a blue beret. Could it be a Chinese adviser? They had been known to work with the NVA before. Still, the hobnailed boot prints had been pretty big to have been made by an Asian, and while the Makarov was used by the Red Chinese, the Tokarev was more prevalent in Chicom inventory.

"Papa-san, think hard now," Barnes said. "This soldier in the strange uniform, what was he doing? Did he seem to be giving the orders, or was he just walking along with the rest?"

"He have box he look at," Papa-san said.

"What sort of box?"

Papa-san shrugged. "He carry box in hands and look at it every little bit. It have black cord connected to big box he carry on back, like radio, but have funny antenna."

"Describe the antenna," Barnes said, feeling a hollow sensation beginning to grow in the pit of his stomach.

Papa-san touched his fingertips and thumbs together in a circle. "It round. Like hoop with net Americans throw ball through."

"Fucking marvelous," Barnes said. "A directional antenna. It must be some sort of portable RDF gear. They must have picked up our transmission yesterday afternoon to Hillsboro, then sent out patrols of trackers equipped with RDF units to try to pinpoint us."

Barnes turned to the indigenous team leader. "Kue, this is a very bad situation. Charlie knows we're somewhere in the area and has sent out patrols to look for us. The patrols not only have trackers, but are apparently also using special radio equipment that'll allow them to pinpoint us if we transmit anything over our radios. It also looks like they may have Chinese advisers or technical troops helping them. This raises the question of what exactly the Chinese are doing here. Do you understand everything I've told you so far?"

"I understand everything, Sergeant Craig," Kue told him.

"Good. Now, then, what I'm about to suggest we do will be dangerous. Very dangerous. We have to be extremely careful or things could get even worse for us. It's extremely important that we know what the Chinese are doing here. The best way I know to find out why they're here is to capture one of the Chinese advisers. Since we know there's a Chinese with the patrol following us, I think it'll be best if we try to ambush the patrol.

"Here's the danger. There are twice as many NVA in the patrol as there are of us. Also we don't know how many other patrols may be looking for us and we don't know if the patrol following us has already alerted these other patrols by radio to the fact that they're on our trail. If we ambush them, and another patrol is nearby, we could suddenly find ourselves out-gunned by four or five to one instead of only two to one and we'll lose the element of surprise. On the other hand, if we wait too long, they may be able to call in other patrols and we could find ourselves surrounded.

"We've got to decide right now whether to risk ambushing the enemy patrol and trying to capture the Chinese or abandoning the mission and getting the hell out. Lying low and hoping they'll miss us and go on past isn't an option if their trackers are as good as Papa-san says they are. I ask you now for your opinion. What do you think we should do?"

"We must attack at once," Kue said. "To delay is only to bring more danger. If we attack now, perhaps we can capture the Chinese and get away to where the helicopters can pick us up before the enemy closes the noose around our necks."

"Terrific," Barnes said. "I was hoping you'd see it that way. We've got to send Cheo and Papa-san ahead to find a suitable ambush site and to scout out the area to make sure there are no enemy patrols in front of us. Then Blooper Man has to make sure the trail we leave isn't so easy to follow as to arouse enemy suspicion, yet clear enough that we don't lose the enemy. The hardest part will be the ambush itself. It's got to be a site that isn't too obvious, but which will ensure we can kill all the enemy except for the Chinese. No one must escape. Do you understand that?"

"I understand. We let no one get away."

"Good," Barnes said. "Now, then, once we've got a good site, we'll have to lead the enemy through it, then double back to set the ambush. I'll set up five claymores to cover the killing zone, but will only fire from two to four. Which claymores I fire will depend upon exactly where the Chinese is in the enemy column. He'll probably be near the center of it, but there's no guarantee of that. With luck the claymores may take out half to two-thirds of the enemy, but some NVA will survive. Those will be the ones nearest to the Chinese. I can't risk detonating a claymore aimed too closely toward him, because the Chinese might be killed also and we want him alive.

"You'll be near the front of the ambush site, I'll be in the middle and Sergeant Searsboro will be near the end. Each of us will have a CS grenade ready. When the claymores explode, whoever's nearest the Chinese will throw his grenade at the bastard. You may have to stand to get a good throw, so if you're the one doing the throwing, get up, make your toss and get back down as quickly as possible. Whoever throws will be exposed to enemy fire for the moment it takes him to toss the grenade.

"Blooper Man and one other Sedang will anchor the extreme ends of the ambush. If any of the claymores misfire, it'll be up to them to compensate with the M-79s, but they're not, I repeat, *not* to fire close to the Chinese. It's imperative that they understand this. If one of them drops a 40 mm grenade in the adviser's lap, all our work will be for nothing."

"I tell them be very careful," Kue assured Barnes.

"Good. Finally, and this'll be the hardest part, we've got to deal with the enemy soldiers closest to the Chinese. All of the men with rifles will shoot at these men first before they worry about anyone the claymores might have missed. The men will fire only on semiauto. No one, and I mean no one, is to fire on full-auto. Semiauto fire only, and they'd better shoot each man at least twice to make sure he goes down.

"Absolutely nobody is to shoot at the Chinese except Sergeant Searsboro, you or myself. We won't shoot at all if we can help it, but if he tries to get away, whoever's closest will shoot him in the legs. Nowhere else, just the legs. Aim any higher and we might accidently kill the bastard. If he isn't close to you or you don't have a good, clear shot, don't shoot at all. Understand?"

"Yes," Kue said. "Only Sergeant Jack or myself to shoot the Chinese, and only whoever's closest, and only in the legs. And we're not to shoot at all unless he try to run."

"And none of the men are to shoot at the NVA close to the Chinese if the NVA are within two yards of him or they don't have an absolutely clear field of fire. It's important that you tell them that."

"I tell," Kue replied, "but what we do about NVA if they stand too close?"

"Then you or I or Sergeant Searsboro will shoot them. Two shots apiece. No one else is to shoot at them."

"I understand and will tell men."

"Good," Barnes said. "Once the CS grenade pops, the Chinese and anyone near him will be gagging, coughing and crying their eyes out. With any luck at all, they'll be so busy being sick they won't even fight. The problem will come if they do. If we miss anybody with the claymores, don't get all the leftovers taken out with rifle fire or the gas doesn't work, we'll have to make an assault, because we can't risk hanging around until more bad guys show up.

"In that case I'll blow one long blast on my whistle, followed by two short ones. Everybody will then have to get up and attack the survivors. Remember, semiauto fire and aimed shots only. We'll have to get down there on top of them and kill whoever's left. Remember, too, that the gas will affect our men as well as the enemy, so we can't fool around. Just get down there, shoot the surviving NVA and grab the Chinese.

"If he doesn't want to come, we'll have to knock him out and carry him with us, but for Christ's sake don't kill him. Whatever you have to do, do it quick if you're the one who has to grab him. The longer you have to stay in the gas, the worse its effects will be and the longer they'll last. Tying a triangular bandage over your nose and mouth may help some, but not for long."

"I tell men to cover faces," Kue assured Barnes.

"All right, then. Explain it to your men and get Cheo and Papa-san started," Barnes told Kue. "Tell them to follow the gravel road and look for an intersecting dirt road or trail. If they don't find anything after five hundred yards, tell them to halt and wait for us to catch up."

Kue hurried off to find Cheo and Papa-san while Barnes made a check of the thicket to make sure no one had left any equipment behind. The area was clean, although it would be obvious to anyone who really looked that several men had spent the night there. What wouldn't be so obvious, given the arrangement of the sleeping positions, was that it had been a dozen men instead of only ten. Barnes wasn't sure what kind of advantage that might prove to be, but he figured it might come in handy to have two more men than the enemy thought you did.

Barnes checked his watch. It was time to go. Just then Searsboro appeared out of the bush and signaled to him. Barnes crawled out of the thicket, not being quite so careful as he had entering it, and went over to his assistant team leader.

"Ready to go," Searsboro reported. "Got all the claymores and managed to pull a couple of the flares. Had to leave the rest of them like you said."

"Good work, Jack," Barnes told him. "Have Blooper Man meet me at the road. Then take the rest of the team and move out. Parallel the road for about fifty yards, then pull out onto it and make some speed."

"You want us to walk on the road?" Searsboro asked incredulously.

"No, Jack. I want you to run. It'll be okay. I had Kue send Cheo and Papa-san ahead to scout. I don't want them picking up the scent too soon, but we've got to get far enough ahead to set things up. We're going to ambush the little bastards."

"Is this a good idea, Craig?"

"I hope so," Barnes said. "They apparently have a Chinese adviser with them and I want him. The only way we're going to get him is if we let them get us right where they want us, and then annihilate them."

"This I gotta see," Searsboro said, rubbing the stubble on his camouflaged skin.

"You will, Jack. At least I hope so. Now get going."

After Searsboro left, Barnes swung out in a wide loop, which brought him back to the road about thirty yards from where they had set up the OP to watch for traffic. The requirement for speed meant he wasn't able to move as carefully as he normally would have, and he left behind telltale but not particularly blatant evidence of his passage, which suited him just fine. He didn't want the enemy to get the idea they'd left in a real big hurry, but he didn't want to be so careful that the NVA lost the trail. Not yet, anyway.

He wanted them to waste a little time following RT Florida off the trail and into the thicket before they picked up the scent again. The trip flares they'd had to leave behind should help with that. If the NVA blundered into a wire and initiated one, they'd have to take the time to check the area very carefully once they'd changed their underwear. And if they found one without triggering it, they'd have to assume the recon patrol they were hunting was still in the immediate area and check things out very carefully, anyway. Either way the NVA patrol would waste a lot of time while RT Florida got ahead and had a chance to set up their ambush. With luck the simple ruse might buy them forty-five minutes to an hour.

Barnes found Blooper Man waiting beside the road and explained the situation to him. The men would leave no obvious prints in the gravel, and it would only be necessary to obliterate the shallow depressions left by their boots where the gravel was loose. The trick was to make the trail difficult enough to follow so that the enemy wouldn't catch on that they were being baited, while making it plain enough that a good tracker wouldn't overlook it.

Barnes and Blooper Man armed themselves with leafy branches and hurried down the road, being careful to rub out most but not quite all of the trail. Every fifteen to thirty yards they left a few boot-sized depressions in the loose gravel, just enough so that the enemy would be able to pick up the track again once they had lost it. They were almost out of earshot when Barnes heard the faint pop and whoosh of a trip flare, indicating that someone had walked into one of the difficult-to-see wires.

For just a moment Barnes wondered if he'd made a mistake. The NVA trackers were undoubtedly out front, and thus it was probable that one of them had initiated the flare. Barnes couldn't help thinking that maybe it would have been smarter to have left behind a few grenade traps or claymores with mechanical detonators hooked up to trip wires. What they planned was very risky, and it might have been a better situation if they had left behind booby traps to kill the trackers and just slipped away. That would have been the safe thing, the smart thing, to do, but it wouldn't have got them a prisoner, and Barnes wanted the Chinese adviser with the RDF gear. He wanted him bad.

They pushed on hard, both men sweating from the exertion of traveling fast with a heavy pack and the added burden of swinging the branches back and forth across the road to level the gravel surface. Once, when Barnes feared they had gone too far without leaving any clues, he took out one of his magazines, stripped a 5.56 round from the top and tossed it several yards back down the road behind them, where it glinted dully in the light filtering down through the overhead canopy of trees.

He hoped it wasn't too obvious a lure. A smart tracker following their trail might realize that such an object, which might have casually fallen from someone's pocket or ammo pouch, was unlikely to be overlooked by whoever was assigned to cover the tracks of the recon team, but it wasn't impossible for such a thing to be missed. After all, Barnes had found the Makarov round.

They had traveled nearly four hundred fifty yards when Kue hissed at them from the bush beside the road. "Up ahead, Sergeant Craig. Maybe twenty yards. Cheo find footpath off side of road. You look. See if okay what you want."

They moved forward to where Searsboro was waiting. "Where's the rest of the team?" Barnes asked.

"Scouting ahead for a suitable ambush site," Searsboro replied. "This trail suit you okay?"

Barnes studied the situation for a moment before answering. "It'll suit me just fine if it's got a good spot for the ambush," he finally said. "Jack, you take Blooper Man and get off the trail. With luck the bad guys will only figure there's ten of us. Stay close enough so that you can parallel us, but be careful you don't leave any signs. You two will anchor the tail of the ambush when we find the right spot. That way, even if they smell something and don't walk into the trap, you two should be in a good position to hit them from near the rear.''

Barnes quickly ran through his basic plan with Searsboro and Blooper Man, then made sure that all evidence of their leaving the trail was carefully removed before he and Kue continued onward. Barnes hoped the NVA trackers wouldn't be good enough to pick up on the difference between Searsboro's size ten medium-width boots and his own size nine narrows. The Sedangs' prints wouldn't be so much of a problem. They all wore narrow boots, either size seven or eight, and Kue and Blooper Man wore the same size.

Two hundred yards along they found the others waiting for them at a perfect spot. The trail made a sharp turn to the right, ran more or less straight for about eighty-five yards and then made another sharp turn to the left before it wound up a hill. There was no ridge or bank, which would have made the site too ideal and might have provoked suspicion in the enemy, but the trees and bushes grew in close along the sides and offered ample hiding places for Barnes's men. The biggest problem would be protecting his own men from the back-blast of the claymores, but Barnes figured he could eliminate most of the secondary missile hazard by placing the mines at the bases of trees.

Barnes placed Blooper Man right at the curve of the first turn where he could fire his M-79 in either direction, then sited a claymore in the overhead branches of a nearby tree, angled downward at about a forty-five degree angle so that it could rake the bottom third of the straight stretch of trail. As an added precaution, he then sited a second claymore to fire down the trail away from the ambush site, placing it about fifteen yards back along the way they'd come and angling it to fire even farther back up the trail. Barnes tested both circuits and then gave the firing control for the extra mine to Blooper Man.

''There are only three situations in which you're to use this,'' Barnes explained. ''First, if the enemy detects or suspects our ambush and either attacks or attempts to go around it. Second, if I'm forced to spring the ambush before all the enemy are in the killing zone. Third, if I spring the ambush and enemy reinforcements arrive. Don't fire the mine under any other circumstance. Understand?"

"Understand," the Sedang told him.

"Good. You know how the mine works?"

"Yes," Blooper Man said. "I use before. To fire, I move little wire square out of way and squeeze lever quick."

"That's right," Barnes told him. "And what do you do if the mine doesn't fire when you squeeze the lever?"

"I pull up lever and squeeze again."

"And what if that still doesn't work?"

Blooper Man smiled. "If that no work, and I have time, can cut off plug, strip wire and hold ends of wire against two flashlight battery, but I no think I have that much time. So if mine no fire when I pull up lever and squeeze again, I use M-79 instead. If that no work, then I think maybe we all in world of shit."

Barnes smiled back. "All right, just remember, don't use it unless you absolutely have to. And keep your head down. Both of these mines are going to be uncomfortably close."

"No worry, Sergeant Craig," the Sedang said. "Blooper Man no lose head over NVA."

"One more thing," Barnes said. "Give me your green cord."

Each man on the team carried a hundred-foot roll of green nylon parachute cord in his left breast pocket. Blooper Man pulled his out of his pocket and handed it over. Barnes made a solid loop in one end and handed it back to the Sedang.

"Loop this loosely over your left hand so you won't lose it. Sergeant Searsboro will have the other end. When you see the enemy, give two slow pulls on the cord to let him know. If the last man in the enemy patrol walks past you and I still haven't initiated the ambush, pull three times like this, slow, quick, slow. If anything goes wrong, give at least five quick pulls. We can't risk breaking squelch on the radios, because we know they've got RDF gear, and if they pick anything up, it could screw up the ambush."

Blooper Man repeated the instructions as he had been taught to do to make sure he had understood them correctly. "Pull two times slow when see NVA. Pull slow, quick, slow if last man pass me and no ambush yet. Pull five times quick if something go wrong."

"All right," Barnes said. "Get situated and get comfortable. We might have to wait anywhere from forty-five minutes to a couple of hours."

Barnes was banking on the NVA following a natural tendency to bunch up when moving in a column on a good trail nearly six and a half feet wide, but he couldn't guarantee that. If the enemy was keeping an interval between each man, the spacing would probably be somewhere between three and five yards. Figuring a minimum of twenty men at three yards and a maximum of twenty-five men at five-yard intervals, he had to be prepared for an ambush that could stretch anywhere from fifty-seven yards to a hundred and twenty yards in length. Since the electrical firing cords on the claymores were only a hundred feet long, he could at best cover something under two-thirds of the maximum distance, although the fragments from the mines should be lethal for an additional fifty yards on either end. That was more than enough to cover the area, but Barnes believed in playing it safe, which was why he had sited the second mine in the tree and angled it to rake the trail.

He got Searsboro into position, made sure the man had good cover, both from incoming fire and mine fragments, and had a CS grenade laid out in front of him with the pin partially straightened, not enough to fall out, but enough to make pulling it easier. Then he gave Searsboro the control for the second mine.

"Jack, I'm counting on you to back me up on this. If things work according to plan, you won't have to do anything but sit back and watch the show. That, and relay Blooper Man's tugs to me on the string. If things don't go according to plan, however, you may have to fire this thing. Use it if I don't get everybody and the survivors try to fall back or if the next clay-more up the line doesn't fire when I pop the rest of them. Don't use it if the Chinese guy's in the killing zone. He should be easy to recognize. Papa-san said he was the only one wear-ing a camouflage uniform, that he had on a blue beret and that he was carrying the RDF gear. If our target's in front of you when the ambush pops, pitch your grenade as close to him as you can get it, then get back down and start shooting at any-one left standing except the Chinese. If he runs, wing him if you have to, but for Christ's sake shoot low. We need him alive. Dead, he can't tell us squat.''

Barnes and the rest of the team then moved along the trail, carefully dusting out some but not all of their footprints, then doubled back to their ambush positions. Barnes set out four claymores, separating each of them by fifteen yards. He tested the continuity of the firing circuit of each mine with an M-40 test set and replaced the combination shorting-plug/dust-covers on the firing lines, then screwed the shipping-plug/priming-adapters with their M-4 electric blasting caps back into place in one of the detonator wells on each mine.

When he finished, he sited his safety mine, another clay-more, on the curve at the head of the ambush, designed to rake back down the trail, as he had placed the mine Searsboro con-trolled at the other end. It could be used in the event the front of the enemy column wasn't caught in the killing zone of the most forward two of the four mines he had placed alongside the trail.

In the meantime Chelsea and Cheo had been sent back to the road to make sure that they left just enough evidence to indi-cate the team had taken the footpath off the road. And Papa-san had been sent to a position beyond the upper bend in the trail as safety man on the left flank of the ambush, while Kue took his spot near the curve, with another Sedang right on the bend, where he could support either the ambush or Papa-san with the other M-79. Like Searsboro, Kue would control the safety claymore at the head of the ambush, as well as stand by with a CS grenade and be ready to shoot any survivors closest to the Chinese.

The rest of the team filled in along the side of the trail between the mines, then got down under cover. When Chelsea and Cheo returned, they took their places in line.

Barnes inspected each man's position individually, stringing a nylon line between Searsboro's and his own position and between his position and Kue's. An additional line ran from Kue to Papa-san to give warning of enemy approach from that direction. All in all, it took about half an hour to set things up properly, inspect the positions and test the firing circuits on the mines. Barnes then returned to his own position and attached the M-57 electrical firing devices to each of the four mines he would control, laying them out in order immediately in front of him.

After that there was nothing to do except wait for the guests of honor to put in their appearance.

3

THREE RIVERS SECRET
ZONE

Barnes lay behind a fallen log of comforting thickness—the firing lines of the claymores running beneath it through the shallow hole he had scooped out—feeling the sweat running down his face and sides. Despite the overhead canopy of the trees, there was no coolness or breeze here. Not even the hint of an occasional gust to bring temporary relief. All around him the jungle was a hot, dark, steaming twilight, broken only irregularly by the brilliant shafts of sunlight filtering down through the leaves.

Yet the jungle was by no means silent. There were the periodic calls of birds and the occasional rustlings of some small animal or snake slithering through the grass now that the jungle's natural inhabitants had decided there was no danger after the disturbance the team had created when they first entered the area. And, of course, there was the incessant whine and buzz of mosquitoes and flies.

Easing back the cuff of his glove, Barnes peeled back the black electrical tape protecting the crystal and bent his head a few inches to consult his watch. It was almost ten o'clock and still the enemy hadn't put in an appearance. Perhaps Florida had done too good a job of covering their tracks, or the expertise of the NVA trackers wasn't as great as Papa-san had believed. In any event, the time was fast approaching when Barnes would have to declare the ambush attempt a bust, roll up the mines and think about moving on.

While the delay could mean the enemy had lost the trail or was simply proceeding with extreme caution, it could also mean they had either smelled the trap and were waiting for reinforcements to arrive or that they were systematically tightening the search area and waiting for other patrols to get into position.

Knowing that the enemy was looking for Florida, and not knowing the exact disposition of NVA patrols in the area, Barnes felt they would be safer to move and look for the enemy than to wait for the NVA to come to them. The ambush, of course, would alert any patrols within earshot when triggered, but while the NVA would be moving toward the sound of the ambush, RT Florida would be moving away. And unless they ran directly into an enemy patrol, Barnes felt they stood a good chance of slipping between the NVA units.

The procedure called for exact timing and a bit of luck, as well as a great deal of skill, but it had been done before. That was all part of the calculated risk Barnes was willing to accept in order to get a chance at grabbing the Chinese adviser. But there were limits. He knew the longer they delayed, the greater the risks. If Charlie and his Chinese friend didn't appear soon, the risk would become greater than Barnes was willing to take. Therefore, he decided he would give the enemy another forty-five minutes and then call it quits.

With Papa-san's alarm of the approaching NVA patrol coming as it had at first light, the men of RT Florida hadn't had time to eat breakfast, take a dump or drain their kidneys—facts that Barnes's stomach, intestines and bladder had been reminding him of for the past hour. Eating or leaving his position to take a squat was out of the question, but having last urinated at around 11:00 p.m., Barnes could no longer ignore the persistent pressure in his groin.

Taking a good, full minute to do so, he slid about a foot to his left, following the gentle, downward slope of the ground, then rolled slowly up on his right side, no more than forty-five degrees, and unbuttoned his fly. Quietly he relieved himself, painfully controlling his muscles so that the urine barely trickled out onto the ground. When he finished, he felt much better and carefully eased himself back into his original position.

Barnes had scarcely relieved himself when he felt two strong tugs on the nylon line looped loosely around his right hand. Searsboro was relaying the signal from Blooper Man that the enemy was in sight.

Barnes gave a single pull in return, acknowledging the message, then picked up the loop of the second line lying near his left hand, took up the slack and gave two firm pulls on it, passing the information on to Kue. A moment later he felt the single tug of acknowledgment from the Sedang leader. Barnes slipped the loop off his right hand and quietly unsnapped the cover of one of the full canteens on his belt, eased the safety of his CAR-15 off and checked that the selector was in semi-auto position.

Laying the weapon carefully beside him, he slipped the nylon loop back over his right hand. There was enough slack in both lines to allow him to reach forward and pick up two of the firing devices for the claymores, and he did so, selecting the first and last. Gently he moved the wire safety bales out of position and put the controls back on the ground. Then he picked up the two middle firing devices and held them reversed in his hands so that he could flick the safety bales down out of the way with the index finger of either hand. As he held them ready, Barnes became aware of a subtle change in the jungle. The birds had stopped squawking. Now only the discordant buzz of the mosquitoes and flies remained.

Barnes realized he had been unconsciously holding his breath and forced himself to breathe shallowly. He could hear the pulse of his own heart thudding in his ears, despite the sound of the insects, and irrationally feared the enemy would somehow hear it, too. He wished with all his might that he could stop the fist-sized muscle beating within his chest for only a minute or two, could temporarily survive without the exchange of oxygen and carbon dioxide in his lungs, so that there would be nothing to betray his presence to the NVA until it was too late. His ears strained to sort out any sound that might give away the enemy's approach from the background drone of bugs now attacking his ears with impunity. After what seemed an eternity, he felt two more tugs on his right hand. Searsboro had now spotted the enemy.

Almost subconsciously Barnes began counting the seconds in his head. He had reached 296, nearly a full five minutes, before he heard a soft footfall on the trail and a faint, metallic clank, like that of a sling swivel against a rifle. A moment later the first NVA, easily distinguished by his gray-green pith helmet, came into view. He walked bent over in a low crouch, intently studying the ground before him, his rifle, an AK-47, hanging across his chest by the strap running over his left shoulder and meeting the buttstock of the rifle under his right arm. Behind him, less than two yards away, walked a second soldier, his rifle held ready in his hands. As he nervously scanned the sides of the trail and the branches overhead, the barrel of his AK followed his gaze, pointing first left, then up ahead, swinging across to the right, then back up and left again. The tracker and his cover man.

Barnes kept his head down and looked at the men out from under the brim of his boonie hat, and then only through slitted eyes and only in quick glances. Like many soldiers, he had a limited but real belief in the supernatural and the paranormal and feared that if he stared at one of the enemy too long, the NVA would, through some sixth sense, detect he was being watched. Yet if the North Vietnamese soldiers' ESP was working that day, it failed them, for they passed Barnes with only a casual glance in his general direction.

As soon as they were past, Barnes tugged twice on the line to let Kue know the lead element of the enemy patrol had now reached him, and felt the answering tug. There was nothing to do now but wait. Barnes counted nine more men pass his position, each with from three to five yards between himself and the men to his front and rear. All were armed with AKs except for one man who carried an SKS with a telescopic sight mounted ahead of the receiver. Then, right about where he had expected him to be in the line, Barnes spotted his man.

It was hard to make out his face through the grass and leaves, and a second man, an NVA, walked beside him, partially obscuring him, but the camouflage uniform was distinctive from the solid dark green of the NVA. As they approached, Barnes caught a brief flash of blue, the beret on the Chinese adviser's head, and the hint of a face masked with camouflage makeup. Then they were directly opposite him and he could see the man's tan leather boots.

The target was passing him by, and still Barnes had had no signal relayed from Searsboro that the end of the enemy column had passed Blooper Man's position. As the two men passed on, Barnes put down the firing control he had held in his left hand and carefully picked up the one farthest to his left—which he had previously removed the safety from—noting as he did so that the target seemed unusually large for a Chinese. It was time for the moment of decision. Should he wait for the signal and trust Kue to get the Chinese, or should he pop the mines now without knowing how many of the enemy had yet to enter the killing zone?

It was then that he felt three tugs on his right hand.

Barnes didn't bother to answer. His reply would be plain enough. Without hesitation he flipped off the safety bale of the firing device in his right hand and squeezed hard on both levers, burying his face in the ground.

The metallic explosions rang through the air almost simultaneously as the first and third mines detonated. Long before the debris had stopped raining through the trees, Barnes seized the control for the fourth mine and fired it, as well. Barnes didn't delay to inspect the results of his handiwork, but yanked the pin from his CS grenade and hurled it with all his might toward the camouflage-suited man with the RDF gear. The grenade hit him square in the back as he darted for cover.

Had Barnes been able to witness the scene from a better vantage point, he would have been both pleased and a little sickened. The effects of the claymores were devastating. As the fan-shaped clouds of steel balls spread outward from the exploding mines, men were literally shredded like tissue paper. Some had a hand or a foot severed. One was cut right off at the knees. Another had his entire left arm reduced to something resembling a heavily tenderized minute steak. Most simply developed a very fatal case of the measles, as though they had been shotgunned with large-bore, double-barreled scatterguns at close range. One soldier was actually torn in half by the blast and expanding cloud of heavy steel balls that had enveloped him.

The air was filled with an acrid blue haze from the detonated plastic explosive of the mines, and the scent of suddenly heated and compressed metal mingled with the coppery odor of fresh blood. For an instant even the flies grew silent, and an eerie quiet hung over the jungle.

The calm was short-lived, though. As Barnes heard the popping of M-16s firing on semiauto, he lifted his head and raised the muzzle of his own rifle over the log. One man was still standing in the middle of the trail, apparently untouched by the claymores, but dazed. Barnes sighted carefully with his CAR-15 and squeezed the trigger twice, putting one round into the man's chest and a second into his right side as he spun toward the ground.

For a moment there was nothing, then another man, stricken by the CS, rose to his knees. He gagged and coughed as he wiped furiously at his face with his sleeve. Barnes sighted again and shot the man in the head and back, the high-speed 5.56 mm bullet carrying away a fine mist of blood and brain tissue, mixed with bone chips as the NVA's head popped, while the second round cut through the man's spine, dropping him like a puppet that had lost its strings.

There were a couple more pops from M-16s, but no return fire from the ambushed NVA. Barnes rose cautiously to one knee, weapon ready, and blew three blasts on his whistle.

Except for Papa-san and Blooper Man, who continued to hold their positions, providing flank security for the ambush, the remainder of RT Florida rose as one man and attacked the ambushed NVA. The Sedang and Americans showed neither mercy nor selectivity. There was no time to determine which enemy soldiers were uninjured, dead or wounded. Any NVA encountered was immediately dispatched with a bullet to the head. None was given the opportunity to surrender. There was only one person RT Florida was interested in, and he had to be taken alive.

Barnes had marked the position of the Chinese adviser just before he triggered the claymores, and he charged directly for that spot, trying to ignore the stinging, choking cloud of CS. The white powder was everywhere. Through tearing eyes, he spotted the huddled form of the camouflage-suited man with the blue beret and ran directly toward him, pausing only long enough to put bullets into the bodies of the NVA he passed. As he reached the Chinese, the coughing man tried to bring up his AK-47. In one fluid motion Barnes yanked his full canteen from its cover and swung it, striking the man alongside the head and stunning him.

Barnes kicked aside the man's AK-47, grabbed him by the straps of his radio and dragged him toward the edge of the jungle, leaving the rest of the team to take care of mopping up. The man was heavy. He felt as if he weighed close to two hundred pounds. With the exertion of dragging the man, Barnes was breathing hard, sucking in great lungfuls of CS, and he'd barely reached the log he'd hidden behind earlier when he had to stop and vomit. His prisoner took no advantage of the opportunity to try to escape, however. He seemed to be having enough problems of his own just trying to breathe. When he had finished puking, Barnes pulled the man to his feet and shoved him ahead, forcing him deeper into the jungle and away from the noxious CS.

When he could run no farther, Barnes collapsed and vomited again. Afterward he felt a bit better. They were clear of the gas now, and its effects on him were beginning to lessen. The prisoner, however, had been only a few feet away from the grenade when it had burst, and his clothing was covered with fine white powder. He showed no interest in anything other than being thoroughly miserable.

Barned uncapped his canteen and used the water to flush his own eyes and rinse the taste of regurgitated LRRP rations out of his mouth. His eyes were still tearing, and it remained hard to catch his breath, but he was functional. He took the little plastic box out of his left breast pocket and pulled out one of the morphine Syrettes, then used his knife to slit open the prisoner's sleeve. He could feel the CS on the man's uniform beginning to get to him. So he worked quickly, pulling back the man's sleeve and taking a look. He was in luck. The man had veins like ropes.

After he administered the medication, Barnes slipped the straps of the radio off the man's shoulders, yanked off the prisoner's CS-contaminated shirt and tossed it aside. Then he forced the man facedown on the ground, pulled his arms behind him and used a couple of feet of parachute cord to tie the prisoner's wrists and elbows together. By then Barnes was ready to vomit again. He did so, then backed away from the CS-dusted prisoner to catch his breath. The prisoner continued to lie facedown on the ground, crying and vomiting at intervals.

Barnes was seated on a tree stump, his eyes still red and moist, when Searsboro, eyes streaming, found him a few minutes later. "You okay?" Searsboro wheezed, coughing and spitting.

"I'm fine," Barnes answered. "At least I will be in a couple more minutes."

"The prisoner?"

"I don't think you could say he's fine, too," Barnes said. "Sicker than a dog is more like it. He's secure. I gave him some morphine sulfate. He ought to prove fairly cooperative if he ever gets done puking his guts out. Did we lose anybody?"

"No casualties," Searsboro reported, dropping beside Barnes. "We got twenty-seven NVA KIA, confirmed. Chelsea and a couple of the Sedangs are checking the bodies for papers and stuff, and Kue is collecting the claymores we didn't use. We ought to be able to pull out of here in a couple of minutes."

"Fine, fine," Barnes said absently. "Tell me, Jack, do you notice anything odd about our prisoner?"

Searsboro blinked away the tears and had a look. "Well, he's not wearing a shirt anymore," he said at last.

"I took that off," Barnes said. "He was covered with CS. Look again. It's so obvious that it ought to leap right out at you. I was so busy just trying to breathe that I didn't even notice it when I shot him up with the morphine. It didn't register until after I got clear and started breathing again."

Searsboro studied the huddled, vomiting form for a moment and then it hit him. "Well, I'll be a son of a bitch. The bastard's Caucasian."

"He's more than that, Jack. Take a good, close look at his uniform. The son of a bitch is a goddamn Russkie."

"Fuck," Searsboro said, "you're right. A Russian paratrooper."

4

FIFTH SPECIAL FORCES, FORWARD OPERATING BASE KONTUM, RVN

Sergeants First Class Ross Hartwick and Bill Killduff of RTs Wyoming and Nevada respectively sat in the PCOD lounge, a long, dark room with a plywood bar running along one end, enjoying a couple of beers. A dreadfully expensive stereo tape deck, its mammoth speakers mercifully silent for the moment, sat behind the bar near the plywood shelves, which held an assortment of liquor bottles.

With its crude furnishings and black-painted concrete floor, the lounge had little to recommend it as a drinking establishment except for two small details. One, it was the only one around, and two, it was air-conditioned. The beer Hartwick and Killduff drank, PBR, had little to recommend it, either, except that unlike Vietnamese beer, it wasn't made with a formaldehyde base and it was the only *cold* beer available at that hour. The bartender, an administrative specialist with the HQ detachment who did double duty shuffling mugs and shots when he wasn't busy typing up requisitions and orders, hadn't finished restocking yet from the previous night.

Staff Sergeant Larry Larsen, Killduff's ATL, had just returned from the bar, bringing them another round of the cold but mediocre beers from the ice-filled cooler beneath the bar, when Hartwick belched, pushed back his chair and folded his hands across his belly, Buddha-like. He belched again and nodded sagely before speaking. "You know, William, I've just figured out what the problem is."

"And what's that, old pal?" Killduff responded.

"It's simple, William. In fact, I'm amazed it didn't occur to me before, what with the powers of my marvelous intellect. Hell, even you should have seen it."

Killduff glared at his friend. "So what's your pearl of wisdom?"

Hartwick squinted carefully, as if to see a distant object better, then raised a finger more or less skyward. "The problem, William, is that the World has gone to hell since John Wayne died."

Killduff nodded thoughtfully, as though he had just received the key to the ultimate mystery and was considering what to do with it.

"What the hell are you guys talking about?" Larsen asked as he set down the beers. "John Wayne ain't dead yet."

"At ease, Wild Larry," Killduff said. "What the Great Rosco means is that since the concept, the role model, if you will, of the Duke has passed onward, it's not so much the Great Man Himself as the life-style he portrayed that's dead and gone."

"Ah, you guys are nuts," Larsen decided.

"Not at all," Hartwick insisted. "The Duke represented the life-style of a simpler man, one who lived by three simple rules. Not to be wronged, not to be lied to and not to be trifled with. He didn't do these things to other people and he required only the same from them in return. The frontier ethic is, I fear, forever dead."

"Ah, that's a bunch of crap," Larsen said, snorting.

"Is it, Wild Larry?" Killduff said. "Just think for a minute. The days of the law of the simple man are gone and with them the days of the exceptional man. We've entered the days of the civilized, common man. Even the Army recognizes it.

That's why they give everybody a full-auto M-16. Only an exceptional man can become a really first-rate rifleman. You have to be good to pick a man off at five hundred yards with a single bullet, but any slouch can hose down the jungle at 850 rounds per minute. He may not hit anybody, but he sure as hell can burn up enough ammo to keep the factories running. We've become so civilized we don't even know how to fight anymore. I only hope we don't civilize ourselves right out of existence."

Larsen studied his beer for a minute, took a careful sip and then quietly said, "I see where you guys are coming from, but I guess I'm still a little confused. I sort of thought *we* were the uncommon men."

"That we are, Wild Larry, that we are," Killduff said. "Which is why none of us has any home but the Special Forces."

"I sure hope you guys are wrong about that," Larsen told him. "I been puttin' away some money each payday. Just a little bit, but enough to make me a down payment on a ranch someday. One of these days I'm gonna quit this man's Army and go back to Cheyenne, or maybe Laramie, buy myself a little piece of land and a few head of cattle and find out whether you guys knew what you were talkin' about."

"Hell, Larry, the way the mining companies have been raping the western states, by then land values will be so high you'll be lucky if you can afford a few acres and a cow," Hartwick growled.

"Maybe. Maybe not," Larsen said. "We'll see."

"Has anybody heard anything about Craig Barnes?" Killduff asked after a moment, changing the subject.

Everybody at the FOB knew that RT Florida had gone out to the Three Rivers Secret Zone, and everybody knew what had happened to Louisiana, Illinois and California the last time they had gone out there.

Hartwick shrugged and shook his head. "The Old Man's as tight-lipped as an unpaid whore these days. You ask me, I think he's worried. The NVA's up to something big and nasty over the border, and he knows it. What he doesn't know is what."

IN HIS OFFICE, a Spartan affair in the concrete administration building, Colonel Charlie Khan, the Old Man, slowly read over the message that had been handed to him by the duty signals supervisor. Then he reread it. When he finished, he dismissed the man, then got up from his desk and went out to speak to his sergeant major, Stewart Baxter.

"Stew," he said quietly, "I want a meeting of all Spike Recon Team leaders and assistant team leaders in the bar in twenty minutes. I'll see the Hatchet Forces leaders and the SLAM Company commanders in the isolation compound briefing room in forty-five minutes. And I want to see all staff officers in my office now."

"Now? All of them?" Baxter asked.

"All of them," Khan said. "The only exception is if they're in hospital or off the base."

Twenty minutes later to the second, Colonel Khan walked into the PCOD lounge with Captain Al Kellog, and the entire room snapped to attention.

"Be seated, men," Khan said. "I won't keep you long. The bar is now officially closed, but only until after the meeting."

Killduff, Hartwick and Larsen exchanged glances. It wasn't customary for Colonel Khan to call an impromptu meeting of most of the FOB personnel in the bar. Whatever the news was, from the look on Captain Kellog's face, it wasn't good.

"I won't bore you with a lot of details," said Khan. "Most of you know that Craig Barnes took RT Florida into Prairie Fire yesterday morning. They were operating in the Three Rivers area. This morning they ambushed an NVA patrol and captured a prisoner, requesting the earliest possible extraction through Hillsboro. A short time later they radioed Hillsboro again, stating they had encountered heavy enemy contact and had been cut off from their designated pickup point. Extraction and Medevac helicopters were then dispatched to the alternate pickup site with heavy gunship escort, but were unable to land due to intense antiaircraft fire. The final message we received from Sergeant Barnes stated that their position was being overrun and that he was going to detonate his remaining claymores and attempt to escape and evade on foot. That last transmission ended in a burst of AK-47 fire. I want two teams to go in there and find out what happened to Florida and bring out any survivors. If there are no survivors, I want the bodies. And I don't want to lose any more men in the process. Is that clear?''

There was a murmured "Yes, sir" from around the room.

"I'll have two Hatchet Forces on five-minute standby and a SLAM Company held in reserve if you get into hot water and need help," Khan continued. Then he paused for a moment and looked at each man in turn. "I hate to ask this of any man, but somebody has got to go out there and bring those boys home. Now, then, are there any volunteers?''

There were twenty RTLs in the room, along with the ATLs. Forty hands stabbed the air.

IT WAS MIDAFTERNOON when the recon teams went in. Hartwick and Kilduff had won the luck of the draw because their teams were the most familiar with the area after Barnes's and the three RTs, California, Illinois and Louisiana, that had had the snot shot out of them a few weeks earlier. In other circumstances either Hartwick or Kilduff might have considered it a questionable honor, but for once both men were glad of the assignment. Somewhere in the jungle below them were recon men who needed help, if they were still alive. They were there of their own choosing. They had volunteered to do it. Besides, Genghis Khan had asked them to do it.

The recon teams were loaded for bear. They carried twice as much ammunition, grenades and claymores as they normally would have, and they only had food for two days. All six Americans had traded their CAR-15s for suppressed Swedish Ks, and each of the indigenous team leaders had been issued with a .22-caliber Ruger semiautomatic pistol whose silencer was so efficient that the weapon produced little more noise than the operation of the pistol's bolt. While the stopping power of the diminutive cartridge left a lot to be desired, a head shot with one of the little .22s was a fast, effective way to take out an enemy sentry, and both safer and quieter than doing it with a knife.

The rest of the operation was similarly upscale. Besides the four helicopters carrying the two teams, there were eight Cobra gunships and two Huey Hogs, UH-1B Aerial Rocket Artillery choppers carrying forty-eight 2.75-inch folding-fin rockets, a 40 mm grenade launcher and two M-60 machine guns apiece. Mindful of the reports of heavy antiaircraft fire, the Army Aviation boys had also brought along a 12.7 killer. Enemy antiaircraft machine guns were usually the Degtyarev-Shpagin 12.7 mm, a gas-operated weapon roughly equivalent in performance to the .50-caliber Browning U.S. heavy machine gun. The 12.7 killer was a specially modified Huey with two 20 mm automatic cannons in pods on either side of the cabin. The 20 mm guns had over three times the range of the 12.7s and fired explosive ammunition. There were two Medevac ships, and Colonel Khan himself rode in the C and C ship with Captain Kellog.

They might as well have left it all at home. The insertions, one each into LZs bracketing the last known position of RT Florida, were cold.

As Bill Killduff and his RTO, Sergeant Phil Grinnell, dropped from the skid of the Huey slick into the high grass along with their four indigenous troopers, Killduff was painfully aware of one bit of unwelcome news. On the way in the radios had been silent on the primary frequency and alternates assigned to RT Florida. Even the Guard emergency frequency had been ominously quiet, and each member of the recon team had carried an AN/URC-10. There might still be someone from the team alive, a man who had lost his radio, or someone whose radio didn't work. Then again, maybe a survivor was afraid to transmit with the enemy so close. Maybe, but Killduff didn't think so. It wasn't impossible, but the odds against it were terrific.

Killduff linked up with Larsen and the rest of the team, then made a quick check of the immediate area. There was no sign of enemy activity.

As rapidly as they could without taking unnecessary risks, RT Nevada headed for the last reported position of RT Florida, while RT Wyoming closed in from the opposite direction. The helicopters could stay on-station for only forty-five minutes or so, after which they would have to break off to refuel. From then on until they could be made ready to fly again, Nevada and Wyoming would be on their own. So that they wouldn't be completely uncovered during that time, four of the Cobras and one of the Hogs would go ahead and break off in fifteen minutes if no enemy contact were made. That way they should be well under way with their refueling by the time the other helicopters had to leave and able to respond on short notice if Killduff and Hartwick ran into major trouble. They would also be able to provide escort for the Hatchet Forces standing by at Kontum.

The real problem would come in a few hours at nightfall. If they hadn't found what was left of RT Florida by then, they would lose their air cover, and a decision would have to be made whether to laager up and remain overnight in the field or extract and have another go at it in the morning. Each situation had its own set of problems. At night it was difficult to coordinate close air support, should the alert aircraft be needed, and it was even more difficult to arrange a successful extraction, particularly if it had to be made under fire. Charlie liked to come out at night because the darkness hid him from U.S. and Vietnamese air power, and RTs Wyoming and Nevada could suddenly find themselves in the middle of a swarming anthill of NVA troops. On the other hand, if survivors of Florida were pinned down somewhere by the close proximity of NVA troops, they might only be able to move at night to slip away, and pulling out till morning would leave them at the mercy of any NVA forces in the area until Wyoming and Nevada could return with the dawn.

Having performed their radio check-ins with Hillsboro and assured themselves that their commo link with the C and C ship, Medevac choppers and helicopter gunships were secure, Wyoming and Nevada thereafter maintained radio silence. The enemy had somehow pinpointed RT Florida in a hurry, and the possibility of NVA RDF capability had to be considered.

Fifteen minutes into the search Grinnel reported to Killduff that he had received the code message "Goodbye, Mr. Chips," telling them that the first of the Hogs and four Cobra gunships had peeled out of their holding orbits and were on their way back to Kontum to refuel. There was no acknowledgment, as none was expected. Thirty minutes later Grinnell again reported, copying the message "Aloha," which let them know that the remainder of the escort, C and C ship and evac choppers had turned back. Again they didn't acknowledge the message.

Wyoming and Nevada now pressed on alone, searching the ground ahead of them and the jungle foliage around them for any sign of Florida, as well as being alert for signs of NVA activity or booby traps. For three solid hours they traveled without rest through the steaming afternoon heat, moving at the maddeningly slow pace required to avoid detection themselves while searching for clues to the fate of their comrades.

It was Cowboy who found the first body.

Cowboy, Killduff's indigenous team leader and interpreter, and Larsen's protégé in the John Wayne fan club, had gone forward to see if he could get the point man to pick things up a bit. He paused to pull off his Air Commando hat, which he wore cowboy style with the brim curled up at both sides, and wiped the sweat from his face. Then, suddenly, he spotted something out of the ordinary and whirled. His hat fell as he pulled his .357 Magnum Smith & Wesson revolver out of the low-slung western rig that he wore in imitation of Larsen and brought the barrels of both it and his M-16 up to the ready position.

Cowboy listened carefully for a moment, then gradually identified the sound and reholstered his revolver. He retrieved his hat and poked cautiously through the bush to one side. As he eased out into the tiny clearing, the buzzing of flies he had heard intensified, and his nostrils flared at the sickly sweet odor of death.

It was one of RT Florida's indigenous troops, a Sedang grenadier nicknamed Elephant Man because of his prodigious manhood. He had been shot several times and was in the middle of a large pool of blood, thick with flies. He had been stripped naked and propped against the base of a tree, with his once truly remarkable equipment now severed and stuffed into his mouth. A crudely lettered cardboard sign hung around his neck from a piece of vine. In Vietnamese it proclaimed Green Beret Lackey Stay Home. Laos Not Your Country. You Come Here, Die Like Cocksucker Dog.

Cowboy wasn't sure what a cocksucker dog was supposed to be, but the sentiment was clear enough. He had seen mutilated bodies before, and worse than this, but Elephant Man was well liked among the Sedang, and Cowboy had considered him a friend. Cowboy was overcome with rage and frustration, and then a feeling of heat and nausea swept over him and he had to step off to one side and vomit before returning to the others to tell them what he had found.

They discovered the rest of RT Florida scattered over half a square mile. The enemy had made no effort to conceal the bodies. Neither had they bothered to move the Florida troopers any great distance from the slaughtering ground. Each of the indigenous team members had been stripped, mutilated and propped against a tree or log, as had Elephant Man, and a few of them had been necklaced with signs bearing the same sentiment as the grenadier's.

The Americans were the last to be located, although that didn't necessarily mean they had been the last to die. The NVA had been slightly more inventive with Craig Barnes and Tim Chelsea, although their grammar hadn't improved, despite the fact that the sign painter had switched to English. After they had cut off the men's penises, they hadn't stuffed them into the corpses' mouths as they had done with the Sedang tribesmen, but instead had placed the Americans facedown and stuck their severed members between their buttocks. Afterward someone had scrawled a message in each man's own blood across his hips. Both messages were the same. They said simply Go Phuc Self Green Beret.

The final corpse was the most grisly of all. His manhood was still intact, but the NVA had cut off his hands and head, which were missing altogether. Killduff squatted near the handless, decapitated body and stared at the scene in puzzlement for some time before he finally got to his feet. "I don't know who the fuck this guy is, but whoever he was he sure as hell ain't Jack Searsboro."

"What the hell are you talking about?" Larsen demanded. "Of course that's him. Who the hell else could it be? The poor bastard."

Killduff shook his head. "Guess again, Larry. Jack Searsboro was born with a double hernia. He had to have surgery on it when he was a kid. I don't know who this guy is, but it isn't Jack. He hasn't got a surgery scar."

"Maybe it healed," Larsen suggested.

"Christ, Larry! I've seen Jack's scar. No scar, no Jack Searsboro," Killduff exploded.

Larsen stared down at the naked body. There was no telltale scar in the groin area.

"Damn it, Killduff, the guy's a fucking Caucasian, for Christ's sake. If it isn't Searsboro, then who the hell is it?"

"I wish the fuck I knew," Killduff said.

Larsen wiped the sweat from his pistolero mustache with the back of his hand. "All right," he said after a moment, "what do we do now?"

"First we call Wyoming and let them know what we've found and haven't found, then have them work over toward us and keep looking for Searsboro on their way," Killduff said after a moment's thought. "In the meantime we get these poor bastards wrapped up in ponchos and cut some poles for litters so we can carry them out."

"We're going to go ahead and pull out, then?" Larsen asked. "Just leave Searsboro alone out here to fend for himself?"

"Not two minutes ago you were convinced *that* was Searsboro, Larry," Killduff said, pointing at the headless body. "I know what you're thinking, and I don't like doing it any more than you do, but we've got to take the practical point of view. First, for all we know, Jack may already be dead or captured. If the former is true, there's nothing we can do for him, anyway, except maybe bury him if we ever find the body. If the latter is true, he's probably halfway to Hanoi by now. Second, if Jack did get away and they haven't caught him yet, then he's doing okay on his own and he'll probably do just fine that way until tomorrow when we can get back in here with more troops and have a better look for him. Third, we're going to lose our light in about an hour and a half. After that, we can't very well go stomping around in the dark calling out his name and looking for him. If we do, we're about as likely to run into the NVA as we are into Jack. And fourth, I don't fancy leaving these guys out here for another day. I'd just as soon get them back where Graves Registration can start to work on them before they get any riper than they are now."

"All right," Larsen said. "How soon do you want the choppers in?"

Killduff looked at his watch. "Say about seventy-five minutes at the primary extraction site. It's the closest."

"That's cutting it pretty fine," Larsen told him. "It'll only leave us fifteen minutes for the extraction."

"I know, but Wyoming's going to need time to get here. We can't carry out all the bodies without their help."

Larsen nodded. "I'll put in the calls."

Half of RT Nevada set up a security perimeter while the other half went to work collecting all the bodies, buttoning them into ponchos and cutting the poles they would need to make the litters. While the dead men were being tucked into the ponchos, Cowboy called out excitedly to Killduff. "Sergeant Bill, come quick! You look, see what I find."

"What is it, Cowboy?" Killduff asked, walking over to where Cowboy stood next to the body of Craig Barnes.

"Not know, Sergeant Bill," Cowboy told him. "Never see anything like. You come look, see. Maybe you tell what is."

Killduff stared down at the object Cowboy held cupped in the palm of his hand. "Where did you find that?"

Cowboy shuddered before looking at his American team leader. "I find there," he said, pointing at Barnes's body. "Sergeant Craig have in mouth, like so," he continued, pointing at his own cheek. "Like maybe he try hide it there. You think maybe he do that?"

"Maybe so," Killduff allowed. "The NVA would have missed it because they didn't give him and Chelsea the same treatment they gave your people. I wonder if . . ." He left the sentence unfinished as he stared first at Barnes's poncho-shrouded body and then at the still-naked form of the headless, handless corpse.

"Sergeant Bill, you recognize?" Cowboy persisted. "You know what is?"

"Yes, Cowboy," Killduff told him. "I know what it is, although I don't know what Craig Barnes was doing with it."

"Then you tell, Sergeant Bill," the Sedang said. "You tell please Cowboy what find."

"It's a qualification badge, Cowboy," Killduff told him. "A qualification badge for a Russian paratrooper."

Cowboy looked puzzled. "What Russian paratrooper do here?"

"I don't know, Cowboy. Maybe Barnes could have told us, but he's dead. I doubt he could have told us, anyway. He probably didn't have time to debrief his prisoner, and I don't know if anyone on his team spoke Russian or not. A lot of guys in Special Forces have studied the language, but it's not exactly a prerequisite for duty in Vietnam, or Laos for that matter. Barnes would have recognized the badge, though."

"So where you think Sergeant Craig find badge? You think maybe his prisoner wear?"

Killduff pointed at one of the poncho-shrouded corpses, the one with no head. "I think he was either wearing it or had it on him."

Cowboy took off his Air Commando hat and scratched his head as he stared at the covered body. "You think this Sergeant Craig's prisoner and he Russian paratrooper? That not make sense. If he Russian, he Communist. If he Communist, then he work with NVA. If so, why NVA do this to him?"

Killduff shrugged. "It's the only thing that does make sense. I don't know who our headless friend here is, but whoever he was he's not Jack Searsboro. We've accounted for everyone else, so this guy must have been Barnes's prisoner. Let's call him Ivan the Headless. Say Barnes or one of his men spotted Ivan here working with the NVA and decided to grab him, or maybe they just ambushed the first patrol that came along, and Ivan turned out to be with it. That part doesn't really matter. What does matter is that once they had him, Barnes probably realized he had a prisoner who could blow the lid off the Soviets' claim that they don't have any advisers working with the NVA. So even if it was a perfect snatch, done quietly and with no witnesses left behind, Barnes probably decided his original mission profile was no longer valid, which meant he had to get Ivan out ASAP. So Barnes radioed for an immediate evac. Only somewhere, somehow, the NVA tumbled to their position before the extraction team could get here, and they ambushed Barnes's patrol. Ivan probably got killed in the cross fire. Maybe the NVA patrol that hit Barnes's patrol didn't know Ivan was with them, or maybe it was a rescue attempt that failed. Either way Ivan was dead."

"So why NVA mutilate Ivan?" Cowboy challenged.

"Think about it for a minute," Killduff said. "They cut off his head and hands. No dental records. No fingerprints. No way for us to identify him. They probably hoped we'd think it was Searsboro, if they knew about him. In any event, they left us with an unidentifiable corpse. The only thing we can say for sure is that it's not Jack Searsboro, and that's only because Ivan doesn't have a scar from a childhood hernia repair. That's the one thing that gives me some hope they haven't got Jack. If they had, they'd know about the scar.

"As to why they didn't just pack out the body, I don't know," Killduff said. "Maybe they couldn't. Could be they had wounded of their own to care for, and with that, plus all the equipment they stripped off our guys, they just didn't have enough people to carry it all. A head and a pair of hands are a lot easier to transport than a 180-pound body. According to Colonel Khan, the extraction team rolled in here pretty quick. Maybe they scared the NVA off, and they just didn't have time to mess with trying to carry away the body. Whatever the reason, I think Ivan was Barnes's prisoner, that he was a Russian paratrooper and that the NVA cut off his head and hands after he was dead so that we couldn't identify him. The only mistake Charlie made was not checking the bodies of all of our guys thoroughly. They probably didn't feel the need to, since they'd stripped them.

"Anyhow," Killduff finished, "at some point Barnes figured they weren't going to make it out and he tried to leave us a clue. Knowing that at the very least the NVA would strip Florida's bodies of their weapons and equipment, Barnes hid the badge in the only place he could think of, a place the NVA might miss—his mouth. The NVA would have found it, of course, if they'd done the same thing to the Americans as they did to your people, but they didn't, and Barnes would have had no way of knowing about that, anyway. I wonder what his last thoughts were, knowing he was going to die, but still having the presence of mind to try to leave a message for us, anyway?"

Both men were silent for a moment. Then Cowboy spoke again. "What you say make sense, but if true, why Sergeant Craig no use radio to tell about Ivan?"

"He wouldn't have initially," Killduff said, "because he wouldn't have wanted the enemy to overhear the conversation and know they'd lost Ivan. He'd have just reported that he had a prisoner and asked for the extraction, which he did. As to why he didn't later, who can say? Barnes wouldn't have been carrying a PRC-25 himself— Chelsea and Searsboro would have had those—and maybe he couldn't get to one of them. Judging from the way the team was scattered, they must have fought a running gun battle with the NVA, although we did find Chelsea fairly close to Barnes. The colonel said that Florida's final transmission ended in a burst of gunfire, so maybe the radio got hit. Barnes would have had an HT-1 and an URC-10, of course, but maybe he just didn't have time to use them. Whatever the deal was, I figure he just had time to stick the Russian's qualification badge in his mouth and hope the NVA didn't find it.''

"So what we do now?" Cowboy asked.

"We deliver Barnes's message," Killduff said. "As soon as the others get here, we're moving to the pickup point."

Killduff took the qualification badge from Cowboy and carefully tucked it into the left breast pocket of his tiger-striped jungle fatigues. It wasn't that he begrudged Cowboy his souvenir, after all, the Sedang team leader had found it, and by the unwritten rule of war booty it belonged to him—but Killduff had other plans for it. If the Army didn't classify it as secret, he intended to see to it that the Russian paratroop badge found its way back to the States and into the hands of Barnes's son, Kevin. It was a poor compensation for a father who would only come home in a coffin, Killduff knew, but the boy was entitled to know how his father had died, and for what.

5

FIFTH SPECIAL FORCES
OPERATING BASE NHA
TRANG, RVN

When Master Sergeant Anthony B. Fetterman checked in with the duty sergeant after a four-day leave, he found a message from Sergeant Major Taylor waiting for him. It instructed him to report to Colonel Bates's office at 1400 hours. There were no other instructions or messages and he was apparently free until the afternoon, so Fetterman figured he might as well get some shut-eye. He'd been on the go from Tokyo, where he'd spent his leave, all night and morning and was dead tired. Some R and R, he thought to himself as he headed to the transient quarters and a bed. Maybe he'd better put in for another R and R so he could recover for the one he'd just returned from.

Once he settled down to sleep, he nodded off instantly. Minutes later, or so it seemed, someone started shaking him vigorously.

"Time to rise and shine, Master Sergeant," a voice said cheerily. "Tony, are you awake?"

The voice wasn't loud, and its owner was standing over him, partially obscured by the top bunk. "Captain Gerber," Fetterman said, sitting up and shaking out his boots before pulling them on. "I'm awake *now*. What time is it?"

"Almost one," Gerber said. "I thought we might get some lunch before we go see what Colonel Bates has in store for us. You didn't spend your whole leave sleeping, did you?"

"No, sir," Fetterman answered truthfully, "although I did spend a good portion of it in bed."

"Not alone, I hope," Gerber said, grinning.

"What do you think, sir?"

Captain MacKenzie K. Gerber of the Fifth Special Forces sat down on the bunk opposite, a smile on his face. Unlike Fetterman, who was a short, dark, balding veteran of three wars, Gerber was tall, fairer, had all his hair and had only fought in two wars—the present one and the Korean. "What was it this time?" Gerber asked. "Blond or brunette or one of each? Or did you conserve energy and time by settling for one of the local girls?"

"Redhead," Fetterman muttered.

A look of puzzlement spread across Gerber's face, and then a light bulb went on somewhere behind his eyes. "Our nurse friend in Tokyo? The one with the steeplejack legs and the Jayne Mansfield grille? Master Sergeant, you are coming up in the world. How did you do it? On stilts?"

"Very funny," Fetterman said. "If the captain will excuse my candor, I'm big enough where it counts, which is more than I can say for you, sir."

Gerber laughed. "Touché, although Robin never complains."

"That's because Ms. Morrow doesn't know you as well as I do, sir. How is our favorite lady journalist?"

"Right now she's pissed. We had a good enough visit, but she wasn't amused with my having to leave early this morning to catch my plane."

"Captain, if I'm not being too nosy, when are you going to do the right thing and marry the poor girl?"

"Right after you retire, Master Sergeant."

"Let's eat," Fetterman said, rubbing a hand through his thinning black hair. "Then we'll go see what the colonel has in store for us."

"Sure, Tony. That redhead really must have worn you out. You don't usually give up so easy trying to convince me to marry Robin."

"Like I said," Fetterman responded, "let's eat. I need to get my strength back."

"COLONEL BATES IS down in the briefing room, Captain Gerber," Sergeant Major Taylor said. "You and the master sergeant are to go straight down. You'll want coffee even if you don't want it."

"Oh, it's going to be one of those sessions, is it?" Gerber said, taking the steaming china mug Taylor handed him.

"It looks that way, sir. The colonel's already been down there for the past two hours with Captain Mauraides and Sergeant Kepler," Taylor said, passing a second mug over to Fetterman.

"In that case," Gerber said, "you'd better give me the pot. They'll be wanting some fresh coffee by now, too."

"Not necessary, Captain," Taylor said. "I just took down a fresh pot about ten minutes ago. Good luck to the both of you, sir, and keep your heads down."

Gerber and Fetterman made their way down the hall to the briefing room, showed their IDs to the armed Special Forces NCO at the door and were admitted. A second guard in the foyer rechecked their IDs before unlocking the inner door and allowing them inside. It was a bit more security than Gerber and Fetterman were used to at this stage of a new assignment, and the fact that both guards were Americans and not the usual Nung tribesmen was itself significant.

The briefing room was actually more like a small theater or lecture hall, with rows of chairs with small folding armrests arranged in descending tiers. The room could normally seat about a hundred men, but today it was vacant except for the three men clustered around a long table spread with maps and papers in front of the bottom row of seats. The chief advantages of the place were that it had no windows, was airconditioned and was electronically swept every morning by American personnel to make sure it was free of eavesdropping devices.

After the ritual handshaking had been performed all around, Bates got right to the point. He went over to a large easel covered with a canvas flap on which *Kin*, the Vietnamese word for *secret*, had been stenciled. Flipping the cover back to reveal a large, brightly colored map of Indochina, he picked up a wooden pointer and began the briefing.

"Kontum," he said, placing the pointer on the map. "And here, just to the northwest across the Laotian border, the Three Rivers Secret Zone." He moved the pointer in a small circle, outlining the area.

Fetterman and Gerber looked at each other. The area was called the Three Rivers Secret Zone because of the three waterways that more or less established its boundaries, and because so little Intelligence was known about it. It was believed to be a sanctuary for the headquarters of the Tenth NVA Division and rumored as well to be the site of a major POW camp where the enemy incarcerated both American and ARVN prisoners, but neither bit of information had ever been confirmed. Part of the main network of the Ho Chi Minh Trail also passed through the area. Although the Royal Lao Air Force maintained a small airstrip at Attopeu, the surrounding countryside was firmly in Communist hands, and the NVA, VC and Pathet Lao operated with relative impunity in the region.

Gerber and Fetterman had been in the region before, and they weren't eager to return. The last time they had gone in with Bob Corbett, a young man loaned to MACV/SOG by the Marine Corps and who was well on his way to becoming one of the top long-distance snipers in Southeast Asia. The mission had been to break up a protocol signing that would have led to a treaty between Hanoi, Peking and the Pathet Lao shadow government, bringing the Red Chinese troops south to protect the Ho Chi Minh Trail. The mission had been accomplished, thanks to some outstanding shooting by Corbett, but the team had barely escaped afterward.

"For the past month and a half," Bates continued, "the area has been the scene of an increased level of NVA activity hitherto unknown. Charlie Khan and his boys out at C and C Central have been running their regular trail-watch operations into the area and have been encountering an extremely high level of enemy security patrols. In fact, they've been getting their butts kicked every time they insert an RT into that area.

"A few days ago RT Florida went in there with the express mission of trying to snatch a prisoner for debriefing and find out what the hell is going on. Apparently they were successful with the prisoner snatch, but the NVA tumbled to them before they could extract with their prisoner. Sergeants Craig Barnes and Tim Chelsea, along with all members of their indigenous team, were killed, and Sergeant Jack Searsboro, Barnes's ATL, is listed as missing.

"When RT Florida stepped into the shit on their way out, Colonel Khan dispatched RTs Nevada and Wyoming to find out what happened to them. They located the bodies of Barnes's team except for Searsboro, but were ambushed themselves on the way out. They lost nine indigenous troops. And Sergeants Philip Grinnell and Larry Larsen were killed during the initial extraction attempt. We also lost one helicopter and the four Army Aviation crewmen and medic on board.

"The teams were eventually able to extract at night with heavy gunship support at an alternate site. They lost four more indigenous troops doing it. Sergeant Ross Hartwick, the team leader for Wyoming, and his RTO, Sergeant Otis Quintin, were also wounded. Sergeant Hartwick died on the way to the hospital. Sergeant Quintin is expected to make it. I believe you men know some of the casualties."

Both Gerber and Fetterman nodded solemnly. For all its size, Special Forces was more like a big family of soldiers, and only the elite of the elite worked for MACV/SOG.

Bates gave them a moment to remember fallen comrades and then went on. "The one hard piece of evidence they were able to gather was this." He put down his pointer and walked over to the table, picked up a manila envelope and shook something out of it. "It was flown in to Nha Trang early this morning along with RT Nevada Team Leader Sergeant William Killduff's after-action report. You gentlemen will recognize it for what it is—a Soviet paratrooper's qualification badge. According to Killduff's report, Craig Barnes had it in his mouth, apparently in an attempt to hide it. Killduff also reports finding the body of a Caucasian male, probably in his late twenties, definitely confirmed as not being Jack Searsboro. The body had been beheaded and its hands amputated so as to make positive identification impossible. At this time, we're proceeding on the twin assumptions that the body is that of Barnes's prisoner and that it also belongs to a Russian paratrooper.

"I need hardly tell you what the possible ramifications could be if the Soviet military has elected to become directly involved in the war," Bates continued. "As everyone in this room knows, there was a previous abortive attempt by the Kremlin to provide Soviet advisers to the NVA and VC in a direct-action role, which fortunately we were able to discourage. It now appears that Ivan may be up to his old tricks again."

Bates looked directly at Gerber and Fetterman. "I want, in fact, I need you two men to take a team in there, find out exactly what the Russians are up to and break it up before it goes any further. I'll see to it that you get all the help I can give you, but it's got to be done quietly. We can't afford to have this sort of thing get into the hands of the Western press. You'll have to operate clandestinely and with minimal direct support. What do you say?"

"I'd say this sounds like something from an episode of *Mission: Impossible,* Colonel," Fetterman said.

"And I'd say we're proceeding on some pretty thin assumptions," Gerber added. "You know what can happen when you start assuming things, Colonel. You said yourself the extra corpse had been mutilated in a manner precluding a positive ID. It might even turn out that it was one of our guys the NVA had captured whom Barnes sprang in his ambush, some Company contract spook we didn't know about on his own mission in the area, or maybe even a French plantation owner or German missionary who just happened to be in the wrong place at the wrong time and got caught in the cross fire.''

"Barnes only mentioned capturing a prisoner, not freeing a POW, finding a wayward priest or stumbling across a French planter," Bates said. "As for the CIA, I've spoken with Jerry Maxwell on the matter and he denies the Agency had any operatives in the immediate area. He checked with the CIA chief of station in Vientiane to be sure."

"Jerry Maxwell is hardly a pillar of veracity," Gerber countered. "What else could we expect from the CIA but an official denial?"

"The denial was unofficial," Bates replied. "Officially it was 'no comment.' Besides, you're forgetting the Soviet paratroop qualification badge."

"I'm not forgetting it," Gerber told him. "I'm just saying that making a quantum leap in logic from a mutilated corpse and a little metal parachute to a Soviet presence in southeast Laos assumes an awful lot. There could be a hundred different reasons why Craig Barnes had that qualification badge, and there's no way of knowing who put it in his mouth. It might even have been some Victor Charlie who did it."

"Mack, I have no intention of making an ass out of either you or me on this one. The nature of the mutilations to the Sedang and American bodies makes it unlikely that the badge was put in Barnes's mouth by anyone else."

Gerber didn't ask what the nature of the mutilations was. He had a pretty good idea from previous experience.

"Colonel, if I may be direct, is there something you're not telling us?" Fetterman asked after a moment.

Bates chewed on his cigar for a few moments, then crushed it in a plastic ashtray on the table and took out a fresh one. He stuck it in his mouth and gnawed on the end for a while, then looked at Kepler, who nodded.

Bates took his time digging out a small box of waterproofed matches, then lit the end of the cigar carefully before continuing. "As a matter of fact, there is," he said at last. "As you know, they're still arguing over the shape of the conference table for the peace talks in Paris. There is some feeling at the cabinet level in Washington that the whole issue of the talks may be only a stalling effort on the part of the North Vietnamese while Hanoi prepares for another major offensive. Precisely where and when, we don't know."

"But there's reason to believe the Russians are involved in some way," Fetterman said. It was more a statement than a question.

"There is reason," Bates agreed. "We've got nothing firm to go on, but certain Intelligence sources inside the Soviet Union indicate something's up. There's not much more I can tell you. Certain sources have picked up some rumblings that could indicate a heightened Soviet interest in events in Southeast Asia."

"What sort of rumblings?" Gerber asked.

"New strains in Moscow-Peking relations, a generalized cooling of attitude on Hanoi's part toward Peking, an increase in contacts between Hanoi's official representatives in Moscow and the Kremlin and a corresponding increase in contacts between Hanoi's unofficial representatives and the KGB and GRU. That sort of thing. There's also a rumor of the formation of an elite Soviet unit, the personnel having been drawn from both the Vysotniki and the Spetsnatz, and from technical troops of the KBG and GRU. The unit is reported to have been issued tropical uniforms and equipment and then secretly deployed outside the Soviet Union. Their exact whereabouts is unknown at this time."

"I can see where those kinds of rumblings could cause a lot of indigestion in Washington," Gerber said, "but where's the connection to Indochina? This special unit could just as easily have been deployed in Cuba, Africa, South America or any other warm-weather hot spot.''

"They could have, but we don't think so,'' Bates said. "It's no secret that the Soviets ship supplies, supposedly of a humanitarian nature, into North Vietnam. The CIA has managed to place an indigenous agent in Haiphong. The agent's cover allows him frequent access to the dock area in Haiphong Harbor. Nearly two months ago he reported the arrival of a number of vessels of Soviet and East Bloc registry arriving within a few days of one another. Part of the cargoes of these vessels was unloaded at night under heavy NVA guard. The agent was unable to determine the nature of the cargo or its final destination, but he did come up with one interesting bit of information. When the Soviet and East Bloc vessels sailed from Haiphong, they left with fewer crew members than they had arrived with.''

"How many fewer?'' Gerber asked.

"Nearly a hundred and fifty men,'' Bates said.

"All right, Colonel, you've got my interest,'' Gerber told him. "But Haiphong Harbor is still a hell of a long way from southeast Laos.''

"It's also at the other end of the Ho Chi Minh Trail,'' Bates reminded him.

"And what, or should I say who, is at the Laotian end of the Trail, Colonel?'' Fetterman asked.

Gerber glanced at the master sergeant to see if he was asking some kind of joke. The look on Fetterman's face convinced him that the man was not.

Bates simultaneously puffed and chewed at his cigar, then rubbed his left eye with the back of his fist before answering. "I said the CIA didn't have any agents in the immediate area of Barnes's patrol,'' he said at last. "They don't. What they do have is an agent in the general area. He's a French national with ties to the Vietcong and Pathet Lao and he owns a cattle ranch on the eastern edge of the Bolovens Plateau and a lumbering operation near Muong May. While visiting his timber-cutting operation last month, he was told by his foreman of a visit by the local Pathet Lao tax collector. The Communist cadre was accompanied by a European soldier dressed in a camouflage uniform and carrying an AK-47.''

"How did the foreman know the man was European?" Gerber asked, suddenly interested.

"He spoke French with an East German accent," Bates said.

"And just how in hell did the foreman know that?" Gerber asked.

Bates looked uncomfortable, then said, "The CIA agent goes by the name of Philippe LeClerc, but he was born Karl Helmut Mannheim in Leipzig, Germany, in 1920. He was an officer in the Waffen SS on the Eastern Front. After the war he joined the French foreign legion. Apparently a lot of ex-Nazis did. The French evidently weren't too particular about that sort of thing, so long as a man wasn't wanted for trial on war crimes charges. Mannheim fought the Vietminh in North Vietnam when the French were in Hanoi, and after five and a half years of faithful service to France, he became eleigible for French citizenship. He was captured at Dien Bien Phu but returned to France when he was repatriated and took a French wife. Subsequently he returned to Indochina and settled in Laos, where he eventually came to a financial arrangement with the Communists. They don't disturb his ranching or lumbering operations and he pays them taxes.

"The foreman of his timbering operation is also an ex-SS man and legionnaire from East Prussia. He had a chance to speak briefly with the European before the Pathet Lao got excited and chased him away. According to the foreman, the Caucasian soldier spoke both his French and German with a heavy East German accent. Also it was stilted, as though neither language was the man's native tongue, but he had learned them from an East German instructor. The foreman, who fought alongside LeClerc on the Eastern Front, thought the man might be a Russian.''

"All right," Gerber said. "You've convinced me of the Soviet connection. At least that there *might* be a connection.

What about this LeClerc? Can he be trusted? How much will he help us?''

"The man has been on the CIA's payroll since 1962 and is considered reliable. He uses the money he gets from the Agency to pay his taxes to the Communists."

"Christ!" Fetterman said. "Now we're subsidizing the guys we're fighting."

Bates shot the master sergeant a warning glance, but made no comment. There was little he could say, and he didn't like the idea himself. Besides, it was the truth.

"As for helping," Bates continued, "LeClerc is willing to help you get into the area and will allow you to establish a base of operations on his timber tract. If you're successful, he'll also help you get out afterward. He's under orders from the CIA, however, to take no direct action against the enemy and to do nothing that might compromise his cover with the Communists unless the safety and success of the mission depends on it. As for trusting him, that goes only up to a point and you'll have to decide for yourself what that point is. The best advice I can give you is to trust no one. You're going to be on your own in there and a long way from any real help if you get into trouble."

"When do we get to meet LeClerc?" Gerber asked.

"Whenever you're ready. You'll stage out of Kontum and be inserted by a night parachute drop into LeClerc's ranch on the Bolovens Plateau. The Ninetieth Special Operations Wing will provide a clandestine ops C-123 flown by Nationalist Chinese out of Air Studies Group here in Nha Trang. LeClerc will meet you when you land."

"What about arms and equipment?" Gerber asked.

"You can have anything you want that we've got in sterile stock here in Nha Trang. I'm afraid there isn't time for any special-order items, although if there's something you can't live without, I'll see if anything can be done. Just give Sergeant Major Taylor your shopping list."

"Men?" Gerber said.

"Again, whoever you want, provided they're available. Make me a list along with any alternates who might fill the bill."

"There are a few I'll definitely want," Gerber said. "I can give you their names right now."

"All right," Bates said. "Go ahead."

"I want Galvin Bocker for communications if he's fit for duty. I also want Justin Tyme for weapons and Sully Smith for demolitions. Those two are musts, since we don't know what in hell we're going up against. I also want a damn good medic. T. J. Washington will do if he's available. Given the situation, an honest-to-God doctor would be preferable if you can lay your hands on one, but only if he's SF-qualified and a surgeon. Otherwise Washington or someone equally experienced."

Gerber looked at Fetterman. "Do those men meet with your approval, Master Sergeant?"

"Yes, sir. As far as it goes."

"Meaning?" Gerber asked.

"We'll likely need a tracker, sir. And he's got to be not just good. He's got to be the best."

"Meaning Sergeant Krung, I suppose?"

"He's the best there is, Captain."

"All right, Krung, then," Gerber said. He would have preferred another choice, but Fetterman was right. Krung could track a cobra through elephant grass on a six-day-old trail. The only trouble was that his skill at following spoor was occasionally exceeded by his hatred of the enemy, which could prove a detriment in an operation that depended on keeping a low profile.

Krung, who wore a tattoo on his chest proclaiming Death To Communists, had reason to hate. His family had been annihilated by the Vietcong, and he had sworn a blood oath not to rest until he had killed ten VC for each member of his family. Krung had kept score by nailing the testicles of the VC he killed to a board in his hootch. Krung had had a very large family. He had eventually satisfied his oath and filled the board, but the VC had then made the very bad mistake of killing and mutilating Krung's friend, Lieutenant Bao. Krung had taken a second oath and started a new board. At last report there were still a few empty spaces.

"We'll want Sergeant Krung if he's still alive," Gerber told Bates. "He's a Nung Tai we've worked with before. He ought to be in the files."

"I'll see what can be done, but that's all I can promise," Bates said. "Anyone else?"

"Yes, sir," Kepler said quietly. "Me. Providing Captain Gerber and Master Sergeant Fetterman are willing to have me along for the ride."

"I thought you had better sense than to volunteer, Derek," Gerber said, smiling.

"I did, too." Kepler told him with a grin.

"This isn't going to be a picnic, Sergeant," Bates said. "And there won't be room for excess baggage."

"Begging the colonel's pardon, sir, but I'm fully capable of carrying my own bags. I'm cross-trained in both light weapons and demolitions and I speak both Lowland Lao and French as well as German, Vietnamese and Russian. And I'm probably more familiar with Soviet equipment than anyone else we have available. At least more so than anyone with the proper training. The captain will need someone along trained to assess any Intelligence he may gather, and we have worked together on many occasions. I really would like to go, sir."

"Okay by you guys?" Bates asked.

Gerber and Fetterman nodded.

"I'll clear it with S-2, then," Bates said. "What about additional personnel?"

"We'll have to see what we're up against before I can give you an estimate of the force needed to carry out a surgical strike," Gerber said. "It could take anything from a squad to a battalion. Any good batch of indigenous troops will do, so long as they're good fighters and already trained. We won't have time to make soldiers out of recruits. Say Nung, Sedang, Rhade, Rengao or Hre. Nung, Rengao or Sedang would probably be best. Whatever you can lay your hands on in a hurry. They'll have to be jump-trained. Once we know what the target is, where it is and have a plan to hit it, we can radio drop zone coordinates and troop strength requirements for the raiding party."

"Not too big a party," Bates cautioned. "We want this done quietly, remember?"

"Colonel, we don't even know what we're going to do yet," Gerber told him. "Once we do know, we can tell you what the target is and how many men we need to neutralize it. Then you can worry about how much noise it's going to make. If the bang is going to be too loud for the ears in Washington, you can always cancel the party. That's a decision for someone other than me to make. I can promise you that I won't ask for more men than I need and that I won't try it with fewer than I need."

Bates nodded. "Fair enough. We'll consider the operation to be two-phased, then. Phase One will consist of the recon you make and it'll terminate when you locate the target and file your report. Phase Two will be the elimination of the target and will commence when I receive your request for additional manpower and supplies. It'll terminate when you and the raiding force are extracted unless terminated sooner by higher authority."

"Fine," Gerber said. "Now, give me everything you've got on LeClerc and the operational area."

"Get yourself another cup of coffee and step on over to the map table, Captain," Kepler said, smiling. "I thought you'd never ask."

6

FIFTH SPECIAL FORCES FORWARD OPERATING BASE KONTUM, RVN

The Caribou transport banked sharply and dived toward the Kontum airstrip as the pilot, who had purposely held the aircraft high as long as possible to stay out of the range of small-arms fire, sought to get the plane onto the runway in the shortest time possible. It almost worked, but not quite. As the pilot shallowed out his turn for final approach, a string of 7.62 mm machine gun bullets stitched a path along the right wing and found the starboard engine. There was a loud bang, followed by a cloud of dense black smoke billowing from the cowling, and the right wing dipped ominously as the crew of the Caribou suddenly found themselves very busy just trying to keep the aircraft from falling out of the sky. Somehow, through a combination of skill and just plain dumb luck, the pilot managed to get the stricken bird down onto the perforated steel planking of the runway and only snapped off a wing tip in the process.

Major Dallas Leighton Reasnor looked at his hands as the Caribou rolled to a stop and noted with a somewhat detached air of clinical interest that they were shaking rather a lot for a surgeon's hands. He made a mental note to find the nearest bar as soon as he deplaned and prescribe himself a large medicinal brandy and then maybe have a serious drink.

This was by no means the first time someone had taken a shot at him. As that rarest of commodities in the Special Forces, an honest-to-God doctor and a surgeon, he had accompanied Special Forces teams on patrols before, had survived an ambush and had found nothing contradictory in shooting the enemy and then trying to keep him from bleeding to death. Such activities weren't part of his normal daily routine, however, and this was the first time he'd been in an aircraft that had taken ground fire. He considered himself lucky to have survived the ordeal, thankful for the philosophically broadening experience and offered up a short, silent prayer to both God and Hippocrates that he should never again have to experience it in quite so terrifying a manner.

"You okay, Major?" he heard a voice asking, and looked up into the dark face and darker eyes of the short, stocky Special Forces NCO who had sat next to him on the ride out from Nha Trang.

"Yes, I'm fine. Thank you, Sergeant. Just a little shaken up, that's all. Was anyone else hurt?" he asked. "I'm a doctor, after all."

That last bit was stupid, Reasnor realized. The man already knew he was a physician. They'd talked about it on the plane ride up from Nha Trang. They hadn't talked about much else. Both had admitted to the other that they were on their way to Kontum for a new assignment, but neither man had discussed what that assignment might be, which was hardly surprising for Special Forces personnel.

"No, sir. I don't think anyone was injured," the sergeant said. "Not unless they had some trouble up front. As far as I can tell, we took a few rounds in the number-two engine, but that seems to be about it."

Reasnor was amazed at how calmly the man seemed to take their near brush with death.

They unbuckled their seat belts as those around them were doing, found their duffel bags and made their way clumsily to the door of the plane, weighed down with their heavy loads. Reasnor had been told that he would be met at the airstrip, although not by whom, and he suspected that the jeep waiting a short distance away had been sent for him. But as they approached it, the Special Forces NCO who had ridden next to him on the aircraft suddenly dropped his bags and rushed forward to meet one of the two men from the jeep. The two men shook hands warmly and slapped each other on the shoulders like a couple of schoolboys.

"Captain Gerber! Damn good to see you again, sir," the sergeant said.

"Likewise, Sully," the officer responded. "I'd punch you harder, but I'm afraid you might explode. Knowing you, there's no telling what you might be carrying in your pockets."

"Honest, Captain, I'm clean," Sully Smith told him. "Not even so much as a one-pound block of TNT or a blasting cap. Used it all on my last assignment."

"Was it a satisfactory blast?" Gerber asked.

A little glint of delight seemed to creep into Sully Smith's eyes, like that of a small child remembering the taste of an ice-cream sundae. "You bet, sir. Might even say it was an inspired piece of work. You should have seen it."

"Well, let's get your bags over to the jeep, then. I guess we'll have to see if Derek can't come up with some new firecrackers for you to play with."

"Derek Kepler? Is he here, too, sir?"

Gerber nodded. "Old Eleven Fingers himself. Flew in with Master Sergeant Fetterman and me early this morning. Haven't even had a chance to unpack yet."

Smith's eyes suddenly narrowed and his face assumed a crafty look. "Who else is here, or is that a state secret, Captain?"

"No one yet," Gerber told him, "but they're coming. Most of what's left of the old crew. Galvin Bocker's due in this evening, and Krung should be here sometime tomorrow. No word on Sergeant Tyme yet, but Colonel Bates promised he'd try to pry him away for us wherever he is."

Smith rubbed his hands in delight. "Ah, the prodigal scorpions return to the nest. Are T.J. and Lietuenant, I mean, Captain Bromhead coming, too?"

"Not this time," Gerber told him. "Bromhead's busy running the camp at Song Be now, and as for Sergeant Washington, he's on R and R in Honolulu. In fact, Bates promised to send me a replacement out with you. Some guy named Reasnor. I didn't catch the first name. Telephone lines are out again and there's some kind of freakish atmospheric condition trashing the ionosphere or whatever the hell it is they bounce radio signals off. About the only thing working right now is HF CW transmissions, I'm told. Supposed to clear up in a day or two, though, so it shouldn't be a problem for us."

"Reasnor, you say?" Smith said. "I rode out with a guy named Reasnor. An SF doc. Sound like your man?"

"Must be," Gerber said, peering over Smith's shoulder. "Where is he?"

Smith turned around and nodded toward Reasnor, still struggling along with his bags and looking as though he had lost someone and was trying to find him.

"Let's go meet the man and give him a hand with his luggage," Gerber said.

They walked over and Gerber introduced himself. Reasnor was a tall, rawboned man with angular features and a carefully clipped mustache that was just over regulation length. He had black hair shot with gray at the temples and wore nonregulation bifocals with wire frames. His handshake was firm but friendly.

"Do you want to be addressed as Major Reasnor or Dr. Reasnor?" Gerber asked. It was a test.

"How about Lee?" Reasnor told him. "It's short for Leighton, my middle name. First name's Dallas, but I never cared for that much. Reminds me too much of Texas."

"You and Master Sergeant Fetterman are going to get along famously," Gerber said. "How much did Colonel Bates tell you about our little group?"

"Said he had some people going on a long walk in the bush," Reasnor replied. "Said it was secret, likely to be dangerous and that they needed a sawbones to patch up the pieces in case anyone got careless. Said you'd fill me in on the details and that he had to have an answer, yes or no, right then as to whether or not I was interested in going along. I was kind of tired of dispensing penicillin to clap-ridden troopers and delivering the local girls' babies when some GI forgot to wear his raincoat, so naturally I said why the hell not?"

"That's not what the colonel told me," Gerber said. "He said he was sending me a first-rate trauma surgeon who didn't have enough sense not to jump out of a perfectly good airplane before the engines had even quit running."

"Then I guess I must be in the right place, although I've no idea why. It's been a while since I jumped, though. Will we have to?"

"It's guaranteed," Gerber said. "You only have to jump once, though. Just make sure the first PLF's a good one."

"Just give me a good, firm push out the door when we're over the drop zone, then," Reasnor replied, "and we'll let gravity do the rest. There's just one little detail I'd like to get clear right from the start, though."

"What's that?" Gerber asked.

"I'm a doctor who happens to be a soldier, Captain. Not the other way around. I'm along to pass out the pills, stick on the Band-Aids and do the stitching if anyone needs it. If need be, I'll even shoot somebody for you, but I've got limited tactical experience and I haven't the foggiest idea what this mission is all about. So if somebody needs medical treatment, I expect you to listen to me, but there'll be no arguments about who's in command. Colonel Bates made it clear that you would be running the show, and I wouldn't have it any other way."

"Thank you, Major," Gerber said, meaning it.

"Lee," Reasnor corrected. "Doc Lee if you feel the need to be formal. I don't suppose there's any chance we could all go get a drink somewhere before we have to go do whatever it is you've had me brought up here for? I'll buy the first round and maybe the second if there's time."

"I think that could be arranged," said Gerber. "Let's get your gear and Sergeant Smith's equipment loaded into the jeep."

IT WAS A LITTLE after ten in the morning and the PCOD lounge had only just opened for business. Some of the chairs were still stacked on top of the tables and the black floor was still wet from mopping. A couple of recon personnel who had come in from a patrol just after dawn were enjoying their breakfast beers at a table in the corner, but otherwise the bar was empty except for the bartender.

Gerber, Reasnor and Smith made their way to the bar. The captain and the sergeant ordered beers, while the doctor ordered the brandy he had promised himself and a double Scotch on the rocks, causing Gerber to raise an eyebrow.

"Are you sure you gentlemen wouldn't care for something stronger?" Reasnor asked, counting out his MPC on the counter.

"Thanks, but it's a little early in the day for me," Gerber said.

"Me, too," Smith echoed. "The beer will suit me just fine."

"Personally I never take a drink before five," Reasnor said, "but I try to remember that somewhere in the world it's always after five." Then, seeing Gerber's expression, he added, "You needn't concern yourself about my being an alcoholic, Captain. I don't drink before operating, and since you said we had time, I assume I won't be doing surgery for the next day or so. The brandy is medically prescribed because we just about got our asses shot out of the air this morning and I'm not used to that sort of thing. The Scotch is because I can't stand the taste of beer, and drinking more than one brandy at a time dulls one's appreciation of a fine liquor."

They took their drinks, retired to a table in the opposite corner from the recon men and were just sitting down when Fetterman came in the door. "Ah, there you are, Captain. Colonel Khan's driver said I might find you here. I've got that man you wanted to talk to outside. Shall I have him come in, or do you want to see him someplace more private?"

Gerber looked around the room again and said, "Might as well bring him in, Master Sergeant. Then pull up a chair and join us. I'll order a couple more beers from the bar."

"I'll get the beers, Captain Gerber," said Reasnor. "I said the first round was on me, remember?"

Fetterman and Smith exchanged handshakes, then Fetterman went back outside to bring in the new man. When they were all settled again, Gerber took another look around and spoke in a low voice.

"Sergeant Killduff, I'm Captain Gerber. You've already met Master Sergeant Fetterman. This is Major Reasnor and Sergeant Sully Smith. We, that is I, would like to talk to you about a little trip we're planning."

"So talk, Captain," Killduff said. "I'm listening."

Gerber studied the man for a moment and almost decided to forget the whole thing. Killduff looked haggard and burned-out. He had dark circles under his eyes, which were bloodshot and puffy, as though he hadn't slept last night or perhaps even longer.

"These men and I, along with a couple of others, are thinking of taking a little trip," Gerber said carefully. "We're going to see if we can't put out a little Prairie Fire."

Both Smith and Reasnor sat up and paid closer attention. Both men knew that Prairie Fire was the code name given to MACV/SOG operations in Laos, and it was the first time anyone had mentioned their possible destination, although Smith had had a strong suspicion as soon as he'd been told the operation would stage out of Kontum.

Killduff picked up his mug and drained about a third of his beer before answering. "In that case, I'd advise you to bring along a couple of engine companies and a pretty good-sized hook-and-ladder truck. Any place particular you had in mind?"

"The Three Rivers area," Gerber said. "I understand you're familiar with the place."

"Captain," Killduff said levelly, "meaning no disrespect, but I don't know any of you people. What areas I might or might not be familiar with is none of your damn business. Just where is this place you're talking about?"

Gerber smiled. "There's no need to act clever about this, Sergeant, but I'm glad you did. If you'd said anything else, this conversation would have come to an abrupt end and you wouldn't be sitting here right now. When we're finished, you can check our bona fides with Colonel Khan. He'll tell you where to find us if you're still interested."

"Intersted in what?" Killduff asked.

"In going along."

Killduff snorted. "Anybody who would want to go there is crazy. Just how much do you know about the place?"

"I know C and C Central has had six recon teams shot to hell there in the past month," Gerber said. "I know you led one of them. And I know about this." Gerber took the Soviet paratroop badge from his pocket and dropped it onto the table in front of Killduff.

The recon man stared at it for a moment, then took another sip of his beer. "I reckon you've established your bona fides well enough, Captain. Just exactly what is it you have in mind?"

"We're going to go in there and find out what the Soviets are up to and stop it."

Killduff laughed. "Captain, you've got a pretty high opinion of yourself. The personnel in all six of those teams, American and Sedang alike, were all good men. Highly experienced men. Some of the best I've ever worked with. Just what makes you think your little crowd can succeed where they failed?"

"Master Sergeant Fetterman and I have been there before, as have the other men who will be joining us later," Gerber said.

"Then you know what you're up against. Why bother me?"

Gerber was beginning to get irritated with the man, but he let it slide. "We've been in the general area, but a bit farther west," he told the sergeant vaguely. "What we need is someone with knowledge of the specific area where your patrols ran into trouble."

"Trouble?" Killduff said. "Is that what you call it? Running into a little trouble? I had eleven other men with me on the team I took in there, Captain. I came out with one. Ross Hartwick did a little better. He brought out four. Of course, he died doing it. All told, we lost fourteen indigenous personnel and four Americans on our two teams. Of the four Sedangs who made it out, two were wounded, as was Sergeant Quintin. They tell me he *may* be able to walk again someday, as soon as he gets used to his wooden legs."

"Look, Killduff," Gerber said, "I'm sorry about what happened to your team and Hartwick's. Just like I'm sorry about what happened to Craig Barnes and his men, and to the twenty dead and wounded from Recon Teams California, Louisiana and Illinois. It's a tough nut to swallow, but that's what war is about. I'm offering you a chance to get some payback from the bastards responsible, at least indirectly, and maybe make a difference in the outcome of the war. Now, then, do you want to be part of it or not?"

"That depends," Killduff said slowly. "You're doing all the talking. Who's in charge of the mission, you or the major here?"

"I am," Gerber said. "Major Reasnor is in charge of medical support. He's going with us, but just to pick up the pieces if need be."

"That right, Major?" Killduff asked, looking at Reasnor.

"That's the way it is, Sergeant," Reasnor affirmed. "Exactly as Captain Gerber describes. I'm a doctor first and a soldier second. My forte is repairing mayhem, not creating it, although I do know how to use a rifle should the need arise."

"In that case," Kilduff said, looking back at Gerber, "you can count me in."

The abrupt shift in attitude caught Gerber a little off guard. "Why the sudden change, Sergeant?" he asked suspiciously. "I didn't think you had any interest in helping us, judging from the way you've been talking."

"I still don't," Killduff said. "My allegiance is to recon, pure and simple. As for making a difference in the outcome of the war, you don't really expect me to swallow that crap, do you, Captain? We're going to lose this war. Not because we can't win it, but because the politicians back home are more interested in public opinion polls than they are in letting us win. And the gentlemen of the press with their sound crews, klieg lights, cameras and padded expense accounts are more interested in outscooping one another than they are in how many lives of American boys getting their story out first costs.

"I don't know if you guys are regular Special Forces, Special Operations or CIA and, frankly, I don't give a shit. I know you're not recon, so I owe you nothing. But I'll go along, just the same. You wouldn't be able to understand why because you didn't see what those Commie bastards did to Craig Barnes and his people. Craig was a friend of mine. So was Jack Searsboro, wherever he may be. All I'm interested in is a chance at some payback, just like you said. So I'll go along for the ride for one reason and one reason only, Captain. That's because judging from the way you talk, I've got a hunch that whoever you are, you're just a big enough bastard yourself to get the job done."

"I don't know when I've ever heard a more moving endorsement of my character, Sergeant," Gerber told Killduff unsmilingly. "You talk the talk. Let's see if you walk the walk. If you'd care to put your money where your mouth is, report to the isolation compound by noon tomorrow. Don't bother bringing any of your gear. You won't be needing it. That's all, Sergeant Killduff."

Killduff got up and left, leaving his unfinished beer on the table.

"You sure you want to take him along, Captain?" Fetterman asked after Killduff had left. "The man could be a problem. He's got an attitude the size of the Mekong River."

"He's also got the only firsthand knowledge of the terrain in the immediate area where six twelve-man recon teams got chewed up into little pieces. I don't intend for that to happen to us. What he knows about the area just might save our asses. I don't care what his attitude is as long as he does his job."

"From what I've heard said, I'm beginning to wish I had someone else to do mine," Reasnor said. "It sounds to me like you need Ben Casey, Dr. Kildare, John Wayne and Superman all rolled into one."

"You want out now that you know what this is about?" Gerber asked.

"Hell, no," Reasnor said. "So far I only know enough to find this intriguing. We doctors get far too little excitement as it is. But having a general idea of our destination, I could use another drink. However, since I've already had two, the second being a double, I think maybe I'll wait until evening."

"In that case," Gerber said, "I'll buy a round. Then we'll go over to the compound and get settled in. We won't start the briefing process until everyone's here, anyway."

7

FIFTH SPECIAL FORCES
FOB KONTUM, RVN

Sergeant First Class Galvin Bocker arrived by helicopter late that afternoon. A tall, well-proportioned man with sandy hair and the hint of a Carolina drawl in his soft voice, he had the look of a Special Forces trooper who had just stepped off an Army recruiting poster. From the precisely positioned flash and crest on his green beret right on down to his spit-shined boots, he was STRAC, yet one cheek seemed a little puffy somehow, as though he had been punched in the jaw recently. The cause of the deformity had nothing to do with injury, however, but was the result of a large wad of bubble gum.

Bocker had massive hands that somehow possessed the ability to tinker with the minuscule innards of a radio with surgeonlike precision. He also had a knowledge of electromagnetic wave propagation theory that would have embarrassed Marconi, Steinmetz and Tesla. Gerber had often felt that if he had given Bocker two seashells and a coat hanger and told him to make a radio, the man would somehow accomplish the task.

For the men of the team this was the worst part of the operation—the waiting. Once the entire team arrived and they could begin the briefing/analysis/brief-back phase of the mission, things would proceed quickly and they would have plenty to do to occupy their time and minds. Ordinarily a Special Forces team was deployed on an assignment as a previously existing unit, but there was nothing ordinary about this assignment, and it took time for the men, each a highly trained and experienced specialist in his own right, to be located and brought into the picture.

In the meantime the men played cards, sipped beers, took care of their personal gear and wrote carefully worded letters to their families or loved ones that contained not a hint about their current assignment and wouldn't be mailed until after they returned from Laos, anyway. The only people who had anything to do to keep them busy were Kepler, who spent a few hours analyzing the latest Intelligence estimates of the target area, and Reasnor, who gave everybody a physical and made sure their shot records were up-to-date.

Krung arrived on the morning plane, dressed in rumpled, tiger-striped fatigues and carrying an M-1 carbine slung over his shoulder. A short, wiry Nung Tai tribesman, he stood half a head shorter than Fetterman, and if anything, looked even more gaunt than the seemingly emaciated master sergeant. Well-known to Gerber, Fetterman, Kepler, Tyme, Smith and Bocker, all of whom had worked with Krung on both their first and second tours, he was known, nevertheless, only by the name of Krung, his family name. As the only surviving member of his family, he claimed the right of sole representation and had abandoned all other names. Krung *was* the Krung family. There were no others, and the revenge for their murders that he had exacted on the Vietcong was the Krung family's revenge. It wasn't merely his alone. It was a matter of family honor.

Sergeant First Class Justin Tyme arrived just before noon, unannounced. Krung and Fetterman, his mentor, were outside the barracks amusing themselves with a little hand-to-hand combat practice when Gerber joined them just as an ancient C-47 droned in from the northeast and began circling the camp. On its second circuit a gaily colored streamer was thrown out, and when the aircraft came around again, a man hurled himself out of the door of the plane.

Krung studied the distant, helmeted figure hanging beneath the billowing light green canopy for a moment, then turned to go inside. "Sergeant Tyme come," he announced over his shoulder. "I go fix meal. He will be hungry."

Gerber and Fetterman stared after Krung for a moment, then squinted up at the tiny, doll-sized figure hanging beneath the parachute.

"Well," Gerber said after a moment, "I sure as hell can't tell who it is."

"Me, neither, sir," Fetterman said, "although he's got about the right build. It *could* be Tyme."

Forty-five seconds later, after a bit of careful maneuvering to correct for wind drift, the parachutist touched down just outside the wire fence of the isolation compound, gathered in his chute and took off his helmet. He was, as Krung had predicted, the light-weapons specialist they had been waiting for.

"Justin, what the hell are you doing jumping into the middle of camp like that?" Gerber shouted through the fence.

"Good morning, Captain Gerber, Master Sergeant Fetterman," Tyme shouted back. "I ran into a bit of trouble getting back from Bangkok and missed my flight out of Saigon to Nha Trang, so I took a later flight to Da Nang and then hitched a ride with an Air America pilot headed back south toward Stormy Weather via Buon Brieng. Only his orders wouldn't let him land in Kontum, so I figured the only way was to jump in. I borrowed a couple of chutes from the quartermaster at C and C North, and here I am."

"Rather a roundabout way to travel, don't you think?" Fetterman asked.

"The orders waiting for me in Saigon said to report here," Tyme said. "They didn't say how I had to get here. Besides, I was afraid I'd miss you guys. I didn't want you leaving without me."

"I might have expected something like this flamboyant display of foolhardiness from Master Sergeant Fetterman,"

Gerber said sternly, "or even from Sergeant Kepler, but I'm surprised at you, Justin. Why, you might have landed on top of someone and injured him." Then Gerber laughed. "Drag that stuff or yours on down to the gate and we'll get you signed in and hidden somewhere before the MPs and the boys in white show up to take you away for a psych evaluation."

Killduff arrived about twenty minutes later, exactly at noon. Gerber was a little surprised to see the recon sergeant. Having heard nothing further from the man, he had half suspected that Killduff had thought the situation over and decided they could all go to hell. As instructed, Killduff had left his personal gear behind and had brought with him only his toothbrush and a heavy Randall combat knife. Introductions were performed all around and then they sat down to lunch.

Colonel Bates arrived in the early evening along with the Area Studies Team, and the briefing process began in earnest. After Bates and Gerber covered the mission in general terms, and Kepler provided the latest Intelligence on the target area, each area studies specialist covered his particular aspect of the briefing. The topics ranged over everything from terrain and meteorological patterns of southeast Laos and ethnic groups likely to be encountered to medical problems endemic to the region, economic and sociopolitical structures of tribal groups and ethnolinguistic and religious customs and taboos.

The session lasted until well past midnight and resumed early in the morning with briefings on the latest available advances in communications and electronic navigation equipment, demolition techniques and materials and sophisticated surveillance and eavesdropping apparatus. It ended with two short refresher lectures on jungle and mountain survival tips as well as land mine and booby trap avoidance. When it was over, they broke for a late lunch of steaks and beer, the last they would enjoy for a while, then retired to various parts of the barracks to pore over their individual briefing packets.

Gerber gave them time to digest it all, then left them alone to sleep on it until morning when he called them all together for a team meeting.

"All right," he said. "You all know what the mission is and what's available to us to accomplish it. You've all had a chance to study the briefing material. Now it's up to us to formulate a workable plan. We've got two days to do it in. That leaves us another two days for training. We go five days from now or we don't go at all. I want to hear general recommendations first, then we'll move on to specifics. Let's start with Derek."

In the end, the final plan presented to Bates during the brief-back was remarkably similar to the one Bates and Kepler had first outlined to Gerber and Fetterman in Nha Trang. They would go in by parachute, a night jump from fifteen hundred feet from a clandestine ops C-123 flown by Nationalist Chinese pilots from the Ninetieth Special Operations Wing. They would use French military parachutes, copies of the American T-10 and reserve, and bury them after landing. They would be met by Philippe LeClerc, who would see to it that the drop zone was properly marked.

After arrival, Bocker would send a brief CW message via a commercially manufactured shortwave transceiver, indicating that all had gone well with the drop and that they had been met. There were other prearranged messages, should the reception committee not be there to greet them or should other problems occur. In no instance was the message to be more than three words long, and the frequencies used, each with three alternates, would be changed according to a daily schedule that each member of the team would commit to memory. Should it prove necessary to send a longer message, the team would take along three small-burst transmitters on which the encrypted messages could be recorded using a tiny magnetic tape that would play back and transmit the message at high speed after an adjustable time delay. The burst transmitters were designed to be carried aloft by a helium-filled balloon so as to drift clear of the team's location on the air currents before broadcasting. They also were equipped with a small self-destruction charge of plastic explosive, which would destroy the transmitter after it had done its work.

They would wear British-made jump boots and Portuguese-manufactured jump pants and jackets, camouflaged with a striped, "lizard" pattern. Their gloves would be rust brown leather handmade in Spain, and their camouflage makeup would consist of a commercially manufactured paste in three colors with an insect repellent base.

To enable them to blend in better with the native population should the need arise, they would all dye their hair black and use a chemical "suntanning" lotion to further darken their skin, although there was little that could be done about eye color, and the heights of Gerber, Bocker, Reasnor and Tyme would tend to mark them as Occidentals if viewed from anything but a distance. No one would carry a wallet or identification papers and dog tags would be left behind. The blood type of each member of the team would be committed to memory by every other man should the need for a transfusion arise.

Once the team had confirmed contact with LeClerc, there would be no further radio contact except in an emergency until the target had been located and studied, and Gerber was ready to make his recommendations regarding the raiding party. In an emergency the team could communicate with Hillsboro or Moonbeam, the airborne command and control center orbiting over southern Laos, but only if the safety of the team was on the line. All other communications would be direct to their control officer, who would be standing by in the commo center at C and C Central in Kontum.

Captain Mauraides, Bates's operations officer, would fill that role and be in direct communications with Bates himself, either in Saigon or Nha Trang. In the unlikely event Bates couldn't be reached and an emergency arose, Mauraides would have full authority, acting in Bates's name, to dispatch as many UH-1F helicopters as were necessary from the Ninetieth Special Operations Wing's Green Hornet squadron to extract the team. The authorization for additional personnel for the raid could, however, come only from Bates. Colonel Khan would be advised of the progress of the mission, but would have neither the authority to extract the team nor to authorize the destruction of the target.

Since the exact nature of the target was still unknown and it was uncertain if the team would be able to neutralize it themselves without the assistance of the raiding party, the team would take a limited amount of demolition equipment with them. Thirty-two blocks of French plastique, similar to American C-4, were to be provided from the special stores warehouse in Nha Trang, along with electric and nonelectric blasting caps, two fifty-foot spools of detonating cord, a fifty-foot roll of safety fuse, half a dozen M-2 weatherproof fuse lighters, two galvanometers, two fuse crimpers, four rolls of electrical friction tape and two five-hundred-foot reels of firing wire, as well as two ten-cap blasting machines. All together the demolition material would weigh about one hundred and forty pounds and would be distributed among the various members of the team to make carrying it easier and to minimize the effect of losing part of it.

Should something unexpected happen to all of the demolition equipment, Smith was prepared to improvise an ammonium nitrate explosive compound from materials LeClerc would probably have on hand at his ranch, or even to compound an improvised plastic explosive or incendiary mixture from materials available commercially in Attopeu, or any decent-sized town. He could even work with matches and medical supplies if he had to, or improvise a gelled incendiary from gasoline and animal blood, he told Bates, and then explained in more detail than was necessary exactly how he would go about doing it.

Reasnor would carry instruments sufficient to perform fairly major surgery, along with drugs and medication to treat most of the infections and treatable diseases likely to be encountered. All of his medical supplies were manufactured either in Pakistan, West Germany or Japan, which wouldn't pose a problem since those countries provided much of the medical world's supply of surgical instruments and pharmaceuticals, anyway, although repackaging of some items would prove necessary.

"Since terrain conditions indicate any contact with enemy forces once we're off the Bolovens Plateau will be at extremely close range and we'll likely be outnumbered, requiring us to respond immediately with a high volume of fire, and since the mission profile dictates the need for equipment sterility, I've given considerable thought to the weapons best suited for the team's use," Tyme said during his part of the brief-back. "Since we'll likely have to carry all the equipment on foot, weight limitations will also be a factor. LeClerc should be able to provide some motorized transport, or we may be able to utilize animal transport, but we can't depend on that. Therefore I've prepared two lists of arms—one that gives us greater advantage in firepower but an added weight burden, and a second intended to maximize portability while still providing adequate firepower if we have to proceed on foot. I've already checked the inventory lists and all of these materials are available from special stores in Nha Trang."

The first list included eight M-3 submachine guns fitted with sound suppressors, ninety-six magazines and 2,280 rounds of ammunition; two cases of French hand grenades; one Belgian-made FN MAG general-purpose machine gun in 7.62 mm NATO with two thousand rounds of linked ammunition consisting of mixed armor-piercing and incendiary bullets; and one RPG-7 rocket-propelled grenade launcher with twelve high-explosive grenades.

"For use against bunkers and fortifications, as well as armored vehicles, should any be encountered," Tyme explained when Bates pointed out that the RPG and MAG seemed to run counter to the notion of the silenced M-3s. "This list assumes transport in some form is available and affords us the maximum flexibility in our firepower response. Should neutralization of the target require the employment of mortars in the firepower plan, these would have to be airdropped in or sent in with the additional raiding personnel."

The second list still contained two cases of grenades and the RPG-7 as the most viable means of dealing with an armored threat or bunkers while maintaining equipment sterility requirements, but deleted the light machine gun and replaced the M-3s with smaller weapons.

"We have a number of the Czechoslovakian-made Skorpion machine pistols in stock in both .32 ACP and .380 caliber, the slightly heavier bullet being favored for our purposes," Tyme said. "The Skorpion is an extremely compact weapon with a folding wire shoulder stock and is well suited to concealment should the need arise. And it's issued with a fairly effective suppressor and a shoulder holster rig, making it convenient to carry and quiet to use. Furthermore, it's reasonably accurate at the ranges we're likely to encounter and it has a rate of fire in the neighborhood of eight hundred rounds per minute cyclic when fitted with the suppressor. The small size and weight of both the weapon and its ammunition means we can carry more ammo.

"With the Skorpions, pistols may be considered superfluous for this mission except as a matter of personal preference, in which case I recommend the German Walther PPK, also in .380 caliber. It's not my first choice as a man-stopper, but it'll suffice if the shots are well placed, and keeping the caliber the same as the Skorpions will simplify logistics. These weapons are also listed on the inventory stock and will take a suppressor with very little reduction in velocity if fitted with a threaded barrel. Fighting knives are, of course, also a matter of personal preference, and the choice of those is best left up to the individual if mission dictates will allow it. I believe Master Sergeant Fetterman will have some recommendations to make along those lines," Tyme concluded. "We are, of course, prepared to utilize weapons captured from the enemy if necessary and have already spent some time on refamiliarization with most of the types likely to be encountered."

"Sergeant Tyme's comment about the individuality of edged weapons is both accurate and relevant," Fetterman said. "To fight well with a knife a soldier must have one that's suited not only to his hand but to his own personal style of fighting. While Sergeant Krung's knife isn't a problem, since it's made locally, the decision whether or not to extend sterility requirements to knives is one to be made at command level.'' Fetterman then gave his suggestions for subsititute knives. When he finished recommending knives, he ran through the additional individual equipment they would need, then turned over the brief-back to Krung and Killduff, who gave short reports outlining their duties as tracker and guide respectively and the importance of their dual roles as scouts to the mission.

When everyone had presented their brief-backs, Gerber outlined his role as mission commander and the conduct of the mission in the field as he saw it. He covered almost every conceivable problem that could arise, from failing to find the drop zone to communications breakdown. He talked about immediate-action drills the team would employ if confronted with the enemy; what they would do if transport wasn't available; how they would proceed if they failed to rendezvous with LeClerc; the search techniques they would use to try to locate the Soviet troops; what they would do if they failed to find them; how the team would respond if surprised during the extraction; and what they would do if the extraction failed or the helicopters couldn't get through for some reason.

Gerber spoke for nearly two hours, and his throat was dry by the time he finished, but Bates and his staff still had enough questions left to grill the entire team for an additional three hours. Some of the questioning was conducted in Lao, French and Russian to determine the language proficiency of each man.

When it was all finished, Bates and his staff conferred among themselves for a few minutes and then Bates said, ''All right, mission plan approved. You're a go. The arms and equipment you've requested will be here sometime tomorrow, hopefully before noon. I probably won't be here to see you off.

8

BOLOVENS PLATEAU
SOUTHERN LAOS

Gerber sat on the troop seat in the darkened interior of the Fairchild C-123 Provider and tried to make out the faces of the other eight men sitting with him in the gloom. It was hard to do.

For four days now each man, with the exception of Krung obviously, had been staining his already suntanned skin a darker shade, and they had all dyed their hair jet black. Tonight, before boarding the plane in Kontum, they had further covered their features in camouflage patterns of bright green, dark brown and black, and the French paratrooper helmets they wore cast dark shadows beneath them. There was little light coming through the windows of the aircraft and even less to reflect it. The outside of the C-123 was painted flat black overall with no nationality insignia or identifying markings, and the interior of the plane was predominantly battleship gray. The parachutes the men wore, and their gear bags fastened beneath their reserve parachutes or strapped to the floor near the rear of the aircraft, ready to be pushed out the door— were dark dark olive green. The men themselves wore charcoal gray coveralls over their jump fatigues to keep their Czech machine pistols and webgear from snagging the canopies or lines of the chutes and help hide them against the night sky.

Fetterman appeared to be asleep, and a couple of the others had leaned their heads against the side of the fuselage, but Gerber didn't think anyone was actually sleeping. It was something he had never been able to do before a jump, though he had often closed his eyes for a few minutes in an effort to force himself to relax and organize his thoughts for those brief seconds of high-stress decision making that could suddenly occur in the next few moments.

A light rain had been falling, which the meteorological boys had somehow failed to predict in their forecast, when the team had boarded the aircraft at Kontum, bearing their newly assigned operational code name of Special Recon Team New Mexico. Gerber had considered the rain a bad omen, as well as a genuine cause for concern. Rain could do funny things to parachutes, like make them not deploy right or collapse them. A rain-soaked canopy could add enough weight to speed your descent and make you hit hard enough to break something, like a leg, back or neck. The rain could soften the ground so that you found yourself buried up to your knees when you hit, and especially here in the mountains of the tropics, it could flood valleys and gullies where you had planned to land and drown you instead. But the biggest nightmare Gerber could think of was trying to struggle out from beneath a heavy, sodden canopy while under fire.

This was by no means Gerber's first jump into Laos, or Fetterman's, and Bocker, Tyme and Krung had been there before, too. It had been raining the last time they had jumped into southern Laos, not too far from where they were going now, and they had lost one man even before the entire team was down. They had lost some others later on and had nearly lost several more. For Gerber the rain was definitely not a good sign.

They had been in the C-123 for nearly two hours now. What would have been only a half-hour flight direct from Kontum had been stretched to almost four times that by the Nationalist Chinese crew, flying first south toward Ban Me Thuot, then turning west to cut across northeastern Cambodia, and finally back north to cross over the Bolovens Plateau from the south. After the drop the plane would then continue northeastward toward Quang Tri Hue before recrossing the mountains and heading due east to Da Nang, finally flying back south down the coast to wind up in Nha Trang, where it had started.

There was good reason for the roundabout flight plan, though Gerber knew no real flight plan had been filed except with a handful of men who would never reveal it. Oficially the flight didn't exist, just as officially neither the aircraft nor the men aboard it existed. Six RTs had gone into the Three Rivers Secret Zone and made successful chopper insertions, a standard practice for most recon teams. All six had gone in from the east, and all six had been shot to hell. Maybe there was a connection and maybe there wasn't, but MACV/SOG Special Operations and the men of SRT New Mexico were taking no chances on it happening again. That was also the reason for the extraordinary COMSEC procedures this time. The six recon teams that had been lost had been following standard COMSEC procedures per their SOPs. Perhaps there had still been a COMSEC breakdown somehow, and perhaps there hadn't, but no one was willing to risk the possibility of repeating the mistakes of several dozen dead men.

Gerber had felt the plane bank to the right perhaps fifteen or twenty minutes ago and knew they must be getting close to the drop zone. He leaned against the fuselage and closed his eyes, willing his muscles to relax and his mind to rid itself of the myriad thoughts running through it. He couldn't completely blank out all the thousands of little bits of information and unanswered questions pertaining to the mission assaulting his neural centers, so instead he forced himself to imagine that he was somewhere else, beside a bubbling brook or a rushing mountain stream, in a quiet glen with Robin Morrow. He carefully picked autumn as the time of year so that the greenery wouldn't remind him of the jungle. The air was crisp and clean and there was a hint of frost in it, but it was a sunny day and winter was a long way off yet. They were lying on a big red-and-black blanket, and Gerber, calling on his college background in botany, was explaining to her the differences in half a dozen leaves spread carefully out on the blanket before them.

The daydream was just beginning to work when Gerber was startled out of it by the Nationalist Chinese jumpmaster placing a hand on his shoulder. The man was dressed in a black flightsuit devoid of any insignia, black boots and a black watch cap. He wore a dark gray Air Force emergency parachute and held a headset consisting of twin earphones and a boom microphone in his hands. When he spoke, his clipped British accent reminded Gerber of Captain Minh, an LLDB officer he had worked with during his first tour in Vietnam.

"We're about ten minutes out from the drop zone, old man," the jumpmaster told him. "Time to start getting your chaps on their feet and ready to go."

Then he moved on back toward the rear of the aircraft and started unstrapping the equipment bundles from the floor and checking that their static lines were hooked up to the steel cable running down the inside of the plane.

Gerber stood and bellowed above the roar of the C-123's engines, "Ten minutes to drop! Everybody stand up! Check equipment!"

The remaining eight members of the team did as ordered without comment, each man checking his own gear first to make sure everything was properly strapped and buckled down and then that the quick-release catches on his parachute were secure. Next he checked the gear of the man in front and the man behind him. Fetterman, who would jump last, waddled over and double-checked Gerber's gear and chute, and the captain returned the favor before the master sergeant waddled back to the end of the line. As they finished, each man handed the other's static line to him, and the men placed the nylon webbing between their teeth to signal they had been checked and were ready to jump.

"Hook up!" Gerber yelled again, and all nine men snapped the metal hooks of their static lines onto the steel cable and tugged on them to show that they were hooked up and the safety covers on the hooks had closed properly.

Behind them the jumpmaster had finished with the equipment bundles and had plugged the long cord of the headset into an intercom jack near the door. "Five minutes to drop zone," he sang out as he unlocked the door and pulled it inward and to the side.

There was a sudden inrush of cool air through the cabin, and the noise level increased considerably. The jumpmaster listened for a moment, holding his right earphone to the side of his head as if to block out the sound of the engines and the rush of the wind, then he cupped his hand over the boom mike and shouted, "Two minutes," as the little red light came on above the open door of the plane.

Gerber turned slightly and shouted, "Move to the door!"

He shuffled down the aisle and stood behind the pile of equipment bundles. The others formed a single file behind him with Fetterman in the rear.

The jumpmaster was leaning forward now. He peered out the door of the C-123, trying to penetrate the blackness with his eyes and make out the drop zone. Suddenly he shouted, "Tallyho!" and began dragging bundles over to the door.

The light changed from steady red to flashing red, and the jumpmaster tensed, one hand on the edge of the door, the other on an equipment bundle. Suddenly the red light went out and the green one next to it came on as the jumpmaster began madly shoving the heavy bundles out the open doorway. As he pushed out the last bundle, he shouted at Gerber, "Action stations! Go!"

Gerber found that amusing. An American jumpmaster would have said "Stand in the door!" not "Action Stations!" or simply "Go!"

Gerber stepped quickly to the open door, brought his feet together on the edge of the deck, tucked in his chin and placed one hand on the outside of either side of the doorway, then gave himself a shove upward and outward into space. Behind him he could hear the jumpmaster shouting, "Go! Go!" at the others.

There was no feeling of falling. Instead, it seemed as if the black shape of the plane had suddenly leaped upward and away from him. Gerber fell automatically into the count. "One one thousand. Two one thousand. Three one thousand."

He heard the flap and rustle as the main container opened and the static line, still firmly attached to the steel cable in the aircraft, pulled the deployment sleeve from the chute, then heard the crack of the air opening the canopy and felt himself suddenly lifted by the harness. Gerber glanced up. He had a full, round canopy with no holes or blown panels showing. A good deployment.

The SF captain slid his hands up the nylon webbing of the risers until he found the steering toggles, then looked down to get his bearings. Off to his left and slightly behind him he could see the lighted arrow on the dark ground that marked the drop zone and he steered toward it.

At three hundred feet, as measured by the altimeter on his reserve chute, he brought his feet and knees together and turned the canopy into the wind, using the lighted arrow as an indicator. The impact, when it came, wasn't as hard as he had feared it might be, and he rolled with it easily, coming up quickly and running forward to spill the air from the canopy and punch the quick-release plate on his chest.

As the harness dropped from his body, he unzipped the coveralls and pulled the Skorpion from its holster, quickly snapping the little wire stock into position and chambering a round, then glancing skyward. The plane was lost against the overcast of the thirty-five-hundred-foot ceiling, but he could see someone coming down near him, and after checking the safety on the machine pistol, he ran forward quickly to assist the man should he need help.

Suddenly Gerber stopped short as half a dozen armed men dressed in black loomed up out of the shadows between him and the descending parachutist. He brought the Skorpion up to his shoulder, snapped off the safety and tensed, ready to fire.

"Don't be afraid. We are friends," a voice said out of the darkness in French. The phrase was repeated in soft, delightfully accented English.

Gerber lowered the machine pistol only slightly and turned a bit to his right to see who had spoken.

"We are friends," the voice said again, and Gerber finally placed what was odd about it. It was a woman's voice.

In the faint glow of the kerosene lanterns that had marked the drop zone, Gerber could see that she was fairly tall and somewhere between five foot eight and ten. She had long, flowing hair, either black or dark brown, covered by an indigo kerchief, and was dressed in a black turtleneck sweater and blue jeans.

She was classically beautiful rather than pretty, despite the charcoal she had daubed on her cheekbones and nose, but there was absolutely nothing either beautiful or pretty about the .45 caliber semiautomatic pistol belted around her slim waist, or the 9 mm MAT-49 submachine gun slung over her shoulder. He guessed her age to be near his own, mid-thirties, although he had always had a hard time guessing women's ages.

"*Excusez-moi, madame,* but who exactly are you and who are these people with you?" Gerber asked.

"I am Monique LeClerc," she said, extending a slender hand. Her grip was surprisingly strong. "And these are my people. They work for me. They are Lao Theung, Mountain Mon-Khmer. We've come to help you. May I know your name?"

Gerber considered that. Would it be a breach of security to tell her his real name? That was something that had never been discussed during the briefing, planning or brief-back. And they had expected to be met by Philippe LeClerc and at most one or two of his hired hands. Not by Madame LeClerc and a small army of Mountain Mon-Khmer. Could the woman be an enemy agent? Had they jumped right into a trap? At least she wasn't North Vietnamese. That much was certain. But where did her loyalties lie? That had been unclear even in the case of Monsieur LeClerc. One could never tell with the French, anyway. Many of them *were* Communists.

"I beg your pardon, Madame LeClerc," Gerber said, "but half of Laos is controlled by the communists and half of that is Lao Theung. How do we know you are who you claim to be?"

She smiled tolerantly. "And the other half of that half are Meo, are they not? Yet I believe your CIA has found little trouble working with them. These Lao Theung aren't Communists, nor am I. They're absolutely loyal to me, personally, and can be trusted."

"Where's your husband, Madame LeClerc? We expected him to meet us," Gerber pressed.

"My husband is dead, *monsieur.* He was shot to death five days ago, ambushed as he drove back from Muong May in his truck. Two of our workers who were with him were also killed."

"Five days ago! Christ! Why weren't we told?" Gerber demanded.

"It's a very remote area, *monsieur.* News travels slowly. I didn't learn of his death myself until yesterday."

"Then who's been making the arrangements for our arrival?"

"I have, *monsieur.* Philippe and I had no secrets from each other. I've often used the wireless to talk to Control in Vientiane."

"Then why didn't you use it to tell us that your husband had been killed?"

"There is, how you say, a valve broken in the set? I don't have the skill to repair it."

"We say tube," Gerber told her. "The Brits say valve. Just when did this tube get broken? Don't you have any spares?"

"*Oui, monsieur.* Many spares. A whole boxful. To me they are all the same. I know the Morse code. I can work the key and understand the di-dahs very well, but I don't know how to repair the wireless. I'm not—" she searched for the right word "—inclined electrically."

"The term is mechanically inclined," Gerber corrected in a somewhat gentler tone. "If you don't mind my saying so, Madame LeClerc, you seem to be taking your husband's death rather well."

She gave a shrug that was positively Gallic. "Would crying help? Would hysterics bring him back? No. I am a pragmatist. The war taught me that. Also, I didn't love Philippe, although I cared for him a great deal. More like a brother and sister than husband and wife. Ours was, you might say, a marriage of economic convenience. When Philippe first met me, I was a prostitute. I'm not ashamed of it. After the war I had nothing. No family. No money. No skills. I was seventeen and I had only my beauty. I soon found that men, be they French or American GIs, would pay for that beauty. When Philippe met me in 1954, I was no longer poor, but neither was I rich. Philippe had money—four gold bars he had stolen from the Nazis during the war and hidden away. Nearly four million francs altogether. I liked Philippe. He was always very kind to me, and when he offered me a better life, I said yes to him."

Gerber found her candor almost shocking. "You said that you and your husband had no secrets from each other, Madame LeClerc. Did Phillipe tell you how he came to be in possession of those gold bars?"

"Certainly. He was in command of the detachment of soldiers detailed to guard the shipment of which it was a part. Yes, *monsieur,* my husband was a Nazi. He was an officer in the Waffen SS."

It was the one thing she could have told Gerber that would prove she was who she claimed to be, if not with complete certainty at least within a reasonable doubt. "Forgive me, Madame LeClerc. My name's Mack Gerber." He didn't tell her his rank.

"Please, you must call me Monique."

"And you must call me Mack."

"Very well, Mack."

She pronounced it more like "Jacques", but Gerber let it pass. Perhaps it would be better if she didn't get it too correct.

"Tell me, *madame*, uh, Monique, is there someplace else we can carry on this conversation?"

"Of course. The ranch house isn't far. We can walk there in about twenty minutes. My workers will help your men bury their parachutes and carry the equipment. I have a jeep, but it isn't working properly, either. Perhaps there is a mechanic among your men? In any event, it would be too small to carry everyone."

"I believe a couple of my men are amateur mechanics. Perhaps Smith or Fetterman can take a look at it for you when we get to the ranch."

"Fetterman?" She said it with difficulty, then rolled the name around her tongue and tried it again. "That is an unusual name."

"He's an unusual kind of guy," Gerber said. "Shall we get this mess picked up and get back to the ranch?"

"You are standing on my ranch, Mack. I only hope you are not standing in it. Come, the house is this way."

When everyone had been accounted for, the extra equipment dispersed among the Lao Theung, the lanterns collected and the chutes carefully buried, Gerber introduced their hostess and they all walked to the house, following a narrow footpath. The darkened trail made Gerber suspicious of an ambush, but the Lao Theung and Monique LeClerc seemed unconcerned about the possibility and chatted amiably along the way. Gerbert sent Krung and Fetterman forward with one of the Lao Theung to check things out, just to be on the safe side.

"Tell me, Monique," Gerber said as they walked along, "why all the guns?"

"My husband was killed, Mack. I don't know by whom. Perhaps it was only bandits. Perhaps it was soldiers. Until I know by whom, I must take precautions, *non?*"

"I thought your husband had an arrangement with the Pathet Lao," Gerber said.

"Yes. It is as you say. And also with the Vietminh and the North Vietnamese. Control knew this and approved of it. He even provided the money used to pay them. They call it a tax, but it is extortion."

"If Philippe had an arrangement with the Communists, why would they kill him?"

"I don't know that he was killed by Communists. This is Laos. The country is full of soldiers. Besides the Pathet Lao, the Vietminh and the NVA, there is the Royal Lao Army, the Meo army of Vang Pao and the CIA. There are even private armies of smugglers and a few Kuomintang and Chinese warlords who were driven out of Mainland China by the Communists. It's said that in the north of Laos there are even Communist Chinese troops. There are also the bandits and the private armies of the drug lords. The opium poppy is a powerful force in Laos."

"What I meant was, where did you get all the guns?" Gerber asked after a moment. "A submachine gun isn't exactly standard issue on ranches where I come from."

"Where do you come from, Mack?"

Damn, she was clever, Gerber thought. She could take almost anything he said and turn it into a question. "What did your control officer tell you?" Gerber asked instead.

"Only to expect a small number of men by parachute, and the date and time to prepare a landing place for you."

"He told you nothing about our mission?"

"Only that it was important and that Philippe was to help you if he could. He can no longer do that, so I will help you now. You are American, yes? Are you here to fight the Communists?"

"You prepared an excellent landing place," Gerber said, avoiding her question. "Where did you learn how?"

"Once before, a man came here by parachute. I went with Philippe to meet him and saw how my husband marked the field. I did as he did."

"You did well. This man who came before, was he an American?"

"No. He was French, but he worked for the Americans. Control in Vientiane told us to expect him."

"What was his name?"

"He called himself Jones, but that wasn't his name. As I said, he was French."

"You're sure of that?"

"Positive."

"What happened to him?"

"He went to Attopeu. He was supposed to be gone only a week, but he never came back. After a month, we got a message from Control asking about him, but we could tell them nothing. We never heard from him again."

"I'm not surprised," Gerber said, "with an alias like Jones. What did this Mr. Jones look like?"

"He was tall, but not as tall as you, maybe ten centimeters shorter. He had brown hair and a mustache and a scar along the side of his face. Philippe thought perhaps the man had once been a legionnaire, as he had, but he didn't say why."

"You're very straightforward, Monique," Gerber said.

"Does my frankness trouble you?"

"Not at all. You've answered almost all my questions except one."

"And you've answered almost none of mine, Mack. Still, I will tell you what you wish to know. What is your question?"

"Where did you get the submachine gun?"

She dismissed the question with a wave of her hand. "This is Laos. There are guns everywhere."

"It's illegal for a private citizen to have a submachine gun," Gerber said. "Even in Laos."

"In Laos nothing is illegal, *monsieur*, if you have enough money. Philippe acquired the guns. I don't know where he got them. Most of them are hunting rifles. There are also three shotguns, two with double barrels and one with a pump, like a trombone, as well as a revolver in the house. It's a .38-caliber Special, I believe."

"Are there any more machine guns around the house?" Gerber asked quietly.

"Yes," she said unexpectedly. "There is a big one. Philippe called it an automatic rifle. It has the two legs you fold down beneath the barrel to help hold it. It's very heavy and quite old. I think he said it was a Browning. There's also another small one. A British gun. Philippe called it a Sten. It has the thing on the end of the barrel to shoot the bullets with very little sound. A silencer, I think you call it."

"Technically it's called a suppressor, but silencer is close enough," Gerber said. "Sounds like a BAR and a Sten Mark VI. Yours must be the best-protected ranch in all of Laos. Monique, for someone who seems to know only a little about firearms, you carry that MAT-49 as though you know how to use it."

"I do," she said firmly, and Gerber believed her. "Philippe insisted that I learn to shoot all the guns, even though I had no interest in hunting. It's with this and the Sten that I am the best. The others, they are either too heavy or the recoil is too uncomfortable."

"That .45 you're wearing can't be very comfortable to shoot," Gerber remarked dryly.

"It isn't," she said, "but it makes a very big hole. It was Philippe's favorite. Perhaps if he'd had it with him when he was ambushed, he would be alive today."

Gerber didn't think a single Colt .45 would have been much help in a well-planned ambush, but he made no comment. Philippe LeClerc was beginning to sound like a very interesting sort of guy. Gerber would have to make it a point to find out a bit more about him.

When they reached the house, a sprawling concrete affair with a tile roof that reminded Gerber more of a Southwestern hacienda than a French villa, and had satisfied themselves that there was no NVA company lurking in the shadows, waiting to suddenly come out in the open and surround them, they went inside.

"May I offer you and your men some dinner, Captain?" Monique LeClerc asked.

Gerber was instantly on the alert again. "What makes you think I'm a captain, Madame LeClerc?"

"Ah, so formal now, are we, Mack?" She smiled. "You're obviously in charge, yet you rely greatly on your Monsieur Fetterman, who is visibly older than you, so you must be an officer and he your sergeant, I think. You are far too old for a lieutenant, so it must be a captain."

"Let's stick with just names, okay?"

"As you wish, Mack. I ask again, may I offer you and your men something to eat?" She seemed amused by their brief exchange.

"We have no wish to impose upon your hospitality," Gerber told her.

"It isn't an imposition. This is a ranch. The one thing we have plenty of here is beef. I will have the cook prepare something. You and your men are welcome to spend the night in my home. There is plenty of room, as you can see, although some of the men may have to share a bed. Philippe always wanted a large house filled with children. I regret that I wasn't able to provide him with that. In the morning we can discuss how best I can assist you in your mission. Now, if you will excuse me for a few moments, I wish to wash my face and change into something that makes me look a little less like a gangster."

Monique LeClerc disappeared somewhere into the big house, and Gerber joined his men in the living room. It was a large, comfortable room, well furnished in expensive woods, but in rather a heavy style for Gerber's taste. There was no denying one thing, however: Karl Helmut Mannheim, alias Philippe LeClerc, had certainly carved out a nice little hideaway for himself in Laos.

"How about it, Captain? Are we going to stay here tonight?" Smith asked when the Americans and Krung were alone.

"We might as well," Gerber said. "In the morning we'll see what can be done about lining up some transportation. We want Madame LeClerc as our guide, anyway, at least until we get to the target area, and she's calling the shots right now, so we might as well relax and enjoy it. I want two of us on guard all night, just the same. One inside the house and one outside. We'll take it in shifts."

"It sounds as if you don't entirely trust the lady, sir," Fetterman said.

"I don't. There are just too many things going on here we didn't know about but should have. Until we get some answers, however, about all we can do is relax and try to get used to all this luxury she's trying to force on us."

"Sounds like real rough duty to me, Captain," Tyme commented.

"Yeah, the kind I'd like to get used to," Smith echoed.

"Well, it's a bit different from the kind of treatment we're used to," Kepler allowed.

"Which doesn't mean we can afford to let our guard down," Gerber said. He turned to Krung. "Sergeant, I'd like you to go find the kitchen and keep an eye on the cook. Don't get in her way or enter into any arguments over recipes. Just make sure she doesn't add any extra ingredients, like maybe a couple of pounds of arsenic. I really don't feel up to a bellyache this evening."

"I watch careful, Captain," Krung said, rising and going off in search of the kitchen.

Gerber noted that Krung's English had improved immeasurably since he'd first met the man, although it still had a long way to go.

"Doc, you and Master Sergeant Fetterman take the first stint of guard duty, if you don't mind. I want both of you outside for now. Once people start getting settled down for the night, we'll post one man outside and the other inside the house," Gerber said to Reasnor. "I don't want a bunch of NVA to come calling while we're all sitting down at the dinner table. I'll make sure we save you something to eat."

"Thanks a lot," Reasnor said sarcastically. "Just what I always wanted. Leftovers."

Fetterman grinned. "Come on, Major. We've got work to do."

"Just one more thing before you go," Gerber told them. "Fetterman, Madame LeClerc says she's got a jeep out in the shed, but it won't run. In the morning I want you and Sully to have a look at it."

"Will do, Captain."

Fetterman and Reasnor pulled on their camouflaged caps and went out the door. Once they were outside, Fetterman took out his machine pistol and screwed the suppressor onto the barrel.

"Time to put your muffler on, Major," Fetterman said. "If we find anybody snooping around and have to take him out, we want to be able to do it quietly."

"Wouldn't it be better to be a bit on the noisy side and alert the others that something is wrong?"

"It would also alert any enemy patrols in the area," Fetterman said. "If things are seriously wrong, I think we can depend on the enemy to make enough noise to alert everybody. If you absolutely feel the need to be noisy, I suggest trying a hand grenade. Try to find a spot where you can watch the front of the house without exposing your back and keep to the shadows. I'll take the rear."

Fetterman moved off, quickly becoming nearly invisible in his camouflaged suit. They had buried the gray coveralls at the drop zone with their parachutes.

"Sully, I want you to go over the demolition equipment and make sure everything's okay," Gerber told Smith back inside the house. Then he turned to Tyme. "Justin, you and Sergeant Killduff break out the grease guns and hand them out. If the shit does hit the fan in the middle of the night, we'll need all the firepower we can get. Galvin, I want you to get a message off to Kontum right away," Gerber told Bocker.

"Acknowledging our arrival?"

"Yes, but don't use the transceiver rig. Use one of the burst transmitters. Tell Mauraides we've landed intact and made contact, but with Mrs. LeClerc. Tell him Philippe LeClerc is dead, ambushed on the road from Muong May five days ago by unknown assailants. Also tell him to get hold of Jerry Maxwell and ask him to have the CIA chief of station in Vientiane pass along any information on an agent they may have had named Jones, a Frenchman who was supposed to go to Attopeu but vanished. He's described as having had dark brown hair and a mustache, about five seven or eight, with a scar on his cheek, possibly a former member of the French foreign legion. Also ask them how much they know about Philippe LeClerc's wife. Monique LeClerc claims she didn't advise Vientiane about her husband's death because their radio transceiver is broken. I'll want you to take a look at it after we eat."

"You want me to fix it or just take a look at it?"

"Just let me know what you find first, then we'll decide."

"All right, Captain."

"What about me?" Kepler asked.

"I've got a particularly tough assignment for you," Gerber told him. "I want you to gather Intelligence on the sleeping accommodations and figure out where we're going to put everybody."

"That, I think I can handle," Kepler said. "What are you going to do?"

"Me?" Gerber said. "I'm going to do the toughest job of all. Try to make some sense of all this." Then he leaned back in his chair and closed his eyes.

9

BOLOVENS PLATEAU
SOUTHERN LAOS

Monique LeClerc looked positively radiant when she joined them at the supper table. She had scrubbed her face clean of the grime she had worn earlier and had brushed her long brown hair until it glowed in the electric light provided by the ranch's own generator. With a cream-colored pleated skirt, she wore a well-tailored, rust-colored blouse with billowing sleeves of silk and a neckline that was just daring enough to be interesting. Obviously she wasn't the sort of woman who required a great deal of makeup, but there was a touch of pale pink on the lips of her slightly too large mouth and a trace of mascara on her long eyelashes. There was just a hint of perfume about her, which Gerber thought he recognized as Chanel No 5.

"But we're not all here," she said as they took their places at the long mahogany table. "Where is the little Montagnard you had with you? And the *monsieur* with the mustache and your Sergeant Fetterman?"

"Monsieur Krung fancies himself an amateur chef," Gerber said glibly. "I believe he's still in the kitchen, trying to learn some trade secrets from your cook. As for Fetterman and Reasnor, they have duties to attend to and will be unable to join us but request that we save something for them."

She arched an eyebrow at that, and a little pout appeared on her lips that conveyed both a slight sense of displeasure and a certain provocativeness. It seemed almost a calculated expression, and Gerber wondered if it was because the absence of the others suggested they didn't entirely trust her, or because she was curious about what they were doing, or perhaps for some other reason entirely, one he couldn't fathom.

"Did you get that little problem taken care of, Galvin?" Gerber asked quietly as Bocker sat down beside him.

"The balloon's gone up," Bocker answered cryptically.

"I don't know that expression," Monique LeClerc said. "What does it mean, the balloon has gone up?"

"It means things are about to start happening," Gerber told her. "I believe it derives from an old circus custom where the show began with a balloon ascension or the release of a number of balloons."

The searching look Madame LeClerc gave him said clearly that she didn't entirely believe him.

"Galvin here knows a bit about radios," Gerber said. "After we eat, I'll have him take a look at yours and see what he can do about fixing it."

"*Merci*. That would be most kind."

Krung appeared moments later with the cook, another Lao Theung. Gerber couldn't follow what she said to Madame LeClerc, but Krung's announcement was succinct if not subtle. "Meal okay. We eat."

It was an impressive meal and was served on fine china. First a salad of tossed greens and radishes, then onion soup, followed by filet mignon and asparagus in béarnaise sauce. The wine, a slightly sweet Pinot Noir, was served in crystal. As Madame LeClerc proposed a toast to her guests, and therefore had had to drink first, Gerber didn't concern himself about the possibility of unwanted additives.

After supper Madame LeClerc showed Bocker where she kept her radio, a British Halicrafters set, and the spare tubes, then excused herself, saying she had to check on her employees and some of the animals before going to bed. Gerber offered to accompany her, but she politely but firmly refused, saying that since it was now her ranch, it was her responsibility. There was no way to push the issue without inviting a confrontation, and as Gerber had no evidence that anything was wrong, only a vague suspicion that something wasn't quite right, he acquiesced. Monique LeClerc then buckled on her .45, took her submachine gun and a kerosene lantern and went out.

As soon as she was gone, Gerber went to check with Bocker.

"It was a broken power tube," the communications sergeant said. "Just like the lady said."

"Can it be fixed?"

"I already fixed it, Captain, but I took the tube back out. You said you didn't want it working until I talked to you."

"She had a spare, then?"

"Two. Got 'em both right here in my pocket. Want me to put one of them back in?"

"Not just yet. I think maybe we'll hold on to them until we're ready to leave. Any trouble finding the right one?"

"No, sir. Not if you know what to look for." He hesitated a moment, then continued. "A person who didn't know much about radios *might* have had a bit of trouble. Mrs. LeClerc said she didn't have a schematic for this thing, and the tube was pretty well smashed. You couldn't read the identification numbers on it."

"Could she have figured it out by trial and error?"

"Sure. Eventually. Anybody could, but it might take a while."

"Were any of the other tubes broken?"

"No, sir. Just the one power tube."

"Doesn't that strike you as a bit odd, Sergeant? I mean, if the radio had been dropped or something, wouldn't some of the other tubes have been smashed, as well?"

Bocker thought for a moment, then shook his head. "Not necessarily. While the odds would favor it, not all tubes are alike, even of the same kind. Not any more than all radios are. Sometimes you get one with a thinner or thicker glass wall than others that can take less or more abuse. It can also be affected by how new the tube is. Every time a current is passed through the filaments in the tube, the resistance of the wire to the energy of the electrical current creates a surplus that has to be given off as heat. You heat a tube up a number of times, it's bound to have some effect on it. Usually the filaments give out first, but if the tube were defective to begin with, say just a little, good enough to work, but with a fault in the body, the reheating over a prolonged period of time could exacerbate the problem just enough to make it let go one day. I don't know how long it would take. That would depend on the tube, the defect and how much it had been used, but over a long period it *could* affect it enough to weaken it to the point where it became brittle and prone to breakage."

"Would six years be long enough for that sort of thing to happen?" Gerber asked, remembering that Bates had told him Philippe LeClerc had been on the CIA payroll since 1962.

Bocker shrugged. "Who knows? I can tell you one thing, though. After six years practically any radio made is bound to have something wrong with it if it's been used very much at all. This radio's been dropped or struck with something at some point. There's a dent in the side of the case."

"All right," Gerber said. "Let's keep this between the two of us for now, and hang on to those tubes. I'm probably just tilting at windmills, but there's no point in taking any chances. If Madame LeClerc asks about your progress with the radio, just tell her you're still working on it."

"Whatever you say, Captain."

After his conversation with Bocker, Gerber was beginning to wonder whether he might not in fact be tilting at windmills. Monique LeClerc had been amazingly frank with them, both about her relationship with her late husband, including each of their sordid backgrounds and the source of their not inconsiderable wealth. She had even volunteered the information that Philippe possessed a number of automatic weapons in addition to the more usual collection of rifles and shotguns one might expect to find around any ranching operation. In fact, she had shown them every kindness and had given them no solid reason to doubt that she was anything other than what she claimed to be. She had a logical explanation for everything Gerber questioned. Yet still he felt vaguely uneasy.

Could the fact that Philippe LeClerc owned a Browning Automatic Rifle and two submachine guns, one of them equipped with a suppressor, simply be attributed to the shadowy life the man had lived as a CIA agent, pretending to be the friend of the Pathet Lao, NVA and Vietcong, or did it have some darker meaning? Had he been involved in smuggling or drug trafficking perhaps? Perhaps unknown to his CIA control, or perhaps even with the guilty knowledge or approval of that man? It seemed like a lot of heavy hardware for an agent to have around. And why would the VC come to a friendly understanding with a wealthy Frenchman who had fought against them in the first Indochina war? Surely not just for the tax money he paid them. There must be some other reason. The more questions he had answers to, the more questions they raised.

But the biggest unanswered question of all was why would any man who feared something so much that he kept three machine guns hidden around his ranch allow himself to be caught in an ambush without even so much as a pistol to defend himself?

FROM HIS HIDING PLACE Fetterman watched as Monique LeClerc came around the corner of the elaborate French ranch house, a lighted kerosene lantern in her left hand. She had apparently bathed and changed into a very attractive skirt and blouse since she had met them at the drop zone, but the .45-caliber semiautomatic pistol and the MAT-49 submachine gun were still very much in evidence. Even without the female Resistance fighter costume she had worn at the DZ, she looked very much the part of one of the Maquis Fetterman had seen in France during World War II. All she needed to complete the effect, he thought, was a scarf around her neck and a beret.

Fetterman thought it a little odd that the captain was allowing her to run around unsupervised. Gerber wasn't a man to play fast and loose with security on an operation of any kind, expecially one this deep in enemy territory, and Fetterman had picked up on the feeling that Gerber didn't entirely trust her, although a certain amount of distrust was normal enough for soldiers in their particular line of work. Still, he had no idea what had transpired inside since he and Reasnor had left the house, and it was quite possible that something had been said or occurred that had put Gerber's mind at rest about her loyalties.

Fetterman watched as she went directly to the big barn behind the house and entered it with her lantern. He thought that a little bit odd, too. A kerosene lantern wasn't the safest thing in the world to take into a barn, and there was an overhead electric line running from the ranch's generator shed to the barn. He waited to see what would happen, and when she didn't reappear after twenty minutes, he slipped quietly from his hiding place and eased over toward the big wooden building, the suppressed Skorpion machine pistol held ready in his hands.

Monique LeClerc was on her knees doing something in a stall at the far end of the barn, the kerosene lantern resting on its base on the concrete floor near her, when Fetterman eased open one side of the big double doors. The door creaked loudly, despite his efforts to keep it quiet, but she didn't look up until he spoke. "Good evening Madame LeClerc."

She made a very creditable show of being startled. "Ah, Sergeant Fetterman. You frightened me, *monsieur*."

"I apologize for doing so, *madame*," Fetterman said. "If I may ask, what are you doing out here?"

"I was looking after the horses," she told him.

"You keep horses here?" Fetterman asked innocently.

"*Oui*. This is a ranch, no? We have horses. Look around you, Sergeant."

Fetterman didn't take his eyes off the woman. He had already noted the half-dozen horses in the stalls. "And have you got a horse back there, too?"

"Come. See for yourself." She motioned with her hand.

Fetterman came forward cautiously. He didn't lower the machine pistol.

"You see," she said. "Such a small one."

Fetterman satisfied himself that Monique LeClerc's hands were empty and that her submachine gun hung loosely at her side before he glanced toward the stall. A newborn colt and his mother lay on the straw. Fetterman relaxed slightly. "That is a young one."

"*Oui.* His mother must have given birth while we were meeting you and your men at the landing place. I didn't expect her to deliver for a few more days yet."

"He's a fine-looking colt. Well marked."

"Ah! You know something about horses."

"I grew up on a ranch out west," Fetterman said. "That is, at least I did until I was fifteen. The western United States, I mean. Madame LeClerc . . ."

"Please. Call me Monique."

"Monique," Fetterman said. "Why are you out here alone? You shouldn't be walking around out here by yourself."

"And why not? This is my ranch, is it not? Should I not go where I please on my own ranch?"

"I meant only that it might not be safe. You said yourself that your husband was murdered and that you should take precautions until you know by whom."

"I am taking precautions, Sergeant Fetterman," she said, tapping the barrel of the MAT-49 meaningfully.

"Still, ma'am, I don't think it's wise to walk around after dark without someone with you. Why didn't you turn on the lights? There's electricity out here, isn't there?"

"Yes. There's a transmission cable from the generator, but the lamps are broken. Philippe was going to change them, but he never got around to it. I would do it myself—there's a ladder on the wall—but truthfully I'm frightened by heights. Do you know the name of this condition?''

"I think it's called acrophobia," Fetterman said. He took an olive green GI flashlight out of his pocket and shone it up at the steeply pitched roof of the barn. "The lights look okay to me."

"When I said they were broken, it was, how you say, an expression of speech? I meant that they don't work."

Fetterman walked back over to the door, pretending to be interested in the overhead lamps while he kept one eye on Madame LeClerc. He flipped the light switch several times, but the overhead bulbs stayed dark. "Probably a loose wire somewhere," he said with relief. "I'll have a look at it for you in the morning if you like, provided there's time."

"Thank you, Sergeant. That's very kind of you."

She stood and raised the hem of her dress to brush away the straw from her knees. Fetterman couldn't help noticing, not even in the light of the lantern, that she had great legs—slender but with a bit of muscle to them, like a dancer's.

"Sergeant Fetterman," she asked suddenly, "have you a first name?"

Since Gerber had placed no restrictions on their giving their real names, Fetterman told her. "It's Anthony."

She gave it the inevitable French pronunciation.

"Antoine, a lovely name. It suits you well. The name of a great leader of men, Marc Antoine, and," she added after a moment, "the name of a great lover."

Fetterman laughed. "But no match for Cleopatra. You do say some odd things, Monique."

She smiled mysteriously in return, then changed the subject. "Tell me, Antoine, have you known Captain Gerber for a long time?"

"Yes," Fetterman said, wondering what she was leading up to.

"And have you fought in many campaigns together?"

"Yes. Many."

"He's a good officer, then, your captain?"

"One of the finest I've ever known."

She shrugged. "I don't think Captain Gerber likes me very much."

"It's not that he doesn't like you, Monique," Fetterman said. "It's just that he's a very careful man. In our line of work we have to be."

"Perhaps it's as you say, but I think it's something deeper than caution. I, too, have learned to be careful, yet I trust you because I was told to expect you by Control. Therefore, I know we're on the same side and I have no secrets from you."

Fetterman wondered if she meant him personally or the entire team.

"Yet Captain Gerber continues to distrust me. Perhaps he's only being careful, as you say, but I think it's that he just doesn't like me for some reason. Do you know any reason why your captain should not like me?"

"I can't think of anything."

Her expression changed and she scratched at her leg with her hand, raising the hem above the knee again. "And what about you, Antoine? Do you like me?"

The question caught Fetterman off guard. "I have no reason to dislike you."

"That isn't what I meant. Do you *like* me?"

Fetterman wondered what she meant, and then slowly realized the import of what she was asking. "I find you very attractive, Monique. Any man would," he told her truthfully.

"Bien!" she said, smiling brightly. "I must go check on my workers before retiring. She stooped and picked up the lantern. As she pushed past him, she impulsively seized the master sergeant and kissed him full on the lips. He was so shocked that he didn't even respond. "I'm very glad you like me, Antoine. *Adieu.*" And then she was gone.

Fetterman stared after her for a moment. "I wonder what in hell got into her."

He, too, started to leave, but then the innate curiosity that he had been cursed with since birth got the better of him, and he turned and walked back to the stall that held the mare and the colt. Taking his flashlight, he knelt down and examined the floor of the stall, brushing aside the straw.

There, on the concrete floor of the stall, where the straw had hidden it, was a dark patch of something unpleasant and very familiar. He tested it with his fingertips. It was sticky but not quite dry, perhaps several hours old. Slowly he raised his hand to his nose and sniffed. The coppery odor confirmed his suspicion.

It was a pool of blood.

10

**LECLERC RANCH,
BOLOVENS PLATEAU,
LAOS**

After he had been relieved from guard duty, talked to Gerber and eaten, Fetterman went to bed, but he didn't sleep, despite the comfortable bed and the restful surroundings. He was in a small guest room in the northeast wing, one of the half dozen scattered throughout the big house. Because the room had only a double bed, he hadn't been forced to share it with anyone, as the others had. It was, apparently, one of three rooms that Philippe LeClerc had intended for the children he never had.

Fetterman lay there for a long time, staring out into the darkness. His mind was filled with thoughts of Monique LeClerc. Why had she kissed him? And why had she told him that she was very glad that he found her attractive? Why hadn't she been able to fix the radio the CIA had given to her late husband when it had proved so simple a task for Bocker? Why wasn't her jeep in running condition, and how long had it been that way? Why where there so many weapons in her house, including illegal automatic weapons? Why didn't the lights work in the barn? And, most troublesome of all, what about the pool of blood in the stall? Was it simply the result of the mare's giving birth to the colt? Or was it something else, something Monique LeClerc had deliberately tried to hide from them? There were just too many questions and not enough answers, and too much at stake if the answers proved to be the wrong ones.

It was all just too confusing. The only thing he could think of was to sleep on it and see if things made any more sense in the morning. He closed his eyes and willed himself to relax, to blank everything from his mind except the image of a black velvet curtain in a dark room. Slowly he brought the curtain closer and closer, growing smaller himself as he did so until he was lying on the surface of it, completely surrounded by it.

He was almost asleep when there was a soft knocking at the door of his room. Soundlessly he rose from the bed and picked up the M-3 grease gun with the long silencer. Holding the submachine gun ready in one hand, he padded across the polished teak floor to the door and flipped it open.

It was Monique LeClerc.

She was dressed in a white lace robe over a long white silk gown that clung to her in a way that left little to the imagination. She looked at Fetterman and then at the M-3 in his hand, and her gray eyes grew wide. "Forgive me, Antoine. I didn't mean to alarm you," she said quickly. "May I come in?"

Fetterman lowered the grease gun and stood to one side. She slipped quickly through the open doorway and closed the door behind her.

"How can I help you, Monique?"

A brief look of anguish passed across her face, then she paced around the room for a moment. "May I sit down?"

"Please. Be my guest."

She laughed tensely. "That's funny, no? It's you who are my guest, yet you tell me to be your guest."

She looked around the room, as if seeing it for the first time, noted Fetterman's jacket and webgear with the Skorpion and sat on the bed. Fetterman put down the M-3, then sat beside her. It was either that or remain standing. There was no place else to sit.

"Now, then, Monique," Fetterman said reasonably, "what's all this about?"

"I don't know how to begin. You'll forgive me, please, if I'm not very good at this?"

"Go on."

"Earlier this evening, when I kissed you in the barn, did it shock you very much?"

"A little," Fetterman admitted. He had a hunch he knew how this was going to end.

"I'm sorry if I shocked you, but you must understand that it's been such a very long time." She reached out and took one of his hands in both of hers. Her palms were sweaty. "Antoine, may I be frank with you?" she asked, her voice suddenly firmer, as though she had drawn courage from the act of touching him.

"Sure."

"First, understand that I didn't love my husband. Ours was a marriage of convenience. I've already explained this to Captain Gerber."

Fetterman did his best to look surprised.

"There's more," she went on quickly. "Say nothing until you've heard it all."

He waited patiently for her to continue.

"I'm not sure whether you heard me say that I couldn't give Philippe children. That isn't entirely true. It was Philippe who was sterile, not I. During his time in the foreign legion, he contracted a venereal disease from a Vietnamese prostitute. The doctor cured him with penicillin, but the disease left him sterile. Philippe didn't know this when we married. After we had tried for many years to have children, but with no success, Philippe insisted that we both be tested for fertility. When he discovered the truth, he became so depressed that he started drinking heavily. I tried to tell him that it was of no consequence, that he was no less a man because of it and that I still cared for him. It was the truth. I was very fond of him, but I didn't love him, and he knew that. In time he became impotent, and that so frustrated him that he became abusive. I think the alcohol contributed to his impotency. He would drink heavily, then take me to bed, and when he couldn't function despite my efforts he'd grow angry and beat me. Irrationally he blamed me for his condition.''

"I'm sorry," Fetterman said, patting her hands with his free one. "Why didn't you leave him?"

She shrugged. "Where could I go? When one has become accustomed to certain things, it isn't easy to leave them for the unknown, even when they have lost part of their attraction.'' She looked down for a moment, then looked at him with tears in her eyes. "You're a kind man, Antoine. I sensed it when I first saw you, although I didn't yet even know your name. That's why I ask you now for your help.''

"What do you want me to do, Monique?" Fetterman asked.

She blushed and looked away. "I want you to help me. To give me what's rightfully mine, but which was denied me these past two and a half years. To give me what is the right of any wife.''

"I'm sorry," Fetterman told her. "I don't understand.''

She looked him squarely in the eye. "I want you to make me a woman again, Antoine. I want you to make love to me.''

Fetterman sighed. "Monique, please don't misunderstand, but . . .''

"Shh, Antoine," she said as she let go of his hand and opened his fly. *"Mon cher,"* she whispered softly in his ear, then lowered her face to his lap.

As he felt her warm mouth close around him, Fetterman shut his eyes and marveled at the knowledge that he was being seduced.

IN THE MORNING, after the Lao Theung cook had prepared a breakfast of vegetable-and-sausage quiche, once again under the watchful eye of Sergeant Krung, Fetterman repaired the lights in the barn, finding, as he had predicted, a loose connection in the switch. It was almost ridiculously easy to fix and only took him about five minutes, but it gave him the chance to carefully examine the barn. He searched for nearly forty-five minutes, but found nothing unusual other than the blood beneath the straw.

Then he and Sully Smith attempted to get Monique's jeep started. After almost two hours, working with tools Monique brought them from the machine shed, they succeeded in finding and correcting no less than five separate problems with the carburetor and electrical system. By then the battery was almost dead and they had to push the jeep to get it started, but it ran.

While Fetterman and Smith worked on the jeep, Gerber and Kepler had a talk with Madame LeClerc.

"My men and I want to go to Muong May," Gerber said. "To your late husband's tree plantation. Can you help us get there?"

"Why do you want to go there?" LeClerc asked, evident surprise on her face.

"We wish to use his forest as a base for our further operations," he told her vaguely. "Didn't your control officer in Vientiane tell you that?"

"No, only that Philippe was to assist you however possible."

"Can you help us get there?" Gerber repeated.

Monique LeClerc seemed to consider the situation. "We cannot all fit in the jeep. Perhaps if your men are successful in getting it to work, I could drive to one of the neighboring ranches and borrow a truck. There's a man named Robert, Paul Robert, a Frenchman whose house is only about thirty kilometers from here. He doesn't own the ranch, but manages it for a German company."

More damn Nazis probably, Gerber thought. He shook his head. "That's no good. I don't want anyone to know about our mission or that we're here."

He didn't tell her that he had no intention of allowing her to go off by herself somewhere and leave them waiting at the ranchhouse to be collected by the first Pathet Lao or NVA patrol that happened by.

"Please think, Madame LeClerc. Is there some other way?"

"Monique!" she snapped at him.

"I'm sorry," Gerber said. "I forgot. Please try to think of something else. We really need your help."

She seemed to soften at that. Gerber had finally expressed an element of trust for her. It actually brought a smile to her lips. She furrowed her brow, as if in deep concentration, then suddenly brightened. "*Oui!* Perhaps there's another way. Tell me, Mack, can your men ride?"

"Ride? Ride what?" Gerber asked.

"Horses! It's the only way."

Gerber suddenly had an image of the nine of them riding off into the Laotian sunset in the style of a grade-B western movie, their ponies loaded down with explosives and rocket-propelled grenades, grease guns tied to their saddles. It was a ridiculous idea, of course. Besides, they would be traveling east into the sunrise, not the sunset.

"You're joking," he said. "There must be some other alternative."

Madame LeClerc wasn't amused. "Of course there's another alternative, Captain. You and your men could walk. It should only take you about a week to get there, provided you don't run into the Pathet Lao or the Vietminh. On horseback we could make it in two days."

"What do you mean, *we* could make it?" he asked.

"I would have to show you the way, guide you. There's a way through the hills that would enable us to make the journey in two days. The route isn't on the maps, but I think I can remember it well enough to lead you through it. I rode it once with Philippe many years ago. To go by following the roads would take three or four days at least, and you'd run an increased risk of encountering the Vietminh and Pathet Lao. They often use the roads themselves, and sometimes they mine them or set ambushes."

"This is the twentieth century," Gerber protested. "Not the nineteenth."

"And it's also Laos, *monsieur*. Much of the country isn't even in the eighteenth century. I ask you again, Captain, can your men ride?"

Gerber sat silently for a moment, then said, "Derek, find out how many of the men have ever ridden a horse."

"Sir," Kepler began, "don't you think it would be better if we . . . ?"

"Just go find out, damn it!" Gerber snapped.

"Yes, sir."

THEY LEFT in the late morning with fourteen horses: ten mounts and two pack animals carrying the extra equipment, food and water. The other two horses were spares in case one of the animals was injured.

Monique LeClerc rode with Gerber near the front of the little column. She had traded in her blue jeans and sneakers for a pair of beige riding pants and brown knee-high boots and wore a khaki bush jacket over a gray tank top that matched the color of her eyes. She had left behind her favored MAT-49 for the silenced Sten Mark VI, but had kept both the Colt .45 pistol and her indigo kerchief. The black turtleneck was tucked into her saddlebags, since the evenings in the foothills of the mountains would be cool.

They would ride for an hour, then walk for fifteen minutes, leading the horses to rest them. By midafternoon they had crossed the Se Kong above its junction with the Khampho River and stopped to water the horses and eat. The atmosphere was almost picniclike, with the water rushing over a small, nearby rapids and the greenness of their surroundings. The presence of the peacefully watering horses added to the pastoral setting in which their weapons and the uniforms of the men seemed an intrusion.

Madame LeClerc's cook had prepared sandwiches of cold roast beef for them before they'd departed and had included cheese and beer, packing in canvas bags filled with ice. Gerber allowed each man a single beer, and they drank it gratefully. Even Reasnor, who professed to detest the beverage.

sampled the Japanese brew and pronounced that perhaps, given enough time and enough thirst, he could develop a taste for it. Krung alone made tea, boiling it in a canteen cup over a tiny bar of trioxene fuel.

Monique LeClerc came to sit by Fetterman while they ate. They didn't speak while eating, but stared at each other often.

"Antoine, I've been thinking a lot about last night," she said quietly when they finished.

"Sometimes it isn't good to think about something too much," Fetterman told her gently. "It can make things lose their luster."

"No," she told him. "It isn't as you say. Even if the book ends other than one expects, the beauty of the prose remains. Should you ever return to Laos, you will find yourself most welcome in my home."

"I'd like that. You'll stay at the ranch, then? You're not going to return to France?"

"No, I won't go back to France. There is nothing for me there. My life is here now, and here I'll remain unless the Communists drive me out. It's a good ranch, and even with the war it's done well. When the fighting ends, I'll make it prosper. The house is a very large one, and I'd like to fill it with children someday."

"Monique...I can't promise you anything," Fetterman said slowly.

"Antoine, say no more. I know, although you can't blame me for having hopes. And now it's time to go. We will travel many miles yet before darkness."

They camped that night south of Attopeu, picketing the horses nearby, and dined on rice and pickled pork. There was a jug of wine, too, but Gerber allowed them only half a glass apiece. They were nearing the area where they could expect trouble anytime, and he didn't want their brains befuddled with alcohol. They built no fire, and Krung had to settle for water to wash down his meal.

After they ate, Bocker strung an antenna for the radio and listened for any word from Kontum, but there was no news, only the routine nine o'clock acknowledgment that Mauraides was listening for word from them in the communications center. Bocker sent his identifier, got a response and carefully tapped out the two short code words on the straight key, telling Mauraides that all was well and that they were proceeding toward their target.

When they turned in for the night, the men wrapped themselves in their ponchos and blanket liners, and Monique LeClerc unrolled her sleeping bag next to Fetterman.

"Our master sergeant seems to have found himself a new girlfriend," Kepler whispered to Gerber.

"Yeah," the captain said sourly. "And that could turn out to be a real problem."

11

FIFTH SPECIAL FORCES
FORWARD OPERATING
BASE KONTUM, RVN

"Captain Mauraides? Captain Mauraides!" the voice repeated.

Captain Bruce Mauraides opened one eye and stared at the Special Forces communications sergeant shaking him gently by the shoulder. He had been up all night in case there was any additional word from SRT New Mexico, and anyone waking him now had better be doing it for something other than to tell him breakfast was ready.

"Please get up, sir. I think this might be important," the sergeant said.

Reluctantly Mauraides sat up and swung his legs over the side of his cot. "What is it?"

"Message for you, sir."

Mauraides opened his eyes wide. "From New Mexico?"

"No, sir. It's from somebody named Winter White. Not listed in the SOI. It's priority one, sir."

Mauraides had no idea who Winter White was. "You'd better give it to me, then," he said, holding out his hand.

"It's not a telex, Captain. It was a Fox Mike voice transmission. Winter White said he was about fifteen minutes out and requested that you meet him at the chopper pad. Said to tell you the White Clam was on board.''

Mauraides knew who that was, even if it wasn't an official code name. ''Tell him I'll be there,'' he said, pulling on his boots, ''and find me some coffee. Black.''

The sergeant scurried off while Mauraides finished lacing his boots, struggled into his jungle jacket and pulled on his beret. He splashed some water from his canteen on his face, slipped his webgear over his shoulders and picked up his M-16. The sergeant handed him a large mug of steaming black coffee as he went out the door of the bunker.

The helipad was a big square of PSP with the corners held down by olive drab rubberized sandbags and a big *H* painted in the center. There was a big, bright yellow windsock on a nearby pole. Mauraides got there early and managed to down about half of the cup of scalding coffee before the blue-and-white Huey with Air America stenciled on the side showed up and tried to blow the beret off his head.

Mauraides turned away to avoid the billowing dust as the chopper settled onto the pad, then turned back in time to see two swarthy men armed with Uzi submachine guns and dressed in white shirts and blue jeans jump out. A moment later they were followed by a man in a rumpled white linen suit and a narrow black tie, carrying a briefcase chained to his wrist.

Jerry Maxwell, CIA chief of station, Saigon, had earned the unflattering nickname, the Dirty White Clam, from the Saigon press corps because he always looked as if he needed a shave and was never seen except in his rumpled tropical suit. The Clam part was because it had proven impossible for the members of the fourth estate to extract any information from him.

''Good morning, Jerry,'' Mauraides shouted over the whine of the Huey's turbine, trying to sound more cheerful than he felt. ''You're kind of far afield, aren't you? What brings you to this neck of the woods?''

"Good morning, hell!" Maxwell grumbled. "I'm here to save your ass. Where can we talk?"

"You mean privately?"

"I mean absolutely two hundred percent secure. I didn't fly all the way out here just to exchange golfing tips."

"I suppose we could use the isolation briefing room."

"Is it secure?"

Mauraides rolled his eyes and looked at Maxwell. "Jerry, for Christ's sake, come on! We use it to mount covert ops practically every day of the year."

Maxwell took a toothpick out of his pocket and chewed on it. "I suppose it'll have to do," he said after a minute. "Let's go."

"Do you want me to post a guard outside?" Mauraides asked when they got to the briefing room.

"Don't bother," Maxwell said. "They'll take care of it." He spoke to the two bodyguards, who took up positions on either side of the door with their Uzis.

Mauraides sat down in one of the chairs. He hated dealing with the CIA. Really hated it. Especially this early in the morning. "Come on, Jerry. What's all this about?"

Maxwell unchained the briefcase from his wrist and unlocked it. He took a manila file folder out and dropped it onto the desk in front of Mauraides. The cover was embossed with the logo of the CIA and covered with Top Secret stamps. "That file doesn't exist," the CIA agent said melodramatically. "You never saw it. I could get my dick in the wringer just for showing you the cover. Understand?"

He loosened his tie and took off his jacket, revealing a Swenson .45 semiautomatic in a shoulder rig. Draping the jacket over the back of a chair, he plopped down a couple of seats away from the Special Forces captain.

"All right," Mauraides said. "I never saw it. In fact, I never even heard of it. What's inside?"

"Just everything we've got on one Etienne Pierre de Oran, alias Daniel Coustea, alias Wolfgang Speer, alias Dr. Carl Weatherspoon, alias Yuri Petrov, alias Henri Fouche, alias

Henry Jones. The man with the scar on his face your people asked my people about."

"A man of many personalities. I take it he was a double agent, as well."

"Single, double, triple, quadruple, you name it. The KGB thought he was working for the Brits. The British Secret Service thought he was working for the French. The French thought he was working for the Germans and the Germans thought he was working for us. We always thought he was working for the Russians."

"Jesus! What a can of worms! Who *was* he working for, Jerry?"

"All of us. Although personally I think he was a Russian agent all along. Not KGB, though. I think he was run by the GRU. I won't bore you with the details. It's all in the file if you really care, although I admit a part of my conclusions are guesswork. There's enough circumstantial evidence in there to build a pretty good case for it."

"I thought the KGB had responsibility for foreign Intelligence collection?"

"They do, but only up to a point. The GRU can become involved if purely military matters are involved."

"It would seem this fellow dealt with matters other than of a purely military nature," Mauraides said, leafing through the file.

"He did. But only so far as it tended to serve his cover and enhance his access to military Intelligence. It's the one thing consistent about the man."

Mauraides closed the folder and looked at Maxwell. "Jerry, why are you telling me all this?"

"I'm not telling you anything," Maxwell reminded him. "This conversation, that file, this meeting—none of it ever existed. But if I were telling you something, it would probably be because of what happened to him."

"What did happen to him?"

"He started working for us about five years ago. He'd already been working for the French and the Germans as well as the British and presumably the GRU. He had worked for the Germans and the British during the Second World War. Afterward things got a bit too hot for him on both sides of the Channel and he had to drop out of sight for a while. He did it by joining the foreign legion, a good place to hide but also very risky. Coincidently, it gave him access to French military information. Then something happened he hadn't planned on."

"The French war in Indochina."

"Precisely. I'm glad to see you're keeping up with me on this one. That's where he met Philippe LeClerc, alias Karl Helmut Mannheim."

"Talk about convolutions!"

"After the Indochina war he went to work for French Intelligence," Maxwell continued. "That's what he was doing when we picked him up. After France decided to pull out of NATO, we needed someone on the inside who could feed us information on the French military Intelligence network. Then the unexpected happened again and the man got posted back to Indochina. This time it was Laos. It wasn't what we wanted, but there was no way around it without tipping the French that he was working for us. So we had no choice but to go with the flow. That's when he was contacted by Odessa."

"Odessa? Who in hell is—wait a minute. Isn't that supposed to be the secret underground organization of ex-Nazis, or something like that?"

"Bingo," Maxwell said. "Odessa wanted to recover a shipment of gold bars lost during the final stages of the war, supposedly when the train they were on was bombed by Allied planes. There were 164 bars, each of them worth about two hundred and forty thousand dollars. A little over forty million bucks was riding on that train."

"No wonder they'd like to get their hands on it," Mauraides said, whistling. "That kind of money could keep a lot of guys happy in Argentina."

"A lot of people would like to get their hands on it," Maxwell said. "As it turns out, Philippe LeClerc was a guard on that train. Odessa seemed to think he might have gotten his hands on part of the gold."

"And did he?"

"Jones said no. Odessa wanted him to go and talk to LeClerc, and the French wanted him to go to Attopeu to meet with the Pathet Lao southern command. Since we were involved in Vietnam by then, and Laos was right next door, we gave him our blessing and told LeClerc, who was by then working for us, to keep an eye on him. We wanted to know what the French were up to, holding hands with the Pathet Lao."

Maxwell pulled a bottle of warm Coke out of the inside pocket of his jacket and opened it on the edge of the desk.

"What were the French doing holding hands with the Pathet Lao?" Mauraides asked.

Maxwell took a big drink of Coke before answering. "We never found out. He sent back his report to us and the Nazi underground, clearing LeClerc, and then left for Attopeu. He was never heard from again."

"You think LeClerc did know something about the gold? That Jones found out about it and LeClerc killed him to keep it quiet?"

"LeClerc knew about the gold, all right. He stole four bars of it. The bombing cracked open one of the shipping crates, and the guards found out what they were guarding. They'd been told it was a new secret weapon that was going to allow Germany to win the war. I doubt if any of them believed that— by then the writing was on the wall—but until the crate broke they didn't know it was gold.

"After the train was bombed, the surviving guards took a look at all that gold just lying there. They all knew the war was going to be over soon, in a few short months at most, and that afterward the citizens of Germany were going to face some very long and difficult years trying to rebuild. Especially those who had lost everything during the war and who had no marketable skills."

"Like soldiers?"

"Exactly. So, like I said, they talked it over, and then they each took a few bars, whatever they could carry, and scattered. Walked away with nearly twenty-five million dollars in gold bullion. Nobody knows what happened to the rest. LeClerc told us all about it when he went to work for us. We were able to track down a couple of the others involved, and they confirmed his story. It wasn't our problem, so we left them alone. Most of the gold had been converted into other assets by then, anyway.

"But I don't think LeClerc killed him," Maxwell said. "He had no reason to. We already knew about the gold, and Jones had given him a clean bill of health. I suppose Jones could have been planning to sell LeClerc out to Odessa on the sly, but what was there to be gained? LeClerc had already invested most of the gold in his ranch and in certain stocks and bonds. There was no gold to be recovered, and even if Jones had been planning a sellout and LeClerc had found out about it, there was no reason for him not to report it to us. After all, he knew we didn't trust Jones. We'd told LeClerc to keep an eye on him."

"So what did happen to Jones?"

"He just vanished into the jungle, like I said."

"That's not what I mean. What do you think happened to him? Did somebody kill him or not? Did he run afoul of the Pathet Lao when he got to Attopeu?"

"You forget that our friend LeClerc was also in tight with the Pathet Lao," Maxwell said. "According to his sources, Jones never reached Attopeu."

"Jerry, I'm beginning to suspect you're being deliberately obtuse for some reason."

"Oh, Jones is dead, all right," Maxwell said, drumming his fingers on the desk. "I'm almost sure of it. In fact, I know it, damn it!" he growled, slamming his fist on the desk. "I can smell it! When Jones got to LeClerc's ranch, he saw something, something he was never meant to see, and he was killed for it. I'll bet my government pension on it."

"Like what?"

Maxwell drummed his fingers on the desktop again, rubbed his chin with his hand and then opened the briefcase once more. He took out another folder, much smaller than the first, and tossed it to Mauraides.

"There were just too many coincidences involved," he said. "Especially after your people sent word that LeClerc was dead, so I didn't just settle for the routine background files. I got on to our people in Paris and had them start digging. It took some doing because a lot of the wartime records of the Bureau of Statistics were lost. But they kept digging until they finally came up with something. When I put it all together and it made sense, I tried to get hold of Bates, but he's in transit somewhere, so I came here. You'll find it all in that file. It isn't much, but it's there."

Mauraides opened the file and looked at the photograph clipped to the first page. It was several years old but showed a very attractive young woman with long dark hair. Mauraides raised a questioning eyebrow at Maxwell.

"How soon can you get a message to your men in Laos?" the CIA agent asked.

"We can't. We have to wait for them to contact us."

"When will the next contact be?"

Mauraides had to think for a moment. He hadn't had much sleep, and everything Maxwell had told him had already overloaded his brain. "It's a sliding schedule. The next window won't be until 2300 hours tonight, and even then there's no guarantee they'll try to contact us. It's just a present time for us to be listening in on a certain wavelength in case they have traffic for us. If they don't have any news, they won't transmit."

"How about broadcasting a request for them to establish contact blind?"

"We could try that, but depending on their situation in the field, they may not even be listening. They're operating independently."

"Terrific. Just fucking marvelous."

"Jerry," Mauraides said, holding up the photograph, "who is this woman?"

"You mean you don't know? I thought you'd have figured it out by now."

Mauraides looked at the name on the back of the photo. "So who the hell is Giselle Giraud?"

"Look at the middle name."

"Monique. So?"

"Giselle Monique Giraud. Monique LeClerc. Get it? It's her maiden name. That's Philippe LeClerc's wife."

"So?"

Maxwell shook his head, as though working with amateurs was a painful experience. "Read the rest of the report. That's LeClerc's wife, all right. No question about it. They were married in Paris in January 1955. We even found the magistrate, and believe it or not, he remembered them because they made such a lovely couple. He positively identified their photos. The only trouble is, Giselle Monique Giraud died in a bombing raid in France in 1940 when she was twelve years old."

12

**THREE RIVERS SECRET
ZONE SOMEWHERE
NEAR MUONG MAY,
LAOS**

Gerber and the others had traveled steadily since first light, following the course Monique LeClerc had mapped out for them. As before, they had alternated between riding and walking in order not to tire out the horses and had stopped around two in the afternoon to water the animals and give everyone a brief break from the heat of the day. It also afforded a chance to rest tired posteriors and eat. Several of the men made the most of the situation by working in a thirty-minute nap.

Gerber had tried to follow their progress on the map as best he could, but the trails they followed, narrow and twisting, didn't appear on the maps, and sometimes there was no trail at all, only Madame LeClerc's unerring sense of direction. She seemed to have little difficulty remembering the way, despite the time she said had passed since the last time she'd ridden the route. Gerber found that, at best, he could occasionally match up a feature on the map with some prominent landmark, giving an indication of their general location. They did seem to be making progress and were traveling more or less in the right direction most of the time.

The landscape varied considerably, from lush river valleys to the rock-strewn hills and dense jungle. Yet it seemed that every time they encountered a new obstacle, or just when it appeared they would have to get out and hack a path for the horses through the dense brush, Monique LeClerc would show them a way around it, or lead them onto a new trail moving in the right direction.

They were getting uncomfortably close to the network of footpaths and primitive roads that made up the Ho Chi Minh Trail now, and they maintained a constant vigilance against ambush. By mutual agreement, if they did ride into trouble, they would attempt to ride through the ambush and then double back to hit the enemy on the flank. Gerber wasn't at all sure how effective the tactic would be, or how the horses would respond to the sound of gunfire or grenades. He felt very exposed, sitting up there in the saddle, making a wonderful target for anyone with a gun, and consoled himself with the thought that any enemy who saw them would probably die laughing before he could pull the trigger.

Krung would scout ahead each time Monique gave them a new direction of travel, then double back to report what he had found. For the most part he reported only empty wilderness, although occasionally he would come across a trail that had seen traffic recently, but always it was a few days or a few weeks ago.

"There are some Lao Theung villages in this area," Monique told Gerber, "but I've tried to keep us clear of them. You said you wanted no one to know you're here, and besides, as you once pointed out, it is difficult to know the politics of a particular village. We're in the zone controlled by the Pathet Lao and Vietminh now."

Gerber approved of the tactic. He had no desire to run into any of the hill people whose sympathies lay with Hanoi. "How much farther is it to your timber holdings?" he asked Monique when they finally stopped just before sundown.

"Not far," she told him. "If we start again at first light, we should reach it before midday. Beyond that second hill you can see in the distance there's a stream that winds along the base of the hill. Follow it north until it makes a sharp bend back to the southeast and then ride due east for a kilometer or so and you'll come to an old, abandoned logging road. Follow it north for another kilometer and a half and you'll come to the road to Muong May. If you take the main road east out of Muong May, about ten kilometers farther on you'll find another logging road running off to the northeast, only this one is in use. Follow it for five kilometers and you'll come to the logging camp. The foreman there is Hans Mueller. If you give him my name, he'll help you. He's a friend of Philippe's from World War II."

"You speak as though you won't be going on with us, Monique," Gerber said.

"I'll ride with you to the camp if you wish. I thought perhaps you might choose to go alone. You said no one must know you're here. I mention Hans only for emergencies. If you leave the horses near the camp, we'll find them. As I said, I'll go with you if you wish. Otherwise I'll leave you when we reach Muong May. We have an office in town there, and I'll be able to get word to Hans that I'm there. He'll see to it that I return to the ranch safely. There are arrangements that I must make regarding Philippe's death."

"I understand," Gerber told her. "How will you explain the horses to Hans? Or for that matter, your presence in Muong May?"

"It was Hans who told me of Philippe's death. He'll expect me, although he knows I'll be delayed because of the difficulty with the jeep. He expected me to send one of my workers to Robert's ranch to seek help in getting to Muong May. I'll tell him that I rode instead and that the other horses are for the Lao Theung who came with me to ensure my safety. I'll tell him that I released them after my arrival in Muong May, with instructions to take their horses to the camp. He'll believe that because he'll find the horses where you've left them. When the phantom workers fail to return, Hans won't find it very unusual. He considers the hill people to be unreliable.''

Gerber had to admit that the plan might work. "Here," he said, "I've got something for you." He took the radio tubes Bocker had given him out of his pocket. "Galvin believes these may work in your set. I'd been meaning to give them to you, but it slipped my mind."

Monique stared at him for a moment, as though wondering whether or not it was some kind of test. Then she smiled. "Keep them for me, please, until we get to Muong May. I'm afraid I might lose them, and I have no need of them until I return to the ranch."

"All right," Gerber said. "Don't let me forget."

"I'll remember to remind you," Monique said. "And if you'll excuse me, I think I'll go down to the stream at the foot of the hill and wash while there's still enough light to see. It's bad enough not to be able to bathe for two days, but not to wash my hair is intolerable."

"Would you like me to send one of the men along to keep you company?" Gerber asked.

"I'll have difficulty enough bathing. An audience will only make it worse. Besides, there's no need. I'm well protected," she said, lifting the Sten gun. "I'll get my things." She went over to her horse and collected the saddlebags. Throwing them over her shoulder, she set off down the hill.

When she reached the stream, one of the many nameless tributaries that flowed down out of the mountains and fed into the Se Kamene before it joined up with the Se Kong, she checked her watch, then took off her boots, stripped and stepped quickly into the cool water, taking a bar of soap with her. She bathed, remembering to wash her hair, then toweled off most of the water and redressed, this time in blue jeans and the familiar black turtleneck. She pulled on socks and struggled back into the high-topped riding boots, buckled the Colt .45 around her waist and bundled up her top and the riding pants inside the bush jacket, tying the bundle with her ker-

chief. She left her hair wet, since that would add to the cred-
ibility of her excuse. Then, picking up the Sten and throwing
the saddlebags over her shoulder, she started back up the hill,
angling away from the camp.

Monique LeClerc made a careful point of passing well clear
of the spot where the others waited with the horses. It was almost dark now, and she worked quickly so as not to lose the
light. Setting down the bundle of clothes, she laid the Sten
across them, then lowered the saddlebags and opened the other
side.

She took out a coil of wire, weighted at one end, and tossed
it over a convenient branch, then anchored the ends, using two
plastic spoons as insulators for the antenna. Taking the small
HF band transceiver out of the saddlebag, she connected the
ground and battery, then looked again at her watch. It was
nearly time. She switched on the set, allowed it to warm up for
a few minutes, then tuned in the frequency, checked her watch
again and reached for the tiny CW key.

"What are you doing, Monique, arranging a little welcom-
ing party for us?" a voice asked softly behind her.

She froze, her fingers inches from the key.

"Just leave the radio the way it is and stand up slowly."

Monique glanced toward the Sten. It was less than two feet
away.

"Don't even think of it. I wouldn't like to shoot you, but I
will if you reach for that Sten."

Sighing, she lowered her hand and stood up.

"Now the pistol. Unbuckle the belt and lower it to the
ground, nice and easy. Use the left hand only, please, and keep
your right where I can see it."

She did as ordered, letting the belt slip through her fingers
the last few inches to the ground."

"All right. You can turn around now. Just don't make any
sudden movements. They could prove fatal."

She turned to face the voice, and there stood Fetterman in
the dim light. He was about fifteen feet away and held one of
the suppressed M-3s.

"Why, Monique? Is it money or politics? Surely not money. Philippe must have had more than enough of that for both of you."

She smiled at him. "The reasons aren't important, Antoine. It's enough that you and I are on different sides."

"Who do you work for? The Russians? The North Vietnamese? Maybe the French?"

She smiled at him again but said nothing.

"All right, we'll try another question. When did you become an agent?"

"It was a long time ago," she said vaguely. "It seemed the thing to do at the time. How long have you known?"

"I didn't until just a few minutes ago. I suspected you, but I didn't have any proof."

"How long have you suspected, then?"

"Since that first night when you came to my room."

She smiled sadly. "Ah, I thought perhaps you had found the blood in the barn. I'm disappointed. I thought it was a very convincing performance."

"I did find the blood," Fetterman told her. "But I thought it had come from the mare. I was going to have Reasnor take a look at it, but it would have been pointless. Without lab equipment he couldn't have told me if it was animal blood or human. Whose blood was it, Philippe's?"

"Yes. He found me in the barn with that." She inclined her head slightly toward the shortwave set. "I buried him beneath the floor of the machine shed. It's dirt there. I'm sorry that it couldn't be in a more restful spot. At least he's buried in Laotian soil. He loved this country, and the ranch, and wouldn't have wanted it otherwise. It's too bad he had to learn the truth. I really was quite fond of him."

"He really was your husband, then? I thought perhaps you'd killed both LeClercs."

She looked shocked. "Oh, no. We were together for many years. I married him in Paris in 1955. He was always very kind to me, and my superiors thought that it would be good for my cover. They didn't know that he planned to return to Laos, nor did I at the time, but as luck would have it, it worked out well, especially after he started working for your CIA. It was quite a joke really. Your agent and ours living under the same roof, sharing the same bed. Things went along quite nicely until Jones came into the picture.''

"What did Jones have to do with it?"

"We'd met before and he recognized me. He was careful not to let on to Philippe, but my superiors were afraid that it might become a problem. Jones had become, shall we say, politically unreliable. There was some concern that the CIA was onto him, and my superiors were afraid he might be pressured into revealing that he knew me."

"You killed him, too?"

"Yes. On orders from my superiors."

"You're going to have to tell me who you work for, Monique. You're going to have to tell me what they know about why we're here."

"I think not."

"If you don't . . ." Fetterman began.

"You will do what? Torture me? I don't think so, Antoine. That's not your way—to torture a woman."

"There are other ways. Reasnor has some sodium pentobarbital in his bag. Maybe he can do something with that."

She shrugged. "Perhaps. But I don't think it will prove effective. We're trained to resist such things. I'm curious, however. Please answer me one question. You said you suspected me from the moment I came to your room. I did it to win your confidence because I thought you and Captain Gerber would be the biggest threats to me, and I didn't think he would respond to such a move. Tell me, please, what was it that I did wrong?"

"Nothing. It was a perfect performance. I especially liked the way you managed to cry and blush on command, but then I suppose the really good ones always can."

"Nothing? Then what was it that made you suspect me?"

"The fact that you picked me," Fetterman told her. "With a whole house full of big, strapping, American studs, any one of whom would have traded six months pay to get into your pants, you picked the shortest, ugliest, oldest one in the bunch. A woman as desperate for a little lovemaking as you claimed to be, particularly a woman as beautiful and as wealthy as yourself, could have had any one of the others just for the asking. But you picked the balding guy. I'm not so infatuated with my own sexual prowess that I'm used to women throwing themselves at me. I've managed a few in my time, but it was usually because I was the only game around and, if I may be just a little bit conceited, because I acted like a gentleman and treated them like a lady. You weren't interested in being treated like a lady, so there had to be another reason. I'll take the guns now. Just step back a little."

He had to admire her style. She stood there quietly, looking beaten, until he crouched to pick up the Sten. Then she lunged. Only the very brave or the very foolish will charge a man with a gun like that. She didn't crouch beforehand or do anything else that might have telegraphed the move. She just suddenly threw herself at him, her left hand jabbing out to seize the suppressor while she brought her right fist up hard from beneath to deliver a paralyzing blow to his right elbow, driving her right shoulder into his solar plexus to knock him off balance, then snapping her head up to butt him under the chin.

Fetterman managed to squeeze the trigger down and hold it before his arm went numb. It was very nearly enough, and the first round out of the muzzle ripped an ugly gash in the side of her cheek, but he hadn't been quick enough. Another four or five rounds ripped through the leaves and thudded into the trunks of the tree behind her, splintering the wood before he lost control of the M-3. He hadn't been caught totally unaware, however, and brought his left hand up, the fingers locked stiffly together in an underhanded knife strike that caught her left wrist and knocked her hand away from the suppressor, sending the grease gun flying into the shadows, where it discharged once more.

Fetterman kicked out with his feet, adding to the momentum of her lunge, and brought a knee up into her belly, pivoting her to the side. As they hit the ground, he rolled away and came up on his feet. LeClerc came up, too, and immediately danced toward him and struck again, sweeping his feet out from beneath him with her right leg and delivering a solid kick to his rib cage as he fell. He rolled away just in time to avoid the heavy right boot descending toward his face.

Belatedly Fetterman remembered how he had noted the muscular nature of her legs when he'd surprised her in the barn at the ranch. He'd thought they'd looked like dancer's legs, but now he remembered something else that also tended to develop the lower extremities—French kick boxing. He felt two more stunning blows strike his hip and side, just narrowly missing the kidney, before he could finish the roll and get completely clear.

LeClerc was between him and the Sten and .45 now, and the M-3 was somewhere out in the darkness. She danced in close again and delivered two lightning-fast strikes at his knees with the heavy boots, which he managed to avoid, but landed a blow with her fist, aiming for the underside of his nose to drive the septal bone up into the base of his brain. The punch missed and caught him on the cheekbone, staggering him. She was surprisingly strong.

Fetterman had killed dozens of men in combat, many of them in hand-to-hand, but he quickly realized that Monique LeClerc was no amateur. She was easily one of the most dangerous opponents he had ever faced.

She moved in quickly. Her face, reflected in the moonlight, had once been a thing of great beauty, but was now contorted into a hideous mask of rage. And that gave Fetterman hope.

He had learned long ago that a man enraged or gripped by fear acts out of instinct, not cold, calculating thought. Those who killed in the heat of passion, any passion, never became killers in the truest sense of the word. Only those who killed in cold blood.

LeClerc used her feet again in a flying pivot kick that Fetterman was ready for. He dodged as it came, blocking the kick with his left hand and chopping down hard with the right, but he connected with only a glancing blow and her kneecap didn't break.

This time it was she who rolled away, and it took her two tries to get to her feet. He hadn't broken the knee, but evidently he'd numbed it.

As she came up off the ground, he caught the glint of light from the sharpened edge of black steel she held in her hand. It had a familiar shape. A British commando knife. She must have had it hidden somewhere in her clothes, perhaps tucked into one of the boots.

Fetterman considered the Skorpion, nestled in its shoulder holster beneath his armpit, but that would be too slow. If he'd been wearing a jungle jacket, he might have tried for it, could possibly have ripped loose the buttons in time to draw and fire the weapon, but the Portuguese jacket he wore had a strong steel zipper that was drawn well up against the chill of the night. There wouldn't be time to pull it down, free the Czech machine pistol, chamber a round from the magazine and fire before she could strike. Gerber and the others would certainly hear it and come to investigate, but they were deep in enemy country, and there was no guarantee that the sound wouldn't be overheard by the Pathet Lao or NVA, as well.

Fetterman drew his own knife, the old Case VS-21 that had served him well through three wars and countless other encounters. Monique circled him warily now. He had anticipated her last attack, and they were equally armed, although she had a slight advantage in reach over the Special Forces master sergeant.

Fetterman saw the rage fade from her face as her eyes assumed a crafty look, and knew that he had better think of something fast. He held one hand high, palm open and fingers spread near the side of his head, his other hand moving the blade from side to side as though preparing for a slashing attack.

She had a handful of dirt that she must have picked up before rising, and she threw it at his face before she lunged at him. But he was ready for something like that. He snatched the cap from his head and blocked most of the dirt, then tossed the cap into her face. As she lunged past, he sidestepped the thrust and struck with his knife. She parried with her hand, and the edge sliced deep into her palm and forearm.

Fetterman didn't escape unscathed. LeClerc's attack had missed its mark but had sliced downward along his side and hip, severing the belt of his webgear and cutting deep into his hip and thigh. He could feel the warm wetness of the blood immediately and knew he'd been hurt, but he had no idea how badly.

LeClerc ignored her own wounded hand, as she had the gouge the bullet from the grease gun had torn from her face, and circled for another try, but Fetterman turned with her and met her head-on. She paused, studying him, seeking another opening to get through.

"What's the matter, Monique? Don't you know how to kill Americans?" Fetterman said quietly. Then he raised his voice. "You're really not very good at killing people, are you? All you know how to do is *fuck* them!"

It did the trick. She lunged at him wildly.

Fetterman was ready for it. He feinted left, then moved quickly to the right and swung his hips out even farther. As she came forward with the commando knife, he parried the blade with his hand, feeling it slice through the skin of his finger all the way to the bone. Then he brought the Case up hard, held with the edges vertical to the ground, and drove it upward and in beneath the lower margin of her rib cage. The blade went in all the way to the finger guard, and when it stopped, he ripped upward with it.

A look of surprise flickered on Monique's face. She had underestimated the American soldier yet again. She felt her fingers loosen their grip on the commando knife and heard it thud softly as it fell to the jungle floor. It was suddenly very difficult to breathe, and the moon seemed to have gone behind the clouds. She felt the hands of the American upon her, holding her, but didn't have the strength to push them away.

Fetterman stood there, holding the woman erect. He knew he should have followed up the killing thrust with a second between the ribs and a third to the kidney to be certain of the kill, but he lacked the strength to do the job. He was spent, totally wasted. In the brief time they'd struggled, certainly less than two minutes and probably less than one, he'd used every bit of energy he possessed. His body was bathed in sweat. He heard her knife drop, then, after a moment he pulled her away from where the weapon had fallen, withdrew his own blade, hearing her moan softly as he did so, and lowered her gently to the ground. Then he knelt beside her, and she looked up at him with unseeing eyes.

"I . . . never had a chance . . . did I?" she gasped.

There was frothy pink blood oozing from the corner of her mouth, and the huge rent in her abdomen and chest made ugly sucking noises with each breath. He tried to cover the wound with his hand to shut off the flow of air into the chest cavity through the wound, but the damage was too great. When that wouldn't work, he tried to hold the sides together with both hands, but that failed, too. There was blood everywhere now and, as he looked at his hands trying to squeeze the sides of the six-inch laceration together, he couldn't tell if it was her blood or his own.

"I got lucky, that's all," he told her. "On another day it would have been me."

She coughed. "You lie very well, Sergeant. I . . . made a foolish mistake like . . . some young amateur. It is . . . you who acted as the pro . . . fessional."

"Monique, I have to know who you're working for. What did you tell them about us?"

"Go . . . to hell . . . *mon cher.*" She coughed again, but smiled at him. "One . . . question only. Your name. Is it really . . . Antoine?"

Fetterman nodded. "Anthony B. Fetterman. Master sergeant. United States Army Special Forces." It couldn't possibly matter what he told her now.

A spasm seized her, and this time when she coughed, blood bubbled from her mouth and splattered his arm. "I had to know," she said. "You...won't believe...me, but I am truly sorry...it had to end this way. You and I...we are much alike, Master Sergeant Fetterman. Had the...countries of our birth...been different...I could have called you...friend."

"Don't try to talk now. There's no need." He knew he wouldn't get any answers from her.

"Antoine! Antoine!" she said suddenly.

"I'm right here, Monique," he told her gently.

Fetterman watched the life seep out of her eyes. She made one last gurgling noise and then lay still beneath his hands.

"Goodbye, Monique," he said softly.

A moment later the night was split by the beams of three different flashlights.

"Tony?" Gerber whispered. "What the hell's going on here?"

"She's dead, Captain," Fetterman said woodenly. "I tried to take her alive, but she wouldn't have it that way. She was an enemy agent. Her husband found out and she killed him and buried the body in the machine shed on the ranch. She killed Jones, too. He'd met her before and recognized her. I don't know what she did with his body. I caught her trying to radio our position to someone."

"Who?" Gerber asked. "Who was she working for? The NVA?"

"I don't know the answer to that. We may never know."

"Are you all right, Tony?" Gerber asked, suddenly concerned.

"I'll live. She cut me a couple of times. I think the hand's pretty bad."

"Here, let me take a look," Reasnor said, pushing past. He examined Fetterman's wounds quickly by the glow of his flashlight. "You're going to need several stitches, but I don't think she hit anything vital," he pronounced. "I'll know more once we get you cleaned up a bit. It looks like she did get the tendon in your finger. I think I can suture it back together, but it probably won't work as well as it once did. Christ, I hate operating under these conditions."

"Can it wait, doctor?" Gerber asked., "If she did get a message out, we could be up to our asses in NVA any moment now."

Reasnor shook his head. "Not if you want him to have full use of the hand. It's got to be done now before the tendon contracts."

"She didn't talk to anyone, Captain," Fetterman said. "I got to her before she could transmit."

"How long will it take?" Gerber asked.

"Forty-five minutes to an hour," Reasnor said. "Maybe more. It depends on what I find."

"All right, get started," Gerber told him.

"I won't have to put you out for this, but I'm going to have to anesthetize that for you, Master Sergeant," Reasnor told Fetterman. "I'm going to give you some xylocaine. It won't make you sleepy, but it should keep you from feeling anything when I go to work on you. It may sting a bit when I give it to you, but that will pass in thirty seconds or so."

"Fire away," Fetterman said. "It can't hurt any worse than it already does."

"Captain," Kepler said, "what are we going to do now? Do we continue on, or do we abort the mission and ask for extraction?"

Gerber rubbed his chin. Infiltration of the mission by an enemy agent was the one thing they hadn't developed an alternate plan for. To make matters worse, they didn't even know who she was working for. It seemed unlikely that it was the North Vietnamese, Vietcong or Pathet Lao, since Philippe LeClerc had been friendly with them. They would hardly plant a spy on someone they thought was one of their own. Or would they? Perhaps she'd been an operative for French Intelligence. The French were often difficult and sometimes less than friendly allies, and they had retained a strong interest in their former colonies in Indochina. But would they go so far as to murder someone known to be an American agent? That would be trying their tenuous relationship with the United States to the extreme. Besides, Monique LeClerc had said that Jones was a Frenchman who worked for the CIA. It seemed unlikely that France had suddenly decided to declare war on the Central Intelligence Agency. The real burning question was what was she doing there in the first place? Philippe LeClerc had worked for the Agency only since 1962, according to Bates, and Monique had known him since 1954, long before he became an agent for the CIA. Or had that been a lie? Yet how could she have been planted on Philippe LeClerc before he even became an agent? Was it possible that he was a double agent and had been working for someone else before the CIA scooped him up? When Bates had told Gerber to trust no one, he'd never expected anything as complex as the present situation.

"We go ahead," he said at last, "but we change our plans a little. We leave for Muong May tonight, just as soon as Reasnor finishes sewing up Tony. Once we get there we'll turn the horses loose and proceed on foot. If Monique did notify anyone to expect us, they'll be looking for a bunch of rodeo clowns on horseback, following the trail she laid out for us, not men on foot moving through the jungle."

"We're going to go on to LeClerc's lumber operation, then?" Kepler asked.

"Yes," Gerber said. "All this helpfulness on the late Madame LeClerc's part to get us there kind of makes me wonder just what in hell is so special about the place."

"You know, if we're not careful, we could wind up walking right into that trap Fetterman worked so hard to keep her from setting for us," Kepler pointed out.

"We could," Gerber agreed, "but you're forgetting something. We've got an advantage."

"What's that?" Kepler asked. "Seems to me the bad guys have all the advantages."

Gerber smiled. "The advantage is that we know it could be a trap and they don't know that we know."

"All right," Kepler said. "I'll head back to camp and have the others start getting the horses ready. What are we going to do about her, though?" he asked, indicating LeClerc. "Want me to hide the body, or are we just going to leave it?"

"Captain," Fetterman interrupted, "I'd like to bury her if there's time. I think we owe her that much. It's a little difficult to explain why, but she was a good agent, whoever she worked for. She kept a lot of people fooled for a long time, and she damn near took me in hand-to-hand. Call it professional courtesy."

For a moment Gerber stared at Fetterman as though he had lost his marbles, then he nodded. "Permission granted."

13

THREE RIVERS SECRET ZONE SOUTHEAST LAOS

After they had collected LeClerc's weapons and shortwave transceiver, and Reasnor had finished stitching up Fetterman's hand and side, they wrapped Monique LeClerc in her sleeping bag and laid her to rest beneath the fertile soil of southeast Laos. There was no ceremony, and no one said any prayers over her grave, nor did they leave a marker except for the pile of rocks over the mounded earth that would help keep jungle scavengers from unearthing her remains. The only tribute paid was by Fetterman, who, when they had finished the task, simply said, "Goodbye, Monique," and threw a salute toward her final resting place.

Bocker examined her radio and was frankly impressed by the compactness and sophistication of the unit. Interestingly enough, it wasn't transistorized. It was vacuum-tube technology, but very well done. But Bocker couldn't determine its country of probable origin. It could have been recent Russian, Czech or Polish work, or a somewhat older German model. It was pointless trying to guess, anyway, since her superiors might well have provided her with a radio of Third-country manufacture.

Gerber gambled that if Monique LeClerc had managed to arrange an ambush for them, the reception committee would be expecting them to adhere to the schedule LeClerc had established for them and wouldn't be prepared for an early arrival. They followed their previous pattern of alternating riding and walking and reached Muong May shortly after midnight. The town was dark except for a handful of lights burning near its center, but they swung wide enough to bypass it nevertheless.

East of Muong May they moved with greater caution. Farther to the east lay Ban Tasseing and the complex path-and-road network of the Ho Chi Minh Trail. When they reached the road to the LeClerc lumber camp shortly before dawn, they unsaddled their mounts, unloaded the pack animals and bid goodbye to their means of transport, leaving the horses to find their own way home by instinct.

Caching what equipment and supplies they couldn't carry, they moved on toward the lumber camp, now following a course parallel and some distance removed from the one Monique LeClerc had given them. But when they arrived at midmorning, Gerber was disappointed. There was absolutely no indication that the camp was anything but what it appeared to be. There was an office building constructed of unfinished, rough-cut lumber, a couple of old trucks and a belt-driven, steam-powered sawmill. Three elephants were chained near the sawmill, and another half dozen were working in the forest nearby under the guidance of their handlers, moving around the logs. About twenty native workers labored at felling and trimming the trees, mostly with axes and bandsaws. The elephants then moved them to either the sawmill or the trucks, depending on whether they were to be rough-cut there or shipped out as whole logs on the trucks. There was a single telephone line running from poles into the office, but no indication of a radio antenna of any kind.

Gerber and the others patrolled the area for several hours, searching for any sign of activity other than what could be attributed to the lumbering operation, but in the end they found nothing of significance and were forced to conclude that there was nothing to be found.

After resting for six hours, they pushed on through the night and by dawn were halfway between Muong May and Ban Tasseing. This was familiar territory to them now. Gerber, Fetterman, Bocker and Tyme had all been there within the past year on a secret mission to disrupt a meeting between high-ranking members of the Peking and Hanoi governments and the provisional Pathet Lao government, headquartered in Samneua in northern Laos. Had the meeting been successfully concluded between the three political factions, it would have brought tens of thousands of PLA soldiers, complete with tanks and surface-to-air antiaircraft missiles, deep into southern Laos to protect the Ho Chi Minh Trail from American air strikes.

They moved with great caution, alert to the possibility of booby traps and mines, as well as ambush and chance encounters with enemy patrols. Krung and Fetterman found a number of punji pits and other primitive traps, but these were heavily weathered and seemed almost to have been forgotten by the enemy. At one point they encountered an extensive bunker complex and tried to detour around it but found their path blocked and were forced to seek a way through the series of half-buried fortifications. In doing so they discovered that the bunker system had been abandoned some months before and that the rotting timbers were overgrown by plants as the jungle sought to reclaim the complex.

They passed within a few miles of the spot where months earlier they had uncovered a secret jungle airstrip hidden beneath camouflage netting among the trees, and not much farther from the spot where the meeting between the Chinese, Viets and Pathet Lao had occurred, but they avoided these locations. It was possible the sites had, like the bunkers, been abandoned by the enemy once their location had been compromised, and if not, there was no sense in looking for trouble. Their orders were to recon the area east of the Ho Chi

Minh Trail where six RTs had been lost or savaged, not to go poking their noses around in old hot spots.

They slept for four hours during the early afternoon, hidden in a thicket of brambles and thorns. The day was miserably hot, and they lay in the stifling heat beneath the thorn-covered branches and vines, bathed in their own sweat. Fetterman's wounds from his fight with Monique LeClerc were beginning to bother him. His hand was sore and stiff and his side ached, and he was running a low-grade fever. But Reasnor was treating him with large doses of penicillin and expected the problem wouldn't become serious.

That night they crossed the Ho Chi Minh Trail. It took them several hours to work through the area crisscrossed by paths, trails and roads, and at one point their advance was held up for forty-five minutes as a convoy of trucks, marching men and bicycle porters blocked their way, heading southward for the enemy sanctuary areas in Cambodia before crossing over into South Vietnam. Gerber counted nineteen trucks and forty bicycles and estimated that there were over a hundred coolies carrying heavy loads or equipment lashed to packboards on their backs. It was maddening to watch so much war matériel pass by and be powerless to do anything about it, especially knowing that it was destined eventually for South Vietnam, but there was nothing the nine of them could hope to accomplish against such a large group of enemy soldiers, at least not without revealing their presence in the area and jeopardizing their primary mission. They could only watch the convoy go by, estimate the amount of equipment and men and report what they had seen later.

Gerber resisted the strong temptation to leave a few booby traps behind for the next convoy that came along. While Sully Smith could undoubtedly have improvised something from his bag of tricks, there remained a possibility that they would need the demolition equipment later, and with what could be spared for a mechanical ambush, they could hope at best to destroy a few trucks and kill a handful of the NVA. Reluctantly they were forced to concede that it was better to leave well enough alone.

Once they were clear of the Trail, they entered what was perhaps the most dangerous phase of the journey. Ban Tasseing was, for all practical purposes, under the control of the Pathet Lao, and the woods and fields were filled with enemy soldiers. Three times they sighted enemy patrols, twice at close range, and two more times they passed close enough to enemy camps to smell their cook fires or hear the conversation of the Pathet Lao. But each time they managed to go to ground and stay hidden until the danger had passed, or else detour successfully around it. Despite the activity of the patrols assigned to protect the Trail, the Pathet Lao and NVA didn't really expect to encounter American or South Vietnamese troops this far inside Laos, and certainly not approaching from the west.

One dangerous incident did occur shortly after dawn when Krung, scouting ahead of the others as usual, was forced to halt by yet another enemy patrol. When Gerber went forward to see what the problem was, he pushed through a thicket and into a clearing at the same time that a Pathet Lao soldier did so from the other side. As the two men came suddenly face-to-face, Gerber immediately raised his suppressed M-3 to fire, realizing that a knife attack would take too long for him to cross the open ground between them. Even suppressed, the M-3 would make a small amount of noise, and there was the possibility that the Pathet Lao soldier's friends nearby might hear it, but there was simply no way for him to get to the man before the enemy soldier could bring his own weapon, a Chicom Type 54 copy of the Russian PPS-43 submachine gun to bear.

The Pathet Lao soldier reacted at the same time, and it was a dead heat between them. Gerber feared that even if he managed to fire, the impact of the heavy .45-caliber bullets from the grease gun might cause the Pathet Lao to squeeze the trigger of his own weapon, thereby revealing their presence. But just as Gerber's finger was tightening on his own trigger, the enemy soldier suddenly staggered and dropped from view.

Krung had approached silently from behind and swiftly dispatched the Pathet Lao with his knife.

Gerber immediately ran forward and crouched near them, watching with a feeling of disgust as Krung claimed the trophy of his kill. They rounded up the others and left the area quickly, carrying the mutilated body of the dead Communist soldier with them and hiding it beneath a bush nearly a mile away. The corpse was quickly searched for any papers or documents before they covered it with branches and leaves, and Tyme added the man's SMG and Chinese stick-type hand grenades to his already overburdened load.

The men had been pushing hard for several days now, with very little sleep, and all were near exhaustion, yet Gerber drove them onward, wishing to be as far away from the body of the dead soldier as possible if it was discovered. When they found a small hill with a site near the crest suitable for an NDP around four in the afternoon, Gerber pulled them into a night laager and they dropped to the ground from sheer lack of energy. They didn't even bother to remove their packs, but fell asleep where they lay without digging in or setting out their perimeter of trip flares and French copies of the claymore mine. Gerber alone, through force of will, stayed conscious to guard them. He managed to keep awake for nearly an hour more before his head finally nodded to his chest and he fell asleep in a sitting position, his back against the trunk of a small tree.

It was dark when he woke suddenly to find Fetterman's hand across his mouth. The master sergeant leaned close and whispered in his ear. "Sorry to disturb you, Captain," Fetterman said, "but it's nearly 2200. Did you want me to wake up Galvin and have him give a listen to Kontum, or just let him sleep?"

"Who's on guard?" Gerber immediately asked.

"Just me," Fetterman whispered. "Krung woke up about 1930 and took it upon himself to watch over the rest of us until about an hour ago, then he woke me up. I told him to go back to sleep and leave the others alone. They need the rest."

"What about you?" Gerber asked. "How are you feeling?"

"Like death warmed over. The hand's the worst part. Hurts like hell. The side only hurts when I bump it with something. Other than that, my eyes feel like somebody poured a bucket of sand in them and I feel like shit, but I'll live, I guess."

Together they roused Bocker, who set up his radio rig and strung an antenna. When he dialed in the frequency for the Kontum communications center, he was surprised by the urgent, almost frantic request for contact. He took the key in hand and was immediately bombarded with an encrypted series of dots and dashes. He acknowledged receipt and took out the cipher pad and decrypted the message.

"What is it?" Gerber asked.

"Message from Captain Mauraides," Brocker said, reading off the pad by the diffuse glow of his red-lensed flashlight. "It's the answer to the query I sent from the ranch. It advises that Jones was believed to be a double agent and that Monique LeClerc may also be an agent. They urge us to use extreme caution in dealing with her. You want to reply?"

Gerber quickly jotted down an answer, which Bocker encrypted and transmitted before burning both the note and the cipher pad page.

When it was decrypted in Kontum it read, "Caution unnecessary. Monique dead. Proceeding target. NM QRT"

Both Mauraides and Bates, who had returned to Kontum as soon as Jerry Maxwell's message had caught up with him, breathed a considerable sigh of relief. The extraction team, which had been on five-minute alert for the past forty-nine hours, was placed on stand-down. There was nothing to do now but wait.

14

TARGET AREA IGOR
THREE RIVERS SECRET
ZONE, LAOS

Gerber had posted only a one-man guard during the remainder of the night, allowing the men to rest as much as possible. With the coming of daylight, they breakfasted on LRRP rations and water, performed the necessary relief chores, burying the evidence, and set out once more. Killduff walked ahead with Krung now, serving as guide to the Nung tribesman, while Fetterman continually checked their trail for signs of enemy pursuit.

"We should be getting close to the area where we found the bodies of Barnes's team," Killduff told Krung. The time was a little past ten in the morning. "I don't think it's much farther. Maybe three or four miles at most."

"I'd say it's more like five," a voice whispered.

Both men froze as a bush about ten yards ahead of them rose up and suddenly became a well-camouflaged man holding a CAR-15. He was gaunt-looking, with several days' growth of beard, his tiger-striped jungle fatigues hanging in tatters beneath the leafy branches he had tied around his waist, chest, arms and legs. It took Killduff a split second to recognize him, though.

"Jack!" he exploded, rushing forward to greet the man. Then, more subdued, he added, "What in the name of hell are you doing here?"

"Waiting for the cavalry to show up and praying for a miracle," the other man said. "I have to admit you're not exactly what I expected, but I guess you'll do. It's damn good to see you, Bill, but what are you doing in that getup? I almost shot your friend here."

"Sergeant Krung, Jack Searsboro, Sergeant Barnes's ATL," Killduff said. "This is Sergeant First Class Krung, a Nung tracker. He's with MACV/SOG Special Ops."

Searsboro stuck out a hand and Krung took it. "Glad to meet you, too, Krung," Searsboro said. "Sorry about the misunderstanding."

Krung left the two men and went to get Gerber and the others.

"We found Barnes and the others, Jack. What happened?" Killduff asked.

"A mess, that's what. Everything was going along decently until an NVA patrol got on our tails. They had trackers and some portable RDF gear. Barnes decided to try to sucker them into an ambush so we could get a prisoner. From the reports of the indigenous scouts, it sounded as it they had a Chinese adviser with them."

"Only he turned out to be a Russian," Killduff said.

"How did you know?" Searsboro asked.

"There were twelve Caucasian bodies, only one of them wasn't yours. We also found the Soviet's paratroop qualification badge. Barnes hid it in his mouth."

"None of the others made it, then?"

Killduff shook his head. "We lost most of Nevada and Wyoming looking for you guys, too."

"Christ!" Searsboro said. "Let me sit down for a minute, will you? I think I'm going to be sick."

Killduff helped Searsboro to sit, then, after a minute he asked, "So what happened after you found the Russian?"

"We got hit on the way to the LZ," Searsboro said, holding his head in his hands. "They must have fixed our position when we requested the extraction. Then they brought in trackers and dogs."

"Dogs?"

"Bloodhounds. We tried to shake them, but we couldn't. They got some of their people in front of us somehow and shot the shit out of us. We lost most of the indgenous troops right then and there. After that we fought a running gun battle with them while we tried to E and E. My radio got smashed up and then they got Chelsea when we ran into a second ambush. I was damn lucky to get clear. Those NVA bastards gunned down the Russian themselves. They did it just to keep us from getting away with him."

"They also cut off his head and hands," Killduff said.

"The others?"

"Multilated. You don't want to know. At least they were all dead beforehand."

"Fucking animals! You said you and Hartwick also lost some people. Who?"

"Ross Hartwick died on the way to the hospital. They got Gilman and Grinnell, to. And Larry. Quintin's supposed to make it."

Searsboro shook his head. "Good God Almighty!"

"Why didn't you try to contact us when we came in with Nevada and Wyoming looking for you guys? We tried to raise you on the radios."

"There was just me left," Searsboro said. "I ditched the PRC-25 when it got hit, and the indigenous TL had the RT-1 with him. When I tried to use the survival radio, it wouldn't work. I heard the choppers come in and knew somebody was in the area, but I didn't have any way of making contact."

"What are you doing way out here, then? I figured if you were still alive you'd try to walk out."

"Curiosity," Searsboro said. "I got to wondering what was so damn important out here that the NVA would use dogs, trackers and portable RDF to protect it. I also got to wondering what the hell the Russians were doing here and decided I might as well try to find out. Also I figured the NVA would expect me to hoof it back to Vietnam, just like you said. I figured they wouldn't expect someone to be stupid enough to try to hang around and figure out what was going on. I was following an NVA patrol with a couple of Russians with it headed in this direction, but I lost them last night. I was just trying to pick up the trail when you guys came along.''

Krung returned with Gerber and the others, and Searsboro was introduced and ran through his story again. Based on his information about the NVA/Russian patrol, it was decided to conduct a thorough search of the area. Nearly two hours later Krung picked up the track.

It wasn't much to go on, just a couple of partial, nearly obliterated footprints in the soft earth. Krung followed it with unerring accuracy, sometimes going as far as fifty yards between prints that the others could see. As the nearly invisible trail wound back and forth Searsboro wasn't even confident that it was the same people he'd been tracking until the trail finally joined up with a footpath and Krung spotted the obscure remains of a hobnailed boot print.

The path joined up with another that eventually branched into several more trails, and it took a while to find the right one, but Krung picked up the scent again. It was slow, tedious work, trying to follow the almost impossible-to-see signs left behind by the patrol while staying alert for the numerous punji pits and booby traps that guarded the trail. They wouldn't have found them all and would surely have lost someone had it not been for Krung's keen senses in spotting the tiniest detail out of the ordinary.

By late afternoon they encountered a chain of heavily fortified bunkers and were forced to wait for darkness to slip through them. As they watched the ring of bunkers from their hiding place, three NVA patrols, two of them accompanied by men dressed in Soviet paratroop uniforms, were seen to enter or leave the area of the bunker line. Gerber was convinced that they were very close to finding what they were looking for.

After the sun had dipped below the horizon, and before the moon could rise high enough to cast shadows, the men of SRT New Mexico, along with Staff Sergeant Jack Searsboro, slipped through the bunker system and its interwoven web of booby traps, crawling nearly two hundred yards on their bellies. Once through the outer perimeter of the NVA defensive positions, they continued to creep forward, following the path in the dim light of the rising moon until the dirt trail opened up into a wide, clear valley between two hills. There they finally came face-to-face with the secret so many men had died to learn, and so many others had died to protect.

It was a huge camp. There were huts of bamboo and thatch and rough-cut longhouses scattered all over the valley floor beneath an almost unbroken canopy of camouflage netting. In its own way it was even more impressive than the secret jungle airfield Gerber and the others had found some months before.

"Good Christ! There must be close to a regiment hidden here," Searsboro whispered.

"Something in the neighborhood of two battalions, anyway," Kepler allowed, "and one hell of a lot of antiaircraft capability. I count at least six SA-2 Guideline mobile launchers and what looks like three batteries of SA-3 low-altitude missiles mounted on ZIL-157 truck chassis. Those big vans would be Fan Song radar for the Guidelines, and the vans with the twin parabolic antennae would be P-15 Flat Face radar for the SA-3s. Looks like there's a lot of construction material and a Caterpillar down there, too."

Kepler shifted his binoculars and glassed the slopes of the hills. "Triple A guns mounted higher on the slopes. A battery of 57 mm S-60 guns and a second battery of 23 mm ZU-23 twin automatic cannon. God only knows how many 14.5 and 12.7 mm heavy machine guns they've got under cover. I can see some of each. Hello!"

"What is it?" Gerber asked.

"Clear on top of the second hill, the higher one to the northeast. It's camouflaged so cleverly I almost missed it. Blends right in with the top of the hill."

"Derek, for Christ's sake, what do you see?" Gerber asked impatiently.

Kepler peered through the binoculars for a moment longer, then lowered them and shook his head, as if disbelieving what he had seen. "I'm no expert at Soviet air defense strategy and equipment, but I know a long-range search radar when I see it. They've got an electronic eye sitting on that hilltop that's big enough to pick up anything flying over half of South Vietnam. That must be what all the Triple A is for—to protect the search radar from an air strike."

"So what's it guarding?" Gerber asked.

"Nothing," Kepler told him.

"What do you mean, nothing?" Gerber muttered. "That's ridiculous."

"Not really," Kepler replied. "Think about it for a minute, Captain. With that long-range search radar they can probably pick up anything flying above small-arms range over all of central South Vietnam. They pass what they see on the scope on to the NVA and Charlie knows immediately whenever we've got planes coming to bomb the Trail. He not only knows when but how many and how high."

"Not only that," Fetterman added. "It'll give them a pretty good idea of the route our planes are following when they go to bomb North Vietnam. The higher above the horizon the aircraft is, the better that thing will work. I wouldn't be surprised if they can pick up everything from Nha Trang to Udorn, Thailand."

"Operation Falling Rain in reverse," Gerber said, referring to a previous attempt to establish a sophisticated U.S. Air Force radar facility in northern Laos, designed to guide American bombers attacking the Ho Chi Minh Trail and targets in North Vietnam.

"Captain, we've got to take out that radar site before it gets operational," Fetterman said, "or if it's already operating, before it starts doing our flyboys some real damage."

"So why not just get on the radio and arrange for a B-52 strike?" Killduff asked. "Blanket the valley with bombs, and poof! No more Russian radar site."

"If that radar *is* already working, they'll see it coming ten minutes after it's airborne and have all that antiair stuff primed and waiting. We could lose half the attacking force," Kepler objected.

"Besides," Bocker added, "the Air Force might not have much luck spotting it from the air. We'd have to transmit a homing beacon to guide them in, and the enemy is sure to pick that up on their RDF gear. I'm not crazy about being all that close to a B-52 strike, anyway. When those guys talk about hitting a pickle barrel from thirty thousand feet, they're talking about a pickle barrel the size of a city block."

"Is that thing operational?" Gerber asked. "We'd have to know that before we even consider an air strike against it."

"No way to tell for sure, Captain," Kepler told him. "It's got an all-weather covering over it, that ball-shaped structure you can just make out beneath the camouflage netting. No way to tell if the antenna inside is moving."

"Agreed," Gerber said. "We'll have to take it out on the ground."

"You're crazy," Searsboro protested. "You'd need a brigade to take that place. There's at least two battalions of men in there, remember? And a hell of a lot of heavy automatic guns. Plus that ring of bunkers we just crawled through."

Gerber lifted his own binoculars and studied the scene before them. "That would be true if we were talking about a conventional assault," he said quietly, "but it might not be the only way to do it."

Killduff snorted. "What did you have in mind? Just walk right up that hilltop and ask them if they mind if we blow up their nice new radar?"

"I was hoping for something a little less obvious," Gerber said, "but basically that's the idea. Sully, how much explosives would you need to make a job of that radar?"

"I don't know, Captain," Smith said, shaking his head. "The antenna alone I could probably topple with what we've got with us. You want to do a thorough job, though, you'd need to take out the generators and display consoles, too, and generally wreck the whole site. No sense in doing the job halfway and leaving them something they can repair or rebuild in a couple of days. It would sure be nice to do something about all those missiles, too, at least the control radars."

"How much stuff would you need exactly?" Gerber asked again.

Smith took Kepler's binoculars and studied the site. "It would still depend on what I had to work with. Say maybe a hundred pounds of TNT, if we had any, plus the plastique we've got. That, and the time to set the charges."

"How much time?"

"The radar vans wouldn't be much of a problem. A single good-size charge of practically any explosive would do the trick, if you could get underneath them and tamp it somehow so that most of the force of the explosion was directed upward. It might not wreck everything, but it'll sure as hell tear the van apart and scatter the contents over the countryside. Say five minutes apiece to do the vans. The big radar is going to be a bitch, though. Maybe twenty minutes to set the charges. Unfortunately I haven't got a hundred pounds of TNT."

"How about some 57 mm artillery shells and a few dozen gallons of gasoline?" Gerber asked, still studying the enemy camp.

Sully Smith smiled. "Now that's a different prospect altogether. I can do some wonderful things with a dozen artillery shells and thirty gallons of gasoline, and if we work it right, it'll even leave us enough plastique left over to do the missiles."

"Of course, we'll have to do something about those bunkers on the way out," Tyme reminded them.

"Not to worry, Justin," Fetterman told him. "They're designed to keep people out, not in."

"You guys are fucking out of your minds," Killduff said. "All it takes is for one sentry to spot us and give the alarm, and the whole camp will come down on top of us."

"We *will* have to be careful," Krung said agreeably. He was in favor of any plan that would kill Communists.

"What do you think, Doc?" Gerber asked Reasnor.

"Oh, I agree with Sergeant Killduff. I think the whole idea's crazy. Maybe just crazy enough to work."

"We're just supposed to find out what's going on and report it," Killduff protested. "The orders to launch a raid have to come from Colonel Bates."

"Our orders were to find out what the Russians were doing in here and stop it," Fetterman said. "Colonel Bates gave us those orders. His approval to act was required only if the nature of the target required a large raiding force, which might provoke an international incident."

"Which it does," Killduff challenged. "Even if there were some way we could go it alone, do you really think that blowing up a lot of Russian hardware, and maybe some Soviet technicians along with it, won't produce an incident?"

"It's been done before," Fetterman said coldly.

"All right," Gerber said. "Anything we do might provoke a public protest from the Pathet Lao. I don't think the Russians are going to want to admit they have military forces in Laos serving alongside the Pathet Lao and NVA. On the other hand, airlifting an infantry brigade in here is something we won't be able to keep out of the press no matter how hard we try, and we all know that's the last thing Bates wants." He turned to Bocker. "Galvin, what are the odds of raising Kontum on the key this close to that camp and getting away with it?"

"We start transmitting this close and their RDF will be on us in a second," Bocker said. "I suppose we might get away with it if we waited until the appointed contact time, if atmospheric conditions are right and if we can keep the message short enough and get an immediate reply, but I wouldn't want to risk it. It would be sort of like a burglar ringing the doorbell before breaking out your bedroom window.''

"Look, we don't even know if that thing's working or not," Killduff tried again, jerking a thumb in the direction of the hilltop radar site.

"Let's not forget that they knew when six different RTs were inserted into the area," Kepler said. "They must have something working."

"What about using one of the balloon-burst transmitters?" Gerber asked Bocker.

"This close to that thing? Oh, the balloon probably wouldn't show on radar, but the transmitter's got enough metal in it to produce a pretty good return. I'd say we might as well send up a flare. Save the NVA time and effort pinpointing our exact position," the commo sergeant told him.

"Well, there it is," Gerber said. "We can either sit here and do nothing until an NVA patrol comes along and finds us, or we can sneak out of here with our tails between our legs and report what we've found, or we can go on in there and try to do something about it."

"I take it you have some sort of plan in mind," Searsboro said quietly.

"Ah, Christ, Jack, not you, too!" Killduff said.

"All I'm saying is let's hear the man out. See if the plan is workable," Searsboro said.

Killduff shrugged. "Christ! I give up. You people are all mad." Then, after a moment he added, "Have you considered what happens if the plan doesn't work? Suppose we all go in there and get ourselves killed and command still doesn't know what the Soviets have got in here or where it is? Then it'll all have been for nothing. What then?"

"I've thought of that," Gerber said. "We'll have Sergeant Bocker encrypt a message giving the coordinates of this place and what we've found, then feed it into the burst transmitters. If anything goes wrong, we'll launch the remaining balloons and do our best to get out. It won't matter if the enemy spots them because, by then, they'll know we're here, anyway. One of the messages ought to get through.''

"And if they don't? Just suppose the enemy is able to shoot down the balloons? Or that nobody's listening for a burst transmission at Kontum? Or that some atmospheric fluke keeps them from picking up the transmissions?''

"We'll time the attack to coincide with the regular message transmission window, which ought to optimize the chances that it will be received. A rapidly rising black balloon isn't the easiest thing to spot and track optically at night, anyway, and if we launch them from two separate locations, we'll make it a lot harder for them. They'll only have a couple of minutes at most before the burst transmission goes out. After that it won't matter if they get lucky with a ZU-23 and knock them down.''

"And if that doesn't work?''

"There's still the transceiver.''

"Right. You're going to stop in the middle of the battle so that Bocker can string his antenna and tune in Kontum. Get serious.''

"And there's still the emergency radios,'' Gerber said. "If all else fails, we can transmit what we found in the clear on the Guard channel. Moonbeam should pick it up.''

"And if they don't?''

"Damn it, Killduff! You've been nothing but a pain in the ass since this mission started,'' Gerber growled, finally losing his patience. "This is a military unit, not a debating society, and I'm in command of this mission. We're going to go in there and have a go at that radar. Now, you can either get off the fence and give us a hand, or you can sit out here with your thumb up your ass and wait with Bocker to send up the balloons.''

"Captain, if I may, sir,'' Bocker said quietly.

Gerber continued to glare at Killduff. "Yes, Galvin. What is it?''

"We'd stand a lot better chance of getting out of here afterward if I could locate their commo center and knock it out.

They might still have some portable stuff, but the main RDF gear is sure to be in the commo center.''

"We need you out here to make sure the balloons go up," Gerber told him.

"Not true, sir. Once the tapes have been fed into the burst transmitters, all you've got to do is turn on the power and set the destruct timer, then just let them go. Anybody could do it. Take me two minutes to show them how. Besides, nobody knows better how to wreck a radio than the man who fixes them.''

"I could do that, Captain," Reasnor said. "I won't be much good to you in there, anyway. You'll need killers with you, not a surgeon.''

Gerber looked from Reasnor to Bocker. "We'll also need someone to cover our retreat if we pull it off.''

"And someone to take out the bunkers covering the trail," Fetterman reminded him.

"Just tell me what you need done," Reasnor replied.

"Think you can handle both the burst transmitters and the MAG?" Tyme put in.

"I've had foreign-weapons familiarization," Reasnor said. "Just give me a quick refresher on how to load and fire the thing.''

"That'll leave me free to deal with the bunkers," Tyme said.

"You'll need help," Gerber said. "You'll have to take the two straddling the trail at the same time.''

"Leave the bunkers to Searsboro and me," Killduff offered quietly. "Neither of us knows a lot about explosives, but I think we can still pitch a grenade down a rathole.''

Gerber stared at the man. He wondered if he'd actually do the job or just bug out when the fireworks started. "That okay with you, Searsboro?" he asked.

"Suits me. Kind of hate to miss the main feature, but Bill's right. We're not demolitions experts. We'll do the bunkers if that's what you want.''

"Here, then, you'd better take this," Gerber said, handing Searsboro Monique LeClerc's Sten gun. "It'll make less noise than that CAR-15 of yours, if you have to use it. You know how?''

"Affirmative. It's covered in the recon manual."

"Take the BAR with you, too. Once you've knocked out the bunkers, you'll have to cover us when we fall back from here," Gerber added.

They had brought Philippe LeClerc's Browning Automatic Rifle with them when they'd left the ranch and had carried it after they'd released the horses.

"The rest of us will take the camp," Gerber continued. "Galvin, you and Justin have responsibility for the commo center. Find it and knock it out. Just don't make any noise doing it until the rest of us are ready. Not unless somebody starts shooting. Then it won't matter how quiet you are. Once you've handled it, drop back here and give Reasnor a hand. Kepler and Krung can take the radar vans for the missiles. That leaves Sully, Fetterman and me to blow the main radar."

"Captain, what about the missiles themselves?" Kepler asked.

"Only if there's time, Derek. The control radar vans come first. The missiles will be useless without them, anyway."

"Sir. I really would like to get a good look at that search radar before Sully blows it up," Kepler said. "Might come in handy later. No telling what Air Force Intel might be able to glean from a good debriefing."

"I've got the other Pentax camera, Derek," Fetterman told him. "I'll take all the nice pictures you need."

Kepler still looked unhappy. "I suppose it'll have to do." Then he brightened suddenly. "If you get a chance to pick up any technical manuals, that would help, too. And it would give me a chance to get a good look at their missiles."

"We'll do what we can," Gerber promised him. "Whatever time allows."

He turned to Searsboro and Killduff. "You understand you're not to hit the bunkers until you either hear an explosion or shooting?"

Killduff grinned. "Don't sweat it, Captain. We won't do a thing until we hear a loud boom. We want to get out of here alive just a much as you do."

Gerber fervently hoped that at least some of them would get out alive. "All right," he said, "let's synchronize our watches. I make it 2015 hours right . . . now. The next window for radio transmission in Kontum is at 2145. That gives us an hour and a half. Galvin, you get Reasnor checked out on the balloon transmitters and encode the coordinates. Then record the following message. Tell Bates we've discovered a Soviet long-range search radar and SAM site and that we're attacking now on my responsibility. Then ask for an immediate extraction at the primary site. As soon as you're set, you and Tyme go find that commo center. Searsboro, you and Killduff wait thirty minutes and then go get set to take out the bunkers. The rest of us will leave now. We'll have to visit the fuel-and-ammo dump down there and borrow a few gallons of gas and artillery shells first."

Smith handed Kepler a box of nonelectric blasting caps and several feet of safety fuse. The Intel sergeant was already carrying two of the haversacks of plastique, a roll of firing wire and one of the electric blasting machines.

"Break the charges in two and put one underneath the center of each of the vans. If you can find something to tamp it against the bottom of the trailer, it'll work better. Stick half a block between the missiles and the launching cradle. That way even if the missile isn't destroyed, you'll ruin the launcher. Anywhere forward of the tail should do. It won't matter if you detonate the warheads or the propellant. I'd string the vans together and fire them electrically, but you'll have to use safety fuses on the missiles. Don't make them too long. We don't want somebody finding them before they go bang."

"Sully, I *am* cross-trained in demolitions, remember?" Kepler reminded Smith gently.

Smith grinned sheepishly. "Right. Just offering a few helpful suggestions."

"If you two are finished comparing notes on rapid disassembly of Soviet equipment," Gerber said, "we need to get this show on the road."

"Good luck," Killduff said as the others rose to leave. "And, Captain Gerber?"

"Yes, what is it?"

"I was wrong about you, Captain," Killduff said. "You're an even bigger bastard than I thought."

"Good luck to you men, too," Gerber answered. He hoped that Killduff was right.

15

TARGET IGOR THREE RIVERS SECRET ZONE, LAOS

It was risky moving into the camp so early in the evening when people might still be up and moving around, but there had been no choice if they were to coordinate the attack with the next communications window with Kontum. They were aided somewhat by the gathering clouds, which had threatened rain since late afternoon and now covered the moon almost continually. In the Laotian jungle there were no high chain-link fence or barbed wire entanglements to be breached, but there were trip wires attached to flares, and while the overcast helped to conceal the men, it also made detecting the alarm wires difficult. There were two very narrow escapes before they succeeded in penetrating the camp, and Gerber hoped the others would be extremely careful. A single flare, accidently triggered now, would put an end to the assault before it ever had a chance to get started. The hum of several diesel generators helped to cover any sound they might make as they slipped noiselessly into the enemy encampment.

There were no electric lights burning outside any of the structures, and Gerber was thankful that the Soviets and NVA were exercising blackout precautions against overflying

American aircraft, although an occasional dim glow did periodically escape from the bamboo-shuttered windows of one of the huts or longhouses, or when someone opened or closed a door to one of the missile radar vans. It made finding what they were looking for an interesting proposition.

They located the fuel dump without difficulty but were alarmed to discover that it was all diesel fuel for the generators. Unruffled by the minor setback, Smith helped himself to four twenty-liter cans of diesel, unscrewed the caps and poured the contents over a number of other cans and drums of the still-combustible oil, then taped a French WP grenade to a full can in such a fashion that the weight of the can would hold down the safety lever of the grenade. Finally he removed the pin.

"Sully, what the hell are you fooling around for?" Gerber muttered.

"If we don't get a chance to hit this thing on the way out, the little surprise I left behind ought to give them something extra to think about the next time they decide to fuel their generators," Smith said.

Undaunted by Gerber's criticism, he took his empty cans with him and went off in search of a truck whose gas tank he could puncture to rob the gasoline he needed while Gerber and Fetterman looked for artillery shells.

Locating one of the 57 mm antiaircraft guns, they found the ammunition bunker for it nearby. There was a single guard standing watch.

Slipping out of his pack and webgear, Fetterman left them and his M-3 with Gerber while he silently stalked the guard. Approaching from behind, he timed his movements to the guard's breathing and inched forward in a half crouch.

The man never heard him coming, and Fetterman snaked a hand over his nose and mouth, pulling the guard backward as he drove the Case fighting knife into the guard's kidney, then again, higher, beneath the ribs and into the lungs. He finished by driving the point of the blade into the man's neck beneath the ear and ripping outward, tearing out the carotid, jugular and trachea, then lowered the guard to the ground and held him until he was still. Only then did Fetterman notice that the guard was a Caucasian.

Fetterman wiped the blood from the knife and his hands on the guard's uniform, then dragged him quickly into the shadows at the bottom of the entrance to the ammunition bunker as Gerber came forward with their gear. To their grief, they discovered that the bunker had a wooden door that was solidly padlocked, a precaution that seemed insane to Gerber on a bunker where instant access to the ammunition inside would be necessary in the event of an air attack. Working rapidly, they solved the problem by scooping the dirt out from under the door enough for Fetterman to wriggle his slight frame beneath.

Once inside the bunker, Fetterman was dismayed to find that all the ammunition was in wooden crates, solidly secured with metal strips. Grumbling to himself, he pried open the wooden boxes with difficulty and passed out eight rounds of 57 mm ammunition to Gerber through the hole beneath the door. Then, taking a hint from Smith's action at the diesel dump, he scooped out a shallow hole in the dirt floor of the bunker and placed two grenades in it, placing a crate of cannon shells on top of it to hold down the levers. He didn't know if the detonation of the grenades would be enough to trigger the cannon rounds or not, but figured it was worth a try. Then he wormed his way back beneath the door and began shoveling dirt back into the hole with his hands. It probably wouldn't fool anybody in the daylight, but it might at night.

"What the hell kept you?" Gerber asked. He had already wrapped the 57 mm shells in their ponchos for carrying.

"Just taking a little hint from Sully," Fetterman whispered. "You never can tell when we might need a diversion."

Picking up their bundles, they made for the radar installation on top of the hill.

KEPLER AND KRUNG PASSED deep into the camp unnoticed. Evidently most of the inhabitants had retired to their quarters after the sun went down, and few were about in the valley. It took them longer than they had anticipated, however, and Kepler decided that a few of the SAMs would have to be spared. There were simply too many of them, and they were too widely dispersed.

They started at the far end of the valley, and while Krung stood guard, Kepler slipped beneath the first of the radar vans for the SA-3s. He had just started work when a Soviet soldier came out of the van and sat down on the wooden steps to have a cigarette, and Kepler was forced to waste seven minutes while the man finished his smoke. They couldn't risk killing him, since he might be missed by those inside.

When the man finally returned to the van, Kepler got on with business. There was no time for finesse now, and he broke open the plastique and split the puttylike material into half blocks with his knife, placing three half-kilogram charges running down the length of the center of the trail upon which the van rested. Kepler laced the charges together with detonating cord, then improvised a time-delay firing circuit from his own watch and the batteries out of his flashlight, setting it to detonate the electric blasting caps in fifty-five minutes. The radar vans were simply too scattered to tie them all together to the ten-cap blasting machine. He would have had to string firing wire all over the compound, and to do the task manually would have required yards of safety fuse, which burned at the uniform rate of forty seconds per foot.

With that done they dropped back to the second van, and Kepler prepared it in a similar fashion while Krung set the charges on a single missile apiece on each of the three nearby trucks. Running all the wires together, Kepler taped his spare flashlight batteries and Krung's together to give another few volts to ensure detonation of the caps, then improvised a second time delay using Krung's watch. He set that charge for thirty-five minutes and then moved on.

Kepler and Krung split the final two vans and hastily slapped charges on a couple of the nearest missiles, connecting one firing circuit to the blasting machine and the other to

a five-minute length of safety fuse. They had no way of knowing how much time remained, but it had to be less than ten
minutes.

BOCKER AND TYME had found the communications center,
another van-mounted unit obvious by its many antennae and
connections to external aerial masts, and by the fact that it had
its own, trailer-mounted generator. Once found, there was
nothing for them to do but wait. Meanwhile, at the mouth of
the valley, Doc Reasnor also waited, nervously checking his
watch. The FN Mag was ready in front of him and the two
balloon tramsmitters lay by his side, their tiny cylinders of
helium attached and ready for filling. It was more excitement
than he had experienced in a long time, and right now he
would gladly have traded it all for a single glass of good brandy
and a quiet corner to drink it in.

SMITH WAS WAITING for Fetterman and Gerber when they
reached the search radar. It was mounted atop the only sub-
stantial structure in the valley, a concrete blockhouse with a
steel door. There were no guards in evidence outside the
building.

At 2115 hours Fetterman tried the door and found it unlocked. He yanked it open and stepped quickly inside.

There were three men inside, two of them playing cards and
the third making a pot of tea on an electric hot plate. Fetterman shot all three with a quick burst apiece, his grease gun
making an ugly ripping noise as the heavy .45-caliber slugs
ripped into the men as if they were rag dolls, sending the two
at the table spinning to the floor as puffs of crimson burst from
their chests, while slamming the third man back against a steel
locker, toppling the hot plate and sending the copper teaket-
tle clattering to the floor.

Fetterman spun away from the dead men and immediately
charged the metal stairway leading to the second floor, but
Gerber was a fraction of a second ahead of him. They reached

the top almost together and found four technicians, two of them seated at radar consoles, the third at a desk and the fourth just starting for the top of the stairs, a look of surprise on his face. Gerber's and Fetterman's M-3s thudded together, and the four Soviet technicians died where they were, stitched and shredded by the bullets as their blood sprayed across the consoles, desk and floor.

Both men changed magazines, and Gerber went back down to guard the door and help Sully Smith bring in his demolition goodies, while Fetterman studied the Russian lettering on the control panel and tried to figure out how to shut down the radar. Until that was done it was too dangerous for anyone to climb the second metal ladder leading to the antenna above. At close range, and unshielded, the high-frequency radio emissions of the radar could prove lethal.

Once he had figured out the right combination of switches to shut down the radar, Fetterman took out the Pentax camera, fitted on the flash and began taking pictures of everything. He burned up four rolls of film in the process.

While Gerber continued to watch the door, Smith set his charges. Working quickly, he removed the fuses from the 57 mm artillery shells and primed them with nonelectric blasting caps connected to detonating cord, placing one shell in each corner of the building on both floors. He then attached a half-kilogram glob of plastique to the backs of each of the consoles and several of the equipment cabinets, tying it all together with detonating cord and priming the det-cord with electric caps. He used three kilograms of plastic explosive on the antenna alone and then placed a block of plastique in the center of each room, with two of the twenty-liter jerricans of gasoline resting on top of each of them. They were just unrolling the firing wire out the door when they heard the first explosion rumble through the valley below.

"Two minutes early," Gerber said, consulting his watch. "Something must have gone wrong."

"Doesn't matter," Smith replied. "We're set here. All we've got to do is back off and fire this thing." He slipped the haversack containing the rest of his explosives over his shoulder and hurried on through the doorway, Gerber and Fetterman on his heels.

"Sully," Gerber said as they hustled down the slope and unrolled the firing wire behind them, "why did you have us take all the risks getting the gas and artillery shells if you had enough to do the job?"

"Didn't know for sure that it would be enough," Smith panted. "Pays to be on the safe side. Besides, this way we've got a little extra. You never know when it might come in handy."

KILLDUFF AND SEARSBORO were ready when the first detonation sounded behind them. Without waiting for a signal from the other, both men entered the rear of their respective bunkers, and with the aid of flashlights taped to the barrels, shot the NVA inside with their silenced weapons. A grenade rolled inside would have been just as effective and a lot safer for the Americans, but it would also have been much noisier, and while the explosion in the camp would put the bunker line on alert, they had no desire to draw the attention of the occupants of any of the other bunkers to their particular part of the line yet.

WHEN THEY HEARD the explosion, Bocker yanked open the door of the commo van and Tyme sprayed the interior with gunfire from his suppressed M-3. Bocker then entered, while Tyme changed magazines, and shot each of the men again to be sure they were dead. While Tyme covered their rear, Bocker placed WP grenades where they would do the most good against the Soviet R-114, R-118 and R-401-N radio relay sets already riddled by the bullets. Then he tied a two-foot-long piece of safety fuse around each to hold down the levers when the pins were removed. It would take about a minute and a half for the fuses to burn down far enough to release the spoons. When he was finished, and Tyme reported that the coast was still clear, he pulled the pins and lit the fuses with his Zippo.

"Let's get the hell out of here," Bocker said.

Across the camp there was a second, shattering blast.

WHEN THE FIRST Flat Face radar van went up, Kepler still hadn't heard any firing or explosions from the main radar site atop the hill. He had tried to set the timer as accurately as he could, but fifty-five minutes was all the diminutive hands of his watch would safely allow. Still, unless something had gone terribly wrong, he knew that the timing would be close enough. If Gerber, Fetterman and Smith hadn't succeeded in rigging the search radar for demolition by then, they would never get it done. He waited until a siren began to wail somewhere and men started to pour out of the buildings, then he had Krung light the safety fuse as he twisted the firing handle of the ten-cap blasting machine. Kepler watched in grim fascination as the Fan Song radar van for the Guidelines leaped upward and descended in a shower of twisted, jagged metal and human bodies. Two of the SA-2 missiles were engulfed in flames.

"Fuse lighted," Krung reported. "We go now?"

"And how!" Kepler said.

AT THE MOUTH of the valley Doc Reasnor heard the first explosion and inflated the balloons. When they were full and he had to hold tightly against their nylon lines to keep them from soaring skyward, he flipped up the safety covers and armed the autodestruct switches, then turned on the recorder/transmitters and released the balloons.

"I hope to God somebody out there is listening," he muttered.

"GET DOWN! Take cover!" Smith cautioned the others when his five-hundred-foot roll of firing wire ran out. "We're going to be closer than I like."

He stripped the insulation from the ends of the wires and connected them to the terminals of the ten-cap blasting machine, checked that Gerber and Fetterman were down, then pressed himself against the ground.

"Fire in the hole!" he called out unnecessarily, then inserted the firing handle into the machine and twisted it vigorously.

The Soviet long-range search radar disappeared in an expanding ball of bent, twisted metal and pulverized concrete as the deafening blast swept over them, squashing them even tighter against the ground.

"Sully, you horrible little man!" Gerber yelled through the ringing in his ears. He had to yell just to hear himself. "You might have warned us you were going to use thermonuclear explosives."

Sully Smith raised himself to one knee and examined the falling debris coming down uncomfortably close to them. There was an almost beatific smile on his face. "Beautiful!" he whispered.

"What was that?" Gerber shouted.

"I said it was beautiful!" Smith shouted back. "Now stop shouting and let's get the fuck out of here!"

As BOCKER AND TYME RAN through the compound, nobody seemed to pay the least bit of attention to them. Suddenly there was an awe-inspiring explosion that knocked both of them flat, and the entire top of the hill where the search radar had sat seemed to disintegrate. As the stunned men picked themselves off the ground, a whole series of smaller explosions ripped through the camp, sending flaming metal upward and men hurling through the air in all directions. Bocker and Tyme struggled to their feet just as half a dozen armed men came running toward them. Without hesitation they leveled their M-3s and fired until the weapons were empty, knocking down the enemy soldiers as if they were bowling pins. Changing magazines, they ran on toward the rendezvous point. Around them the scene was an inferno.

Pandemonium reigned in the Communist camp. There were fires everywhere, and the screams of wounded and dying men, punctuated by secondary explosions, rent the air. When bewildered gun crews, fearing an air attack, rushed to unlimber their automatic cannon, the booby trap Fetterman had left behind claimed another seven lives as the 57 mm bunker blew into bits. Curiously there still hadn't been any gunfire except for the muffled reports of the suppressed weapons carried by the Special Forces troopers. Running through the camp toward the mouth of the valley, Bocker and Tyme ignored the mass destruction around them, pausing only to aim and fire when actually confronted by an armed foe.

The enemy guns finally opened up, but their muzzles were all directed skyward. Having heard no small-arms fire, the NVA and Soviet gunners were shooting at phantom aircraft they imagined overhead.

Tyme and Bocker, having the farthest to run, were surrounded by the enemy, but the Communist soldiers seemed oblivious to their presence. There was so much noise now that the muted discharge of the M-3s was scarcely audible above the cacophany.

REASNOR WAITED behind the machine gun, a sweaty palm clenched around the pistol grip while his left hand held the ammunition belt draped over it to feed smoothly into the weapon. He was so keyed up that he almost opened up on Krung and Kepler when they came running up the slope. There was generalized firing in the camp now, but not at any real targets. Frightened, confused men were just putting out rounds, shooting at shadows and at their comrades who, in their terror-filled minds, had been transformed into silhouettes of the enemy by the flickering inferno encircling them.

As soon as all of the men were accounted for, Gerber ordered them to move to the bunker line. Killduff and Searsboro were waiting for them, but as they passed between the bunkers set astride the trail, they came suddenly under machine gun fire from a third, previously undetected, bunker.

Killduff immediately returned fire with the BAR from atop his bunker, but the enemy gunners, well protected behind the log-and-earthen walls, pinned them down.

Reasnor got the MAG going, and the armor-piercing incendiary rounds in its belt seemed to have a better effect on the interest of the NVA gunners, but only momentarily. Alarmed by the Belgian machine gun, they shifted their aim and came looking for the doctor. Reasnor ducked as the heavy slugs sliced over his head.

Tyme finally got the RPG-7 unlimbered and loaded, and when the NVA gunners shifted their attention back to the persistent hammering of Killduff's BAR, he was able to rise up for a clear shot and put one of the rocket-propelled grenades into the front of the bunker. While the smoke was settling he reloaded and fired again, destroying the enemy machine gun emplacement totally.

The bunker was no longer a problem, but the position of SRT New Mexico was no longer a secret. As they fled the area, they were aware of an increasing volume of small-arms fire behind them, but it wasn't aimed, since the enemy was still trying to pinpoint their location.

They moved swiftly, the need for speed and distance now outweighing the necessity for caution. If they encountered a Communist patrol, they would have to shoot their way through. If they ran into booby traps or mines, well, that was always a risk, and moving slowly was no guarantee of spotting them. They couldn't afford to crawl along looking for trip wires. Behind them were still several hundred very angry men, and the Americans and their Nung tracker all knew that very soon those same angry men would relish someone to vent their hostility on.

After pushing hard for over two hours through the dense bush, Gerber finally slowed the pace. They walked quickly now, perspiring under the strain of their heavy loads of equipment, arms and ammunition, but had at least disposed of the burst transmitters and their helium cylinders, not to mention the bulk of their demolition equipment. They would stop every few minutes and listen, but there was no sound of pursuit. Gerber was almost ready to call a halt and give them a fifteen-minute break to catch their breath.

Then, in the far-off distance, they heard that sound most feared by any reconnaissance patrol deep in enemy territory: the baying of hounds.

16

TARGET IGOR THREE RIVERS SECRET ZONE, LAOS

"I think we'd better do something to make it hard for those guys to keep following us and easy for them to quit," Gerber said.

Working quickly they set out grenade traps, using both WP and CS to maximize the psychological effect on their pursuers. The grenades were set out in a wide, semicircular pattern designed to cover both the front and flanks of the pursuing enemy. In order to ensure positive results, they tied their canteen cups to the trunks of small trees and wrapped the trip wires around the bodies of the grenades, securing one WP and one CS grenade at either end of the wire. The grenades, with pins removed, were then placed in the canteen cups, with one WP and one CS grenade in each cup, and the twin wires stretched to a second cup containing another two grenades.

Anyone or anything blundering into the wires would pull both of them, dropping both a WP and a CS grenade on either side of him. Once the grenades were pulled free of the canteen cups, the spoons of the grenades, which were held down by the walls of the cups, would fly free, and the grenades would detonate three to five seconds later. The combination of the terrifying WP and the choking CS would induce maximum panic in the enemy and perhaps cause them to flee blindly into the additional traps set on their flanks. Whether the grenades produced any casualties or not didn't matter. They would at least slow down the pursuit and cause the enemy to move with greater caution while the Special Forces team increased the distance between them.

Once the grenades had been set out, Gerber and the others ran quickly, pushing through the undergrowth and cursing the thorns, creepers and wait-a-minute vines that tore at their faces and clothing and entangled their feet, sometimes sending them sprawling to the ground.

Fifteen minutes later their efforts were rewarded by the distant detonation of grenades, and a minute or so later by the sound of additional detonations and the confused yapping of dogs.

At 0200 hours, with the men and himself near exhaustion, Gerber called a halt in the light drizzle that had begun to fall. Then he had Bocker break out his radio and attempt to contact the MACV/SOG base at Kontum. When the commo sergeant tapped out their identifier on the key, the response was almost immediate.

"Ref prev QSO action approved. Target status? NM status? Bates," the message read when decrypted.

Bocker quickly encrypted and replied with the following: "Primary target destroyed secondary extensively damaged. Some pursuit, but believe thrown off. All NM OK. What about pickup?"

The reply wasn't what Gerber had hoped for.

"Good job. Brass much relieved. Pickup delayed due to weather. Will try for dawn at primary."

At Gerber's urging Bocker radioed back, "Any possibility earlier pickup? Request earliest."

The response was a terse "Negative. Birds weathered in. Dawn soonest."

Bocker tapped out an acknowledgment and signed off, then took down his antenna and repacked the set.

"What do we do now?" Fetterman asked.

"We'll rest for half an hour and then move on and secure the LZ," Gerber told them. "There's not much else we can do."

At 0330, as they neared the primary LZ, the distant baying of hounds resumed.

"Shit! We didn't get all the dogs," Smith muttered.

"Either that or they picked up our transmission to Kontum and brought in a second team," Bocker said.

"Well, at least we slowed them down some," Gerber told them.

"Captain, we can't just sit at the primary and wait for them to come and pick us up," Fetterman said. "Those guys behind us will be there long before dawn."

"You're right about that, Tony," Gerber agreed. "Bocker, how long to set up the radio and contact Kontum?"

"Five minutes tops if they're listening."

"Do it. If Charlie's using radio direction finding to pinpoint our signals, I'd rather we send from here and then move on. Tell them pursuit has been resumed and we're shifting to the alternate LZ. Repeat the request for immediate pickup and tell them it's urgent."

"You want to set out some more booby traps?" Smith asked.

"You think the same gag will work twice on these guys?" Gerber replied.

"What else can we do?"

"Captain Gerber, I've got an idea," Reasnor said.

"I'm open to suggestions, Doc. Right now I'll take anything."

Reasnor rummaged through his medical bag with one hand, holding the other cupped around the end of a penlight, and extracted a sealed plastic vial of white powder. Scraping a shallow trench in the moist earth with his hand, he opened the vial and poured the powder into it, then rolled up his sleeve and took out an alcohol pad and a Betadine wipe and swabbed his forearm with the antiseptic and disinfectant. Unwrapping the foil covering of a sterile scalpel blade, he made a small cut in his own arm and allowed the blood to drip onto the powder, then spread a thin layer of soil over the mixture.

"What is it?" Gerber asked as Reasnor squirted some antibiotic ointment from a tube onto his self-inflicted laceration and dressed and bandaged the wound.

"Cocaine," the doctor told him. "One good snort of that stuff and those hounds will be chasing their own tails."

"What are you doing with cocaine?" Gerber asked him.

"Believe it or not, we doctors use it for controlling severe epistaxis, among other things. That's a fancy name for a bad nosebleed that won't quit," Reasnor told him as he rolled down his sleeve. "It doesn't control the bleeding itself but acts as a topical anesthetic when absorbed through the mucosa of the nose. We can then go in and cauterize the bleeding vessels, either electrically or chemically with silver nitride swabs, something the patient wouldn't stand for otherwise."

"Using it to throw off the dogs is a pretty neat trick," Gerber said. "Did you learn that in medical school?"

"Actually, I saw it done in a movie once. I believe it was a World War II picture."

"Bocker, how are things coming with the radio?" Gerber asked.

"Just packing it up now, Captain. Got through to Kontum on the first try. They're monitoring continuously for us now. They acknowledged the alternate LZ, but say morning is the best they can do. Everything flyable is socked in, either by heavy rain or fog. Until the weather lifts they can't get a bird in."

"Let's move, then."

Minutes later as they left the area they had the satisfaction of hearing a terrific din made by howling dogs.

"I'd say the field test has proven my theory sound," Reasnor observed, panting heavily with the strain of their forced march.

"Thank God for that," answered Gerber.

"Captain, there's a stream near here if we're where I think we are," Searsboro told them. "How about we make a little detour through the center of it for a few hundred yards? It might throw the dogs off a bit if they pick up the trail again.''

Gerber told him to lead the way.

It took Searsboro a few minutes to find the stream, not much more than a shallow creek, and they followed it for nearly half a mile, wading up the middle of its sandy bottom. It was easier walking than pushing through the brush, despite the slippery rocks that occasionally cropped up underfoot, and the banks hid them from view, although Gerber knew it would be a bad spot to be in if they were ambushed. When the stream finally made a sharp bend away from their desired direction of travel, they climbed the gooey clay bank, doing what they could to obliterate the signs of their exit, and struck off through the jungle again.

It was nerly 0500, and the sky was beginning to lighten with the false half-light that preceded dawn, when they heard the hounds pick up their trail again.

''Captain, we're going to have to kill those dogs,'' Fetterman told him. ''There's no other way we're going to lose them.''

''You have a plan?'' Gerber asked.

''If the maps are accurate, there should be an open field near here. We'll lead them across it. When we get to the other side of the field, Krung and I will stay behind with the BAR. With the cyclic set for three-fifty, I ought to be able to squeeze off some single rounds fairly accurately. You guys go on and secure the LZ. We'll meet you there.''

''The plan sucks, Tony. You guys stay behind, you might not make it to the LZ. What if they're too smart to cross the open ground? Suppose you get cut off and can't make it to the LZ?''

''They'll be following the dogs, Captain. The NVA might be too smart to cross the open field, and that's just fine by me, but the handlers will have to let the dogs track us across it or risk losing the trail again. They know morning is coming and our side will be trying to get a chopper in here to pick us up. If anything does go wrong, Krung and I will E and E on our own. If we don't make the alternate LZ, you can try to pick us up later back at the primary. Besides, there's no other way."

"What do you have to say about this, Sergeant?" Gerber asked Krung.

The Nung tribesman's answer was simple and direct. "Sergeant Tony right, Captain Mack. It only way. We stay."

They diverted for a half a mile and once again risked ambush by crossing the open ground. There was no surprise gunfire to greet them, and when they reached the other side, Fetterman took the BAR from Killduff, and the master sergeant and Nung tracker dropped off at the edge of the tree line while the others angled back toward the LZ, still a couple of miles distant.

Fetterman quickly set up the BAR on its bipod and raised the tangent leaf rear site, adjusting it for four hundred yards, about the distance he estimated to the far tree line, and peered through the sights. Krung's M-3 would be next to useless at that range, as would his own, but the distance was well within the capabilities of the .3006-caliber cartridges of the BAR. There was barely enough light to see the sights clearly, and Fetterman hoped that the enemy wouldn't appear for another fifteen or twenty minutes. By then things should be bright enough to see the targets clearly.

Fetterman checked to see that the magazine of the automatic rifle held a full twenty rounds, eased open the bolt to make sure a round was chambered, then pulled a second magazine from the bulky BAR belt lying next to him and laid it alongside the weapon. He didn't anticipate needing more than twenty rounds to do the job, but if something went wrong, like a magazine malfunction, he wanted a spare ready. He set the safety and moved the selector switch on the big rifle to 350.

The field they had just crossed hadn't been selected as a possible LZ precisely because it was such an obvious site for one. It was nearly square, about four hundred yards on each side, and covered only with high grass. If the enemy held off until the light was good enough, Fetterman had confidence he could make the shots. They wouldn't be easy using the BAR, he would have preferred an M-21 or even an M-1 Garand, but it wasn't impossible. Krung would make sure no one slipped up behind them while Fetterman was shooting and would spot for him, using the binoculars. Fetterman had already passed the camera and film he had exposed in the Soviet search radar facility to Kepler as a precaution.

Tensely the two men waited, hearing the baying of the dogs growing ever closer. At last Krung touched him lightly on the shoulder. "Sergeant Tony, they come. They follow our trail exactly," the tribesman told him.

Fetterman folded up the butt plate on the Browning and steadied the stock against his shoulder with his free hand. Slipping off the safety, he rested his finger on the front of the trigger guard.

The enemy patrol halted just at the edge of the clearing. For a moment the handler seemed uncertain as to whether he should cross the open ground or not, but then started across. The slight Vietnamese strained against the pull of the two huge bloodhounds.

Fetterman hadn't counted on the grass being so high. He could barely see the dogs moving ahead of the man through the sea of waving green. He sighted carefully, took his best estimate on the position of one of the dogs and squeezed the trigger, feeling the old automatic rifle buck back against his shoulder.

Fetterman immediately released the trigger to keep the BAR from cycling another round and was rewarded by a yelp of pain from the wounded animal. With what seemed like agonizing slowness, he shifted the clumsy weapon on its bipod and fired twice more, hitting the second dog. The baying of both animals stopped abruptly and was replaced by a dreadful whimpering.

Fetterman quickly moved the selector to 550 and sprayed the tree line with automatic fire, splintering wood from the trees and sending a cascade of shredded leaves down upon the men cowering below. When the BAR ran empty, he hit the magazine release and jammed in the spare magazine as soon as the spent one fell clear.

"Let's move!" he shouted to Krung.

As the two men got up and turned to run, Fetterman emptied the second magazine into the tree line. He didn't really expect to hit anyone. He just wanted them to keep their heads down for the few seconds it would take them to get away. He knew that the NVA and their Soviet friends, if they had any Russian advisers with them, would never attempt to cross the open field now. They would detour cautiously around it, try to flank the position where the automatic rifle fire had come from, and when they found nothing, try to pick up the trail again.

Fetterman also knew that if they had another tracker with them, a human tracker, the man would probably get the job done eventually. He and Krung would have to move too quickly now to adequately cover their tracks. But it would cost the enemy some time, a very precious commodity if the NVA hoped to catch the men they were chasing, and it just might prove to be enough. In any event, no human, not even Krung, could track a man as well or as swiftly as the dogs could have.

Fetterman could hear the sound of the choppers in the distance as they neared the LZ and prayed that they would make it in time. It should only be another few hundred yards ahead of them through the trees. They ran desperately now, gasping for breath as the sound of the rotors grew louder. Abruptly Fetterman flung aside the twenty-one-pound BAR.

"Drop your pack!" he ordered Krung. "And get rid of the BAR belt. We're not going to make it otherwise."

Krung threw the heavy canvas ammunition belt into the bushes and shrugged off his pack, still running. They could hear the rotors popping now as the helicopter descended toward the LZ where the others were waiting. Ahead of them a cloud of violet smoke billowed skyward from a smoke grenade. Through the trees he could just make out Tyme's huge frame in the distance.

Suddenly an NVA soldier popped up out of the bush at the side of the trail, an AK-47 in his hands, and fired almost at pointblank range.

Fetterman saw him coming up off the ground. There was no time to work his M-3, so he swung the weapon hard, feeling the jarring impact as the submachine gun knocked aside the enemy's rifle.

The master sergeant felt the searing heat as the bullets ripped past him and then a numbing sting in his side, but he didn't falter. One-handed, he switched his grip on the grease gun and beat the NVA in the face with it, hitting him again and again and rendering the M-3 useless as he turned the man's face into a bloody pulp.

Fetterman scooped up the AK just as the second NVA showed himself and emptied the weapon into the man, stitching him from crotch to chin and hurling him backward into the bushes as chunks of bloody flesh flew from his torso. Tossing aside the empty AK, Fetterman yanked down the zipper of his jacket and pulled out the Skorpion, chambering a round with his numbed fingers. Quickly he spun in a full circle, searching for further threats, but there was no sign of any other enemy.

Krung lay bleeding on the jungle floor.

Heedless of his own wounds, Fetterman scooped up the Nung tribesman and draped him over his shoulder. Staggering beneath the weight of Krung, he pushed forward. The choppers were coming in to land now. There were only seconds left.

Fetterman, carrying Krung, burst from the tree line onto the LZ just as the others were loading into the helicopters. Overhead, armed Hueys prowled, looking for targets.

There was a shout from one of the helicopters, and Tyme leaped from the open doorway and ran back toward them. Gratefully Fetterman felt the weight of Krung taken from his shoulder as Tyme lifted the tribesman with strong hands. Then they were at the chopper, rising, and other hands were helping pull them aboard.

Fetterman sank down heavily on the steel deck of the cargo compartment and leaned his head against the cool bulkhead as the Huey picked up speed, then he passed out.

It was only then that Reasnor noticed that the master sergeant's uniform was covered in blood that wasn't Krung's.

EPILOGUE

Gerber and the others were crowded onto the wooden bench and standing along the wall of the antiseptic-smelling hallway. Both Colonel Bates and Captain Mauraides were with them and, somewhat surprisingly, Jerry Maxwell. All bore very worried expressions on their faces. They had flown directly to Nha Trang after the choppers picked them up, instead of going back to Kontum, and Bates and the others had joined them there.

Sergeant Krung was resting comfortably in the indigenous ward. He had been hit in the arm, but it was only a flesh wound. The second bullet had grazed his scalp and stunned him momentarily. He had banged his head on a rock when he hit the ground and had a mild concussion but was otherwise undamaged.

After a moment, Major Reasnor came out of the intensive care unit to talk with them.

"How is he, Doctor?" Gerber asked immediately.

"Oddly enough, Master Sergeant Fetterman's wounds aren't all that serious," Reasnor told them.

"He'll be all right, then?" Bates asked.

"I didn't say that," Reasnor told them. "I said his wounds aren't all that serious. He's suffering from septic shock, apparently from the wound he sustained in the knife fight with Madame LeClerc. He must have been going on sheer willpower alone these past couple of days. We're treating it with massive doses of antibiotics and intravenous tranfusion to keep his blood pressure up, but so far he's not responding to the treatment."

"*Will* he be all right, Doctor?" Gerber demanded.

"It's too early to tell. We'll have to wait and hope the antibiotics do the trick. If he makes it through the next twenty-four hours, then he has a fighting chance."

Gerber felt as though someone had struck him in the face. "Can we see him? Talk to him for just a few minutes?"

"I'd rather you didn't. He needs to rest."

"Please, Doc. Just for a couple of minutes," Tyme said. There was a catch in his voice, and his eyes were red and moist.

"All right. But only for two minutes. And only one of you. You'll have to choose which one."

"You go, Captain," Tyme said, and the others agreed.

Gerber got up off the bench and entered the hospital room. Fetterman looked even more pale and shrunken than usual. There were IVs plugged into both arms, and he had a catheter in place and a cardiac monitor beeping away at his bedside. An oxygen cannula was stuck in his nostrils.

Gerber walked slowly to the bedside and stared down at the master sergeant, who opened his eyes.

"How you doing?" Gerber asked.

Fetterman smiled weakly. "Kind of rocky, I guess, but give me a couple of days and I'll be ready to stand you a beer."

"Colonel Bates and the gang are outside. Major Reasnor says you're going to be here for a while."

"How's Krung doing?"

"Just fine. He's in the indigenous ward."

For a moment they said nothing.

GLOSSARY

AAA—Antiaircraft Artillery.

ACADEMY PROTECTIVE SOCIETY—A clandestine organization, the existence of which is officially denied by the U.S. military, which seeks to promote and protect the careers of U.S. service academy graduates.

THE AGENCY—The CIA.

AIR AMERICA—Airline and air freight service actually owned and operated by the CIA in Southeast Asia. It served as a useful cover for clandestine air ops and supply flights to covert Green Beret teams in Laos and Cambodia.

AIR STUDIES GROUP—Air operating arm of MACV/SOG. It was composed of the Ninetieth Special Operations Wing and included a squadron of U.S. Air Force UH-1F "Green Hornet" helicopters, a squadron of USAF C-130 transports, a covert operations squadron of C-123s flown by Nationalist Chinese pilots and the South Vietnamese 219th Sikorsky H-34 helicopter squadron. It was headquartered at Nha Trang.

AK-47—7.62 mm Soviet assault rifle.

AN/PRC-25—Portable radio.

AN/URC-10 RADIO—Compact VHF transceiver.

AO—Area of Operations.

ARVN—Army of the Republic of Vietnam. South Vietnamese army. Often disparagingly referred to as Marvin Ar-
vin.

A-TEAM—Basic ten-to-twelve-man operational detachment
of Special Forces advisers.

ATL—Assistant Team Leader.

AUTHENTICATION TABLE—Alpha-numeric grid used
to establish that the person you are talking to on the radio really is who he claims to be.

BAR—Browning Automatic Rifle.

BIRD—Any aircraft.

BOOM-BOOM—Term used by Vietnamese prostitutes for
sexual intercourse.

BUSHMASTER—Soldier highly skilled in jungle warfare.
Also a large poisonous snake not native to Vietnam.

C-47—U.S. World War II vintage twin-engined transport aircraft. An attack version, the AC-47, equipped with
miniguns and parachute flares for night operations, was
known either as "Spooky" or "Puff the Magic
Dragon."

C-123—Fairchild Provider. A twin-engined cargo plane developed from the design of a World War II glider.

C and C—Command and Control. May refer to MACV/SOG
command and control special operations units, i.e., C
and C Central at Kontum, or simply to the aircraft carrying the operational mission commander, who may or
may not actually land and participate in the mission on
the ground.

CAR-15—Common name for the Colt XM177E2 submachine
gun, actually a sort of carbine version of the M-16 with
a shortened barrel and a telescoping buttstock.

CARIBOU—Twin-engined transport aircraft called CV-12 by the Army and C-7A by the Air Force when it took over responsibility for fixed-wing transport in January 1967.

CHARLIE—From the phonetic alphabet Victor Charlie, the letters VC. The Vietcong.

CHICOM—Chinese Communist.

CIDG—Civilian Irregular Defense Group. Indigenous mercenary troops under direct Special Forces command.

CLAYMORE—U.S.-made directional mine. It can be either command-detonated by a small hand-held generator or other electrical device or mechanically detonated by a trip wire. Fires 750 steel pellets in a deadly, fan-shaped pattern, considered lethal out to fifty meters but can produce casualties out to 250 meters.

COLD—Usually said of an LZ but may apply to other situations. A Cold LZ was one from which no enemy fire was received.

COMINT—Communications Intelligence. Troops engaged in or the process of monitoring radio waves in the hopes of overhearing enemy transmissions.

COMSEC—Communications Security. Efforts to prevent the enemy from monitoring friendly transmissions by using codes and ciphers, scrambling, burst transmitters and limiting the frequency and duration of messages.

CONTROL—CIA case officer to which a field agent reports.

CS—Powerful form of tear gas available as a powder for dusting trails or tunnels or in grenade form. CS was widely used in Vietnam.

CW—Continuous Wave. Morse code radio transmissions.

DA—Department of the Army.

DET-CORD—Plastic cord filled with a powerful explosive approximately equal to nitroglycerin in strength.

DEUCE-AND-A-HALF—Six-wheel drive, two-and-a-half-ton truck used by the U.S. military.

DZ—Drop Zone.

E and E—Escape and Evade or Escape and Evasion.

FAN SONG—Van-mounted targeting and guidance radar used in conjunction with the SA-2 Guideline surface-to-air missile.

FLASH—Colored cloth patch denoting one's Special Forces Group worn on the beret.

FLAT FACE—Soviet truck-mounted target acquisition and control radar used with the SA-3 GOA surface-to-air missile.

FOB—Forward Operating Base. A subdivision of an SFOB. In Vietnam FOBs were located at Da Nang, Kontum, Ban Me Tuot and Can Tho.

FOX MIKE—FM. Frequency modulated radio transmission most commonly used for voice communications.

GRU—Soviet Military Intelligence Directorate.

GUARD EMERGENCY FREQUENCY—243-megacycle frequency monitored as an emergency channel for air-sea rescue. It is the channel to which the AN/URC survival radio is preset.

HATCHET FORCES—Composed of five U.S. personnel and thirty indigenous troops. Hatchet Forces were used by MACV/SOG to perform larger missions than the twelve-member Spike Recon Teams, especially raids and ambushes, and to reinforce spike teams that were in trouble.

HILLSBORO—Call sign of the Airborne Command and Control Center aircraft that orbited over Southern Laos and served as a radio relay link and to vector jet fighter-bombers to targets in the panhandle. At night the call sign was switched to Moonbeam. Cricket/Alleycat performed a similar function over Northern Laos.

HOT—An LZ or other area from which enemy fire was received. It could also refer to unloading wounded or other passengers with the engine of the helicopter still running and the rotors turning. A potentially dangerous situation.

HT-1—Small single-channel hand-held transceiver used by recon teams for short-range communications.

HUEY—Bell UH-1 helicopter and its subsequent variants. Probably the most widely used helicopter of the Vietnam War.

HUMINT—Human Intelligence. That branch of intelligence dealing with human resources, such as the debriefing of prisoners or defectors, or the operation of agents in enemy-controlled territory.

IN-COUNTRY—Said of U.S. Troops serving in Vietnam. They were all in-country.

LAAGER—Circular defensive position or encampment.

LAO THEUNG—Mountain Mon-Khmer people living principally in southeast Laos.

LEG—Derogatory term for nonairborne personnel.

LLDB—Luc Long Dac Biet. South Vietnamese Special Forces.

LRRP—Pronounced Lurp. A long-range reconnaissance patrol, usually made up of U.S. Army Rangers who conducted reconnaissance patrols lasting several days or weeks in enemy territory inside Vietnam. The closest regular Army equivalent to the MACV/SOG RTs.

LZ—Landing Zone.

M-1 GARAND—U.S. .30-caliber carbine capable of either semiautomatic or full-auto fire. It was widely issued to Vietnamese and Montagnard troops, especially early in the war.

M-3—U.S. .45-caliber submachine gun. An extremely compact weapon with a telescoping wire stock and a slow rate of fire (about 550 rounds per minute, cyclic). Also called a grease gun.

M-16—Common name for the 5.56 mm assault rifle used by U.S. forces in Vietnam.

M-21—Highly accurate version of the M-14 7.62 mm semiautomatic service rifle, fitted with an automatic ranging telescope and sound suppressor. Used as a sniper rifle in Vietnam.

MAC—Military Airlift Command. The USAF air transport service.

MACV—Military Assistance Command, Vietnam. The U.S. advisory effort to South Vietnam.

MAG—Belgian-made 7.62 mm general-purpose machine gun.

MAT-49—9 mm M1949 French submachine gun.

MEO—Widely used but incorrect name for the Hmong people. The term Meo derives from the Chinese Miao, which means barbarian. The Meo (Hmong) are Montagnards.

MONTAGNARD—Member of an ethnic minority group inhabiting mountainous regions in Vietnam and Laos, often employed as mercenaries by Special Forces or the CIA. Most had no love for the Lowland Lao or Vietnamese, but were intensely loyal to their American commanders.

MP—Military Police.

MPC—Military Payment Certificates. Also called script and Monopoly money. Brightly colored paper certificates issued to U.S. personnel in Vietnam in lieu of U.S. currency.

NCO—Noncommissioned Officer. A corporal or any of the various ranks of sergeant.

NDP—Night Defensive Position.

NVA—North Vietnamese Army. Also known as the PAVN (People's Army of Vietnam).

OP—Operation. A military mission. Also an Oberservation Post.

PATHET LAO—Military arm of the Laotian Communist Party.

PLA—People's Liberation Army. The Chinese Communist military, including naval and air forces.

PLASTIQUE—French plastic explosive similar to U.S. composition C-4. A puttylike substance with a shattering force greater than that of TNT and about the same handling sensitivity.

PLAYBOY CLUB—PCOD Lounge in Nha Trang. PCOD was a Special Forces acronym for Personnel Coming Off Duty. Special Forces officers and enlisted men alike shared the PCOD Lounge.

PLF—Parachute Landing Fall. Technique used by parachutists to lessen the force of impact on landing.

PRAIRIE FIRE—Cover name for U.S. Special Forces covert operations in Laos.

PRC-25—Portable Radio Communications 25. The AN/PRC-25 backpackable FM radio transceiver.

PSP—Perforated Steel Planking used for surfacing runways and helipads.

PUNJI PIT—Concealed pit containing sharpened bamboo stakes used as a booby trap.

QRV—Ham radio shorthand for ready to copy, i.e., ready to receive transmission.

QRT—Ham radio abbreviation for "I am shutting down my radio."

QSO—Ham radio abbreviation for a communication via radio.

RDF—Radio Direction Finding or Range and Direction Finding. Said of radio receivers designed to locate or home in on a radio transmission, especially RDF receivers intended for locating enemy radio transmitters.

RPG—Rocket-Propelled Grenade. Usually refers to the RPG-5 or RPG-7, a Communist Bloc antitank weapon somewhat similar to the bazooka.

RTTY—Radio Teletype.

RT—Reconnaissance Team. Particularly one of those operated by MACV/SOG.

RTO—Radio Telephone Operator.

S1, S1, S3, S4—Four staff sections of a regiment or smaller unit representing personnel and administration (adjutant), intelligence, operations and training and supply; or the officers in charge of these sections. At division level and higher they are known as G1, G2, G3 and G4.

S-60—57 mm automatic cannon. The mainstay gun of Soviet air defense artillery.

SA-2—Also called SAM-2 or Guideline. Soviet medium- to high-altitude air defense missile. The principal SAM used by North Vietnam.

SA-3—The Soviet SAM-3 or Goa low altitude air defense missile, similar in role to the U.S. Hawk missile.

SAM—Surface to air missile. An antiaircraft missile used for air defense.

SEDANG—One of two principal montagnard groups living in the highlands around Kontum. They were superb jungle fighters and were often employed as mercenaries by U.S. Army Special Forces.

SF—Special Forces. Elite U.S. troops trained in counterinsurgency and unconventional warfare.

SFOB—Special Forces Operating Base. The SF Headquarters at Nha Trang.

SKS—A 7.62×x 39 mm semiautomatic carbine with a fixed, 10-round magazine, and usually equipped with a folding bayonet. The forerunner of the AK-47. It was widely used by the Communist forces throughout Indochina, and was produced by the Chinese Communists as the type 56 rifle which often caused confusion with the AK-47 which the Chinese also called the Type 56 but designated as a submachine gun. SKSs were used throughout the Vietnam war, but were largely replaced by the AK-47 in first line NVA units and some VC units by the end of the conflict.

SLAM COMPANY—Acronym for Search Location and Annihilation Mission Company. Company sized MACV/SOG units composed of U.S. led indigenous personnel whose mission was to exploit promising contacts made by Spike Teams or Hatchet Forces.

SMG—Abbreviation for submachine gun.

SOI—Signal Operating Instructions. The book listing radio callsigns of military units and the frequencies to be used as well as authentication tables.

SOG—Studies and Observations Group. Cover name for MACV special operations group that conducted covert and clandestine operations in Vietnam, Laos, Cambodia, North Vietnam, and even China. Mostly made up of U.S. Army Special Forces personnel.

SPETSNAZ—Elite Soviet troops similar to U.S. Rangers or British Commandos but also trained to conduct clandestine or unconventional operations.

SPIKE TEAM—A 12-man MACV/SOG Recon team consisting of 3 Americans (usually U.S. Army Special Forces NCOs) and 9 indigenous troops.

SPOON—Military slang for the safety lever on a handgrenade.

SRT—Special Reconnaissance Team. A Recon team formed for a one time only or limited duration mission.

STORMY WEATHER—Army code name for clandestine operations in Cambodia.

STRAC—Abbreviation for Strategic Army Command. A term used to describe having everything well-ordered and in its place.

SWEDISH K—Karl Gustav Model 45B 9 mm submachine gun. It was similar in appearance to the U.S. M-3 "Grease Gun" .45-caliber SMG, and was often fitted with a silencer, more properly called a sound suppressor. It was widely used by Special Forces engaged in covert or special operations.

TECHNICAL TROOPS—Soldiers with specialized technical training such as those trained in radio operations and interception; radar; computers; or chemical, biological, and radiological warfare.

TRAIL, THE—The Ho Chi Minh Trail over which the NVA and VC brought supplies and men down from North Vietnam through Laos and Cambodia and into South Vietnam.

UH-1—See Huey.

UZI—Israeli made 9 mm submachine gun, with a folding metal stock. It is extremely compact and well balanced, and is very reliable. The magazine fits in the pistol grip. Rate of fire is about 550-600 rounds per minute cyclic.

VC—Viet Cong. From the phonetic alphabet Victor Charlie. A contraction of Viet-Nam Cong Sam, the Vietnamese Communist Party. VC guerillas and Main Force units did most of the actual fighting in South Vietnam until they were destroyed as an effective force in their disastrous Tet Offensive in early 1968. Afterward most of the Communist troops were units of the North Vietnamese Army.

VIETMINH—Original National Liberation Army led by Ho Chi Minh and under the direct command of Vo Nguyen Giap that drove the French out of Indochina in the early 1950s.

WEBGEAR—Soldier's basic load-bearing equipment consisting of a canvas or nylon shoulder harness and pistol belt from which canteens and ammunition pouches can be hung.

WHIP—VC booby trap in which a sapling is bent back under pressure and designed to spring across a trail when a trigger is released by a vine or tripwire, impaling the victim on sharpened bamboo stakes.

WORLD (the)—The United States.

WP—White Phosphorous. An extremely hot, burning compound used as an incendiary in rockets, shells, bombs and grenades, and for casualty and screening efforts. It produces intense heat and dense white smoke and is sometimes referred to as a smoke round. It is often used to mark targets for air strikes and artillery fire.

ZIPPO—Well-made, windproof cigarette lighter favored by GIs. Also, sometimes used in Vietnam as slang for a flamethrower.

ZU-23—Soviet 23 mm automatic cannon on a two-gun, towable mount, used for air defense by Communist forces in the Vietnam War and the secret war in Laos.

DON PENDLETON's

MACK BOLAN.

The line between good and evil is a tightrope no man should walk. Unless that man is the Executioner.

Phoenix Force—bonded in secrecy to avenge the acts of terrorists everywhere

SEARCH AND DESTROY $3.95 ☐
American ''killer'' mercenaries are involved in a KGB plot to
overthrow the government of a South Pacific island. The
American President, anxious to preserve his country's image and
not disturb the precarious position of the island nation's
government, sends in the experts—Phoenix Force—to prevent a
coup.

FIRE STORM $3.95 ☐
An international peace conference turns into open warfare when
terrorists kidnap the American President and the premier of the
USSR at a summit meeting. As a last desperate measure Phoenix
Force is brought in—for if demands are not met, a plutonium
core device is set to explode.

Total Amount	$ _____
Plus 75¢ Postage	.75
Payment enclosed	$ _____

SPF-AR